CAMP VALOR

SCOTT McEWEN

and

HOF WILLIAMS

St. Martin's Griffin
New York

This is a work of fiction. All of the characters, organizations, and events portrayed in this novel are either products of the authors' imaginations or are used fictitiously.

CAMP VALOR. Copyright © 2018 by Scott McEwen and Tod H. Williams. All rights reserved. Printed in the United States of America. For information, address St. Martin's Press, 175 Fifth Avenue, New York, N.Y. 10010.

www.stmartins.com

Designed by Omar Chapa

Library of Congress Cataloging-in-Publication Data

Names: McEwen, Scott, author. | Williams, Tod Harrison, author.
Title: Camp Valor / Scott McEwen and Hof Williams.
Description: First edition. | New York : St. Martin's Griffin, 2018.
Identifiers: LCCN 2018004986 | ISBN 9781250088246 (hardcover) |
    ISBN 9781250088970 (ebook)
Subjects: | CYAC: Spies—Fiction. | Military education—Fiction. |
    Adventure and adventurers—Fiction.
Classification: LCC PZ7.1.M43455 Cam 2018 | DDC [Fic]—dc23
LC record available at https://lccn.loc.gov/2018004986

Our books may be purchased in bulk for promotional, educational, or business use. Please contact your local bookseller or the Macmillan Corporate and Premium Sales Department at 1-800-221-7945, extension 5442, or by email at MacmillanSpecialMarkets@macmillan.com.

First Edition: July 2018

10 9 8 7 6 5 4 3 2 1

This is dedicated to our kids. We have left you a difficult world but can only hope we have given you the skills within it to survive and thrive.

CAMP VALOR

PROLOGUE

April 14, 1984, Night
Private Mooring off the Island of Eleuthera, Bahamas

It was day nine of a ten-day cruise aboard the Honduran mega-yacht
La Crema, a dream vacation for most families. Not a drop of rain,
seas glassy, humidity low, and yet the boys, both high-school
freshmen, had hardly left their rooms. The culprit: video games.
Donkey Kong, to be exact. And Colonel Victor Marvioso Madru-
gal Degas had had enough.

The Colonel yearned to barge into his son's stateroom, rip
the Nintendo from the wall, and hurl the console through a porthole, right into the Caribbean, where the boys should have been
swimming and snorkeling all along. But his son, Wilberforce,
or Wil, as he had started calling himself in boarding school in
the United States, seemingly had no interest in any activities outside of electronic games. And the Colonel's wife, Claudia, would
probably have dove in after the video game, lest, god forbid, they
deprive their son of the mighty Kong.

So, with a measure of self-control highly unusual for a man who cut his teeth running death squads, the Colonel patiently sipped rum, smoked thin little cigars, and cheated at poker until 10 p.m., when he rose from the card table and told his guests he would be returning shortly. He jerked his chin to signal Claudia and two bodyguards to follow. Vámonos. Time to put women and niños to bed.

The boys didn't hear the door open but the scent of rum and cigarillos flooded the room. Neither moved, both hunkered down in front of the pixilated screen, listening to Prince's "Purple Rain" on Wil's jam box. The Colonel cringed. That music was for weirdos.

Wil's mother entered first, swaying more than usual. She accidentally stepped on the back of Wil's leg, spiking his calf with her high-heeled shoe.

"Jeez, Mom, watch where you're going!" Wil said.

Claudia planted a slobbery kiss on her son's cheek, muttering an apology about Dramamine and wine. She staggered out into the hallway, long nails clawing at the walls for support, and bumped her way down to the master stateroom.

"Niños," said the Colonel, clapping his hands. "It is ten o'clock. Time for bed."

"No, Daddy. Please, no. Just one more game. Please," said Wil. "I'm up against my personal best."

But Wil's friend rose. "Wil," the boy said, "we promised we'd stop at ten. It's time." He yawned. "Plus, I think you'll do better in the morning."

"Good call." Wil snapped off the game and then the radio.

"Thank you, Wil," said the Colonel, patting his son's head, but secretly irritated that Wil had been far quicker to obey his friend's request than his own. "Okay, you should brush your teeth, put on your PJs. And you—" the Colonel said, pointing to his son's friend, "Manuelito will escort you to your room. Goodnight."

As soon as the boy was out of earshot, Wil asked, "Why can't Chris stay in my room? Why does he have to sleep in the back of the ship with the servants?"

"Because you are almost fifteen. Too old for sleepovers and . . ." He motioned to the Nintendo. "Video games and that make-believe game you play with wizards and strange things."

"You mean Dungeons and Dragons?"

"Yes," said the Colonel. "All of that childishness will end. As soon as it is safe for you to return to your own country, I'll send you to live with Abuela," the Colonel said with a smile, fondly recalling his youth. "You will be raised in the village where I grew up. You will attend military academy during the day, and your abuela will take care of you, whip you into shape, and make you strong. Like she did with me." The Colonel drew in a breath, puffed out his chest, and struck a proud pose.

But Wil's abuela scared him. She wore a nightgown all day, had a thick mustache, and smelled like a wet diaper. "Then I hope it is never safe to return home!" Wil said.

The Colonel's fist moved faster than his mind. The boy's head snapped back—a good right cross—and Wil collapsed at the Colonel's Gucci slippers, blood seeping from the gash on his chin, courtesy of the Colonel's pinky ring—a hunk of gold and a large pink diamond. Wil began to moan a slow, loud wail that reminded the Colonel of old-fashioned fire alarms. The Colonel was disgusted. Cry like a man, he wanted to say, and then he tried to imagine a context in which it was acceptable for a man to cry—an Olympic podium, perhaps? Instead, the Colonel said what fathers always say, "We'll discuss this in the morning." He stepped over his bawling son and left the room.

"Lock him in," the Colonel said to the guard waiting in the hallway. "Same with his friend in the back of the boat. And make sure neither leaves their room tonight."

The Colonel turned on his heels, enjoying the silky feeling of his slippers on the plush coral carpet, and headed back to the Game Room. He was eager to return to his beloved gambling, but an unpleasant thought nagged at him. It wasn't that he didn't like Wil's friend, whose name he could never remember. Ken, Carl, Chris? Something boring like that. Chris Gibbs. Yes, that was his name.

No, Chris was okay by the Colonel. In fact, the Colonel thought the Gibbs boy was a decent kid—healthy, tall, thick head of hair, good teeth. He was athletic in that wiry kind of way, which makes for good baseball pitchers and fútbol goalies. Chris was the kind of boy the Colonel wished his son would emulate. What bothered the Colonel about Wil's friend was that he couldn't figure out *why* he was friends with his son. Wilberforce was different. Strange. He was a Latino teenager with no fire, pale and gloomy. He had yellow, crooked teeth, absentmindedly pulled out his own hair, and smelled funny. Why would this normal upstanding American boy spend time with his weird little son? Was the boy using Wil for access to money and power? Perhaps. The Colonel himself had exploited and ultimately betrayed every friend he'd ever had. Even that would be understandable. But even more troubling, what if the boy wasn't using his son for gain? What if the friendship was the result of something else? Something unnatural? Their friendship did not feel natural. The Colonel couldn't quite place what it was that bothered him about the boy, but he was absolutely certain something wasn't right. As helpful and friendly and polite as the boy seemed, the Colonel sensed a threat, and the Colonel had excellent instincts in such things.

The Colonel was right to worry. The boy, whose real name and identity were classified Top Secret and known only to the highest levels of the U.S. military, climbed into his bed and waited until the guard locked the door from the outside, effectively trapping him in his room.

The boy rose, crept to the door, and pressed his ear to it, listening for the guard's retreating footsteps, but he heard nothing. The Colonel must have ordered the guard to stay outside, and the boy was fine with that. The team that had prepared him for this mission had planned for every conceivable eventuality, including this one.

Thumbing the radio beside his bed, the boy found a crackly reggae channel broadcasted from Nassau. He moved to the window, noticing heat lightning flickering along the western horizon. The porthole was about ten inches wide and two feet tall, just wide enough to fit through. It was, to a degree, fortunate that the Colonel had put him in a staff cabin in the rear of the boat. The nicer staterooms in the bow had much smaller portholes, too small for a boy to fit through. The only challenge with the portholes in the staff cabins was that they were secured by brass tumbler locks. But this was another obstacle for which the boy had been prepared. He pulled a Trapper Keeper from the bottom of his backpack and removed a strip of metal and a hairpin from the spine. He bent the strip of metal, inserted the short end into the lock, followed by the hairpin, jiggling them both until the lock clicked open. So far so good. The boy released the battens and, leaning his shoulder into the glass, popped open the window. Fresh ocean air poured in. The air smelled faintly of ozone. He noted the distant thunder. Rain was imminent.

The boy moved quickly, yanking the sheets from the bed and tying them together in a square knot. He secured one end to the bed frame and lowered the other out the window, the fabric fluttering almost to the waterline. When that was done, he stripped to his bathing suit and removed a pair of snorkeling fins and a diving belt from his luggage, noting that he hadn't even used his snorkeling equipment this trip because Wil never wanted to swim.

The boy then stuck his head out the window and looked up toward the main deck. He could see light flickering as guards paced back and forth, some twenty feet above him. The sentries were not looking down, at least, not straight down. He squeezed his body through the window like a rat through a crack in a wall, rappelled silently down the sheet-rope, and slipped into the warm water of the Caribbean. It felt good to be in the sea, instead of sealed in a stateroom with Wil, a video-game addict and farting machine.

Taking a deep breath of fresh air, the boy dove down, and following the deep hull of the ship, he swam underneath the boat and surfaced on the other side, exactly fifteen feet beneath the private balcony of the Colonel's suite. From a hidden pocket in the diving belt, the boy removed two suction cups, which he stuck to the side of the boat. Then, slipping off his flippers, he separated the footholds from the rubber fins—both of which looked like normal snorkeling gear but were specially made for this mission. He strapped the fins to his knees and looped the footholds over the suction cups, pulling down until they clicked into place, creating handgrips. Using the suction cup handgrips and the rubber kneepads, he scaled the port side of the yacht, making tiny squeaks as wet flesh brushed against the polished fiberglass.

The French doors to the balcony had been left open, and the

silk curtains undulated in the breeze. The boy hovered outside and listened. Along with the distant rumble of thunder, he heard Claudia snoring away inside, the Valium he'd slipped into her drink at dinner clearly working. As for the Colonel, he would be at the card table, as he was every night until early morning.

The boy lowered himself onto the balcony and slowly peered inside. A human lump lay flat on her back in bed, sweaty skin glistening in the moonlight, still dressed, her eyes covered by a velvet eye mask and an expensive perm puffing out at the sides. The rest of the room was dark, faintly lit by a single reading lamp and the twittering lightning. Using his hands, the boy squeezed the water off his skin, and it pooled at his feet. He leaned past the curtains and looked about the room. Almost instantly, he smelled the thin scent of cigarillos and froze, scanning for signs of the Colonel, but seeing none, he made his way to the gold-plated phone on the Colonel's desk. His intention was to remove the transceiver he'd placed in the mouthpiece the first night of their voyage. The transceiver broadcasted a weak radio signal that was picked up by a Nagra reel-to-reel recorder hidden in a game cartridge back in the boy's room. He had used the hidden transceiver and Nagra to record numerous conversations between the Colonel and Latin American and European leaders, conversations that would be enormously valuable to the U.S. government, so long as the recordings remained secret and the tapes were safely transferred to the U.S. intelligence community. The key to a successful operation was not just getting out with intelligence but doing so unnoticed. Which was why the boy was debugging the Colonel's room. All he had left to do was toss the transceiver over the side of the boat and return to his room, and the mission would be another resounding success for Camp Valor.

The boy was reaching for the gaudy phone when lightning

flickered once more. He saw his own shadow on the floor ahead of him, but there was another one with it. A shadow of a figure pursuing him from behind. A man's silhouette. A gun clearly leveled at the back of the boy's head.

Instantly, the boy's training took hold. Instead of moving away, he jumped back, closing the distance between them. He slammed his hand onto the top slide of the gun, but the barrel didn't move. The hammer bit down onto the webbing between his thumb and his index finger, slicing his flesh. It hurt like hell, but the gun didn't go off.

The boy could see the figure now. The Colonel. His eyes wide and a little whiter than usual—shocked. The boy clamped down on the Colonel's gun, and the hammer fell a second time. The boy did not wait for a third, yanking the gun away.

"Heeellll—" The Colonel began to yell for help, but the boy threw a fist into the Colonel's solar plexus. Breath exploded from the Colonel's throat, the wind squarely knocked from his lungs. He tried to tackle the boy, but the boy ducked and, executing a simple grappling maneuver, slipped behind the Colonel, putting the man in a chokehold. He kicked the Colonel's legs out from under him and dug his forearm into his carotid artery, simultaneously cutting off his breath and the flow of blood to his brain. And that was pretty much it.

The Colonel couldn't believe it. He'd lost the advantage so fast. It didn't seem fair or real. He deserved a do-over. Like he was in one of his son's video games. But this kid, this boy from los Estados Unidos, was not playing. He was a pro. The Colonel knew he was going to die and he couldn't do a single thing about it. If he could have spoken, he would have begged for his life. Begged like the thousands before who had pleaded with him for their lives.

I've had a pretty good run, the Colonel admitted to himself. And now this kid, this little turd, has me in a death grip.

He almost had to respect it.

An hour or so later, the boy was back in his berth in the stern of the boat, lying on top of the bed. The radio on, the guard snoozed in the hallway. Everything was back in place—the sheets on the bed, the porthole glass fastened, the flippers and diving belt stowed away. Like he never left.

And yet nothing was right. A body drifted in the Gulf Stream, weighted down by a lead doorstop. A body the boy had put there. Yes, there was one less mass murderer walking the planet, but there was also one less thug to keep the others in check. One less crappy husband. One less father.

The boy lay awake, listening to the rain, wondering what the chain of events he had just set in motion would look like in the coming days and years. What changes would the Colonel's death bring? What would happen to Wil, to the Colonel's country? Most pressing, the boy wondered if he had perfectly covered his tracks, or if he would be caught in the morning.

He couldn't say for sure, but he held a small packet of cyanide weighing heavily in a sweaty hand, just in case he'd made a mistake.

PART ONE

CHAPTER 1

Early June 2017
Millersville County, U.S.A.

With two days left before summer break, Wyatt was restless. Sleep evaded him. He had the window open, the fan aimed at his bed, churning at full speed. But the air coming in wasn't all that much cooler than the boiling stuff going out. And it smelled of concrete, tar, and whatever sat cooking in the garbage can a few paces from the windowsill—remnants of whatever Wyatt's aunt Narcissa had gobbled up and flung out the door with a well-practiced flick of her sausage fingers. A Styrofoam container slimed with sesame chicken, empty egg roll wrappers, a can of SpaghettiOs, a box of pigs in a blanket, BBQ short ribs sucked clean and bone white.

Aunt Narcy and her pile of bones hadn't always been there. It wasn't that long ago that Wyatt's mom made pancakes shaped like superheroes for breakfast and brought lemonade to Wyatt and his little brother's baseball games. She drove carpool, helped with math homework. But those days had ended eight months ago, when Wyatt's dad packed a bag, climbed into his rig like he did every month, and pulled out. But this time he never came home. No word. No call. The days passed and holidays went by— Thanksgiving, Christmas, New Year's Day. Wyatt tried every trick he knew to scour the Internet to find his dad, conducting Boolean searches, sourcing the deep Web. Not a trace. The Millersville police weren't much help. They filed a missing persons report, of course, but they couldn't even locate his truck. And since money kept appearing in his mother's bank account every month, the police assumed they were not dealing with a homicide.

"Mrs. Brewer," the lead investigator told his mother in the kitchen one afternoon, "you need to prepare yourself for the likely possibility that your husband is alive, but wanted to disappear."

The idea of abandonment destroyed Wyatt's mom. She took to her bed for days on end, no more pancakes, and eventually, no more cooking or cleaning at all. School became an afterthought. Her sister Narcy moved in, supposedly to help. But Narcy just made things suck even more. She talked trash about Wyatt's dad and made his mom think the worst. "I wouldn't be surprised if he had another family," Narcy whispered to his mother one afternoon.

Another family? Wyatt couldn't stop thinking about it in his bed later that night. He was lying there, bathed in sweat and a fog of garbage stink, eyes wide open, when he noticed a little pool of light playing on the wall, glimmering at the end of the bunk bed he shared with Cody, his younger brother.

Wyatt leaned over and peered down at the bottom bunk to see if Cody was awake. His brother lay on a sweat-stained *Star Wars* bedsheet in his underwear, slick with perspiration, long hair stuck to his face, twitching a little. Likely having a nightmare, a regular occurrence these past eight months.

Wyatt snatched up the phone and hopped from the bunk. "Hello," he whispered.

He could hear the smile in his friend Derrick's voice. "Of all my boyz to answer my call in a pinch, you do. I'm glad we gonna get in a year at Maple."

Maple was the local high school. Wyatt was going to be a freshman and Derrick a senior. The fact that Derrick was an all-state running back helped mask that he was also a complete degenerate. Wyatt himself had always been a little on the wild side, but his grades never showed it. Up until his dad disappeared, he'd finished each semester at the top of his class. Then, after his dad left, Wyatt turned punk with a vengeance. It didn't take long for Wyatt to transition into the kind of kid you'd watch so he wouldn't shoplift, the kind you'd walk on the other side of the street to avoid. You wouldn't think that, as an eighth-grader, he tutored high-school kids in math and computer science, specifically coding in CSS, HTML, AJAX, and some of the other basic languages. Tutoring high schoolers was how he met Derrick in fact. The jock and the renegade with a hacker's flare for math and rule-breaking. The bond was instant.

"And lemme tell you, homie," Derrick went on, "I need a friend right now. I neeeeed a lil bad boy like you I can trust. I ain't gonna lie, bro, I'm in some trouble, and I want you to help me get out. Can I count on you, homie?"

"'Til the end of time," Wyatt said, noticing he'd begun pacing, a little thrill building inside him.

Wyatt cracked the door and saw Narcy sitting on the couch watching QVC, the back of her head silhouetted in the bluish light from the flat screen. Her frizzy, short hair glowed like a deep-fried halo, her hand dipping down to the bowl at her side and then rising up to her mouth. Crunch.

The TV volume was set low enough for Wyatt to hear the chewing and lip-smacking and a hum that sounded like a moan. The tube had sucked her into the vortex, all right, but still Wyatt had to be careful. Narcy might have been slow on her feet, but she had bat ears and a voice like a smoke alarm. Wyatt needed to move ninja quiet. He dropped to his knees, pushed the door open, and crawled out nice and slow.

The hallway carpet was dirty and completely worn down in some places. The bare spots creaked if you so much as breathed on them, so he crawled on the soft, cleaner edges of the carpet until he reached the vinyl kitchen floor. Wyatt rose to his feet and padded to the mug on the kitchen counter. Rather than fish the keys out, he took the mug with him and disappeared out the back door.

Narcy's ride, an old Lincoln Town Car parked in the carport, had once been a car-service limo. Narcy had clocked over 150,000 miles on the odometer, her bulk flattening the springs in the driver side. Still, Wyatt was tall enough to physically drive the car and his father had let him tool around parking lots and back roads so that he wasn't scared to drive. The problem was getting the beast out of the carport without making any noise. He'd have to push it.

Wyatt gingerly opened the door, slid in, and put the car in neutral. He hand-rolled the window down and, reaching in to hold the steering wheel, he pushed against the doorframe. It didn't budge. He was getting ready to push again when he heard the kitchen door to the garage open behind him. Wyatt froze, bracing himself for Narcy's yell.

"Wyatt," a voice whispered. Cody. Whew. Cody stood in his tighty-whities scratching his stomach. "Had a dream. Daddy was in a deep pit and you were trying to get to him and you fell and landed on a bed of knives." Cody rubbed his eyes, blinking awake.

"It's okay, bud," Wyatt said to his brother. "Just go back

to bed. Put a story on if you have to." Wyatt handed him the phone, queuing up an audiobook. "Try . . . *Huck Finn*."

This was Wyatt's old standby. When Wyatt was young, his dad would sometimes take Wyatt and Cody on short trips. They'd ride up high in the rig and to keep the boys from getting bored, he'd play *Huck Finn*, over and over. It was Wyatt's favorite book now, and listening to it was how the brothers fell asleep many nights.

"Just make sure to plug the phone in or it'll be dead when we go to school in the morning."

"Okay." Cody took the phone and rubbed his eyes. "But why are you out here? What are you doing with Narcy's car?"

"Borrowing it for a quick spin."

Cody looked confused. "But you can't drive."

"Clarification," Wyatt said. "I'm not *allowed* to drive. That doesn't mean I can't. I need to help a friend. Come help push."

Cody was only eleven and looked young and delicate with long hair like Wyatt, but his appearance was deceptive. He was tall and strong and shared some of Wyatt's natural athletic gifts. But unlike Wyatt, the coaches always said Cody had the self-discipline of a true athlete. And so he gravitated to sports, which helped keep him out of trouble.

"C'mon and put your shoulder into it," Wyatt said.

Cody stepped toward the car, still thinking, gears turning. He shook his head. "I have a bad feeling about this. You were in my nightmare. You can't go." He crossed his arms, scowling, trying to swallow a bitter taste. "Nuh-uh. Not tonight."

"I'll be right back. C'mon, just give a push."

Cody stood there staring, unmoving. Wyatt knew it was pointless to argue with him when he got this way. "Suit yourself," he said, turning back to the car. Wyatt squatted down, leaned and pushed with every ounce of strength he had.

The Town Car inched forward, rolled a little bit, then started down the drive. Once it built up momentum, the car pretty much took off, silently slipping out into the night like a pirate ship. It moved so fast that as the car sailed down the short drive, it got ahead of Wyatt, who sprinted to catch up.

Cody ran down the sidewalk in his undies, hissing Wyatt's name. "Wyatt, Narcy's gonna kill you! Catch the dang car!" The back left bumper scraped across the rusty pickup parked on the opposite side of the street. The mash-up of the cars created a metal tearing scream.

Wyatt dove halfway into the front window, jerked the wheel hard to the right, and the tires squeaked, metal grinding against metal. He pulled himself the rest of the way through, scraping the hell out of his chest before scrambling up behind the wheel and steering the car into the center of the street. Wyatt hit the brakes and the car lurched to a stop a block from his house, a new, long scratch down the side of Narcy's Town Car to add to the plethora of dents and dings. Cody ran up on the sidewalk, jaw hanging down. "Dude," he said. "The car! Let's get it back up the street."

"No turning back now," Wyatt said, putting the keys in the ignition. The Lincoln's engine hummed.

"Wyatt, don't leave me," Cody begged. "Please. If something happens to you . . . I can't lose you. Not you, too."

Wyatt looked at his brother. "Everything'll be fine. I'll be right back. You can trust me," Wyatt said. "I'll never leave you for good."

With that, Wyatt dropped the car into gear and peeled out. In the rearview, he saw Cody running on the sidewalk back up the hill toward their house, his undies glowing against the dark night.

CHAPTER 2

Early June 2017
Millersville County, U.S.A.

The still air gushed in around Wyatt as the Town Car glided down the blacktop. Since Wyatt was well under the driving age and had no license, he kept to the back roads that paralleled the interstate. A thin layer of cool sweat clung to the back of his neck, little electric jolts of fear and excitement trickling through him. It was good to be out in the quiet night, Wyatt thought.

Then, without warning, two cop cars came flying up over the hill behind him, sirens squealing, racing toward Wyatt. He swore under his breath and hit the brakes. Heart hammering, he swerved the Town Car off to the side of the road, praying to God the cops would not arrest him for joy-riding and maybe let him go with a slap on the wrist.

But instead of pulling Wyatt over, they swerved around the Lincoln into the oncoming lane. They tore past, going a hundred miles per hour or more. Maybe an accident, Wyatt thought, breathing a deep sigh of relief. He swerved back onto the road, letting his heartbeat ease down as he drove on to meet Derrick.

The old rail yard had the dingy feel of a bad horror movie, full of junked parts, beer cans, rusting heaps of metal, and scattered piles of discarded clothes. And this time of night, it was dead quiet. Unnervingly quiet. Wyatt rolled the windows up and angled the Town Car down a row of train cars, moving slow, tires grinding gravel, the beams of his headlights spilling into dark, dirty, sordid spaces.

Wyatt knew the yard well. He and Cody would sometimes ride out there on bikes to smash bottles and burn the stuff left by the hobos who camped in the nearby woods and slept in the train cars in the yard when it rained. But the rail yard at night was a different thing entirely, especially when alone.

Wyatt drove in as far as he could and parked. Derrick could be anywhere. Wyatt instinctively groped for his cell phone and then he remembered he'd given it to Cody. He stared into the beam cast by his headlights. Where was Derrick?

Wyatt opened the door. "D? . . . D? . . . You there?"

He knew it was quite possible Derrick couldn't see Wyatt's car. Or maybe Derrick thought he was a cop—they often patrolled the yard, rousting bums.

Wyatt checked in the glove box for a flashlight. Nothing. Wyatt left the car running and got out, careful not to step on broken glass, a syringe, or even a sleeping homeless person. He thought of the time he'd found a dead animal in the middle of the yard, where it had been rotating on a spit inside a makeshift camp. The carcass of the animal was still on the spit, half-eaten, pieces of meat evidently trimmed off as the animal sizzled, licked by fire. A meal for hobos. Wyatt couldn't immediately tell what kind of animal it was. Then he saw a dog collar in the smoldering ashes beneath the spit.

After that, Wyatt swore he'd never come back. Certainly not alone. And yet, there he was. Wandering out into his own headlights.

"Derrick!" Wyatt whisper-shouted.

He heard a rustling and a low moan. He looked out into the dark woods, trying to follow the sound with his eyes.

"Hey, is that you?" he said.

Wyatt heard an unfamiliar voice. "It's me. But I don't know you." Two eyes blinked on the ground, from behind a blackened face. A bottle glimmered nearby. The hobo rocked like he was going to try to get up. Then his face wrinkled, and he growled, "Rrrrrrrraaaaaaaaaaahhhhh!!!" His body trembled with rage and he began to push himself up, but his eyes rolled back into his head and he collapsed in the dirt.

Wyatt ran, hearing other stirrings in the woods, other voices waking up. Maybe half a dozen or so hobos were out in the woods, rousing.

Forget this, Wyatt said to himself. He spun around and started back for Narcy's car. And then, as if on cue, Derrick materialized, stepping out from a shadow.

"What are you doing?!" Wyatt asked.

"Had to make sure it was you," Derrick said, running at an angle, light and fast like how he ran on the football field. His muscles, slick with sweat, rippled in the high beams. He wore shorts and his legs were dirty and badly scratched. He carried a small green fanny pack.

"Man," Derrick said, "let's go. Go. Go. Go." He beat Wyatt to the car and dove into the back seat. Wyatt got in front and fired up the engine. Derrick was talking, but before Wyatt could hear him, he smelled him. The odor moved with the speed of a sonic boom. He didn't just smell bad, like body odor or a fart, he smelled like a chemical accident, acrid and faintly of burnt rubber. It reminded Wyatt of how his cat, Tony, smelled the time his mom put the cat in the trunk and drove to the vet. When they arrived, the cat was scared stiff, claws stuck in the carpet, and a horrible odor—not just pee, but pee and fear—clung to everything. That was how Derrick smelled now.

Derrick lay flat on the back seat. Wyatt rolled the window down a notch and gunned it in reverse, kicking up a cloud of gravel and dust.

"Go back to bed, ya dirty bums!" Derrick yelled out the window.

"So what's up, man," Wyatt asked when they were back on the highway. "What kind of trouble are you in?"

"I'll get to that later. For now, man, appreciation." Derrick tapped the back of Wyatt's seat. "I knew you'd come. I owe you, homie. Tell you about everything in a bit."

Derrick rested the green bag on his chest, closed his eyes, and sunk into the pleather on the back seat.

Wyatt drove in silence, listening to the radio and steering the silver front end of the Town Car into the oncoming darkness.

The song wound down and the news came on. "Time for your 10-10-Wins Weather and News report. Every hour on the hour. Tonight is going to be a hot one for the tri-county area, with temperatures reaching in the mid- to upper nineties and humidity at ninety percent. . . ."

In Wyatt's hometown, talk radio was always the same: bad weather, cheap deals, and sports teams that could never seem to find a basket or a goalpost. Wyatt reached to shut the radio off when something piqued his interest.

"Police advise residents to be on alert after the Citgo Gas

Station and Car Wash in Millersville was robbed by a masked assailant. The assailant fired two shots in the commission of the crime, critically wounding the attendant before fleeing on foot. Police and state troopers are searching the area. Local residents are warned not to pick up hitchhikers and to report any suspicious behavior. The victim was taken to St. Mary's Hospital and is in critical condition."

Wyatt's mind flashed to the cop car that had raced past him earlier that night. He looked into the rearview mirror.

Derrick lay perfectly still, eyes closed, pretending to sleep. But he couldn't contain his smile. "I shoulda told you to keep the radio off," he said without opening his eyes. "Nuthin' good is ever in the news."

"You should have told me what was up."

"I was going to tell you at some point. Just wanted to be sure you'd show." His smile lengthened. "Don't worry, Wyatt, we gonna split the money. Now, I ain't givin' you fifty percent, but you'll get your cut."

"I don't want a cut," Wyatt said. "Not from this. This is too far. I don't want this trouble. I don't want the money."

"Don't want the money, huh?" Derrick grinned, moving his butt around, getting comfy on the back seat. "Too good for it. That right?"

Wyatt said nothing.

"I bet your daddy'd take the money and run for the hills."

"Shut up," Wyatt said, hitting the brakes. "I want you out of the car."

"Hold on. This getting serious now." Derrick's playful smile faded. He cracked an eye and slid his hand into the green bag, removing a shiny silver revolver with brown grips. "You see it?" He wiggled the gun. "Tell me you see it. I want to make sure we got an understanding." His voice cooled and sharpened. "You are in *it* whether you want in *it* or not. . . . Do we have an understanding?"

Wyatt held Derrick's gaze in the rearview.

"Yeah, you get it," he said, smiling again. "Now take me home and turn the radio back up."

Derrick lived on the east side of a little rise. As they drove up the western slope, Wyatt saw lights revolving in the treetops. They crested the hill, and below, Derrick's entire front yard was awash in a sea of cop lights. There were at least four cruisers parked out front. Cops were everywhere, shining flashlights in the bushes, chatting in a cluster, lighting cigarettes. Two cops stood at the door talking to Derrick's parents. Derrick's mom stood hunched over in a grubby pink nightgown, her hair a jumble of flattened curls, her face gummed with tears, makeup, and confusion as she squinted through the cloud of cigarette smoke pouring out of her nostrils and mouth. Derrick's dad had a cocky, drunken smirk and stood in the doorway, scratching his balls. Wyatt's headlights reflected off the bald strip of skin that sliced down the back of a cop's head.

Derrick dropped like a rock and angled his revolver up, pressing it into the back of Wyatt's neck. "You best go straight now. Don't move, don't slow."

The cold barrel poked into Wyatt's skin, in the nook between neck and jaw. He kept driving, trying to act normal. Badges gleamed against the dark uniforms in his headlights. Derrick's dad was the first to look over, squinting dumbly toward the car. Then, in unison, the cops followed his gaze. Time elongated and the car rolled past. The cops' necks stretched as they turned, watching Wyatt. He could feel their eyes studying the dents in the side of the car, scrutinizing his long hair, and somehow detecting that he was only fourteen. And really scared.

The slow stretching of time snapped and all the rubbernecking cops sprung into action, scrambling for their cruisers.

Wyatt put the pedal to the floor and the Town Car lurched.

"What ya doin'?!" Derrick tumbled to the floorboard, swearing up a storm.

"They know!" Wyatt raced up another hill.

"Did you rat me out?"

"How could I have?" Wyatt yelled back.

The Town Car crested a hill. Wyatt and Derrick had a little lead on the cops, and as they came down the back side, Derrick peeked up. "There's a little hidden turnoff ahead. Pull over!"

Wyatt came up on it fast, cranked the wheel hard to the left and jammed on the brakes. Derrick—not belted—slammed into the back of the passenger seat, and the gun shook free from his hand. It landed on the seat next to Wyatt, going off with a deafening crack. The passenger-side window shattered.

Wyatt cut the motor, ears blaring, heart going ballistic, and without thinking, he snatched up the gun. Wyatt felt the pistol grip in his palm and fingertips. The gun felt heavier than he imagined and awkward to hold.

Derrick pushed himself up off the back, frowning. "Damn. My bad."

Wyatt turned. "Get out!" He surprised himself by how firmly he spoke and pointed the gun at Derrick, right between his eyes.

Derrick stared at Wyatt hard. "Man, you ain't gonna do this—"

"Out!" Wyatt repeated, on the verge of hysteria.

Derrick took a moment, then smiled big and wide. "Good luck, homie," he said and bolted from the car. He loped into the woods. Even with the ringing in Wyatt's ears, he could hear

Derrick's laughter shouting, "Now it's on you!" as he dissolved into the foliage.

In the rearview mirror, a pair of lights raced past the turn-off, blazing down the highway. Another cruiser followed. Then two more whizzed by in quick succession.

Wyatt slid down into his seat and thought of what to do. The gun. I've got to dump the gun and get home. He gripped the steering wheel and reached for the ignition. Whatever happened after he got home, he'd deal with later.

Then he glanced in the rearview and saw it—Derrick's green bag, resting on the back seat of the Town Car. The cash, sprayed with blood, poked out of the zipper. So he had the gun and the money. Not good. He leaned into the back seat to grab the bag and fling it out the window, just as a pair of headlights appeared behind him.

The car, a cop car, pulled off on the shoulder, then slowed to a stop so the car was perpendicular to the turnoff, blocking Wyatt off from the main road. The cop flipped on his searchlight. A beam cut like a sword across the landscape and raked its way through the woods toward Wyatt. Wyatt hoped the light would pass right by like in the movies. But the light stopped on Wyatt's car and the interior flared like a lightbulb with Wyatt in it. Wyatt could see the cop radioing inside his cruiser.

No time to wait. Wyatt twisted the key and jammed on the gas. The engine revved and the car shot forward, continuing down the turnoff, which ran up a little hill then abruptly intersected a dirt road. Wyatt turned right, knowing only that he was headed toward town. Other cop cars were gaining on him, adding links to the growing chain of police cars trailing the Lincoln.

A giant cloud of oil and dust rose up in the Town Car's wake, enveloping the police cars in a brownish dust cloud that pulsated with the multicolored cop lights like a glowing, undulating caterpillar.

Wyatt rounded a turn and to his left he saw two sets of sagging bleachers on either side of a sunbaked football field ringed by an uneven track. He now realized exactly where he was. Earlier that day, he had been walking around the track during gym class. On the far side of the middle-school football field, Wyatt saw his school building. He pumped the brakes, turned the wheel, and drove right out onto the field, flattening the backstop. Wyatt headed for the parking lot on the far side of the school, and as he hooked around the vice principal's office, he saw flashing lights coming directly at him.

He swerved, hard. The Town Car lurched to his right, narrowly avoiding a police van, which, in an effort to avoid the police cars behind him, hit the brakes, spun out of control, then flipped on its side and smashed into the brick Millersville Middle School welcome sign, which read, CONGRATS, YELLOW JACKETS, HAVE A GREAT SUMMER!

The school and pileup behind him, Wyatt skidded out onto the main road, pegging the pedal to the floor. The long rattail of cop cars still trailed him, but he felt a rush of confidence heading down the downtown streets he'd haunted by skateboard and BMX bike almost every day since he was six years old.

Eastman Cemetery was not far ahead, and if he could get there in one piece, Wyatt figured he had a slim chance of getting away. A couple turns and the stone wall entrance to the cemetery appeared on Wyatt's left. He hopped the curb and tried to brake, but the tires skidded across the wet grass and the car careened into the wall, the stonework pretty much shaving off half of Narcy's Town Car, which had finally come to a rest, T-boned against the cemetery wall.

Wyatt grabbed the green bag, stuffed the gun inside, and

jumped out the passenger side. The police came screeching up on the driver side. Using the Town Car as a shield and step ladder, Wyatt hopped onto the hood and leaped for the top of the wall. He was just able to loop his arms over the top, but couldn't make it over. He pumped his legs and scrambled.

"Freeze," the cops got out of their cruisers and shouted in unison. Bullets whizzed through the air and ricocheted off the stone, spraying Wyatt with rock fragments. It suddenly dawned on Wyatt with sickening clarity—the police weren't trying to stop him, or even catch him. They were trying to kill him. Wyatt had seen videos of teenagers chased by police who opened fire. Never did he believe that if he were in that situation he would keep running, nor did he believe that the cops would shoot a teenager in the back. The terrifying realization gave him the boost of adrenaline needed to sail over the wall.

Wyatt's feet touched grass and he took off straight down a row of headstones, the green fanny pack tucked under his arm like a football. Cops scrambled over the wall behind him. Wyatt reached the end of that section of graves and ran up into the woods. Sprinting under the big oaks, Wyatt noticed the huge, broad, gnarly branches begin to sway. A thudding wind swept toward him and the trunks creaked. A bright light tore through forest canopy searching for Wyatt. The light confused Wyatt and his mind flashed to aliens.

Then Wyatt realized it was a helicopter. *A friggin' helicopter.*

Wyatt finally reached his destination—the Cachoobie River. He ran up the bank and pitched the green fanny pack out as hard and as far as he could. The bag arched, its belt twisted through the darkness above the swirling river. He didn't stop to watch the bag land in the water, but pivoted and sprinted upstream, trying to get as far away from it as possible. He ran on a footpath beside the river. To his left, police flashlights pinballed through the woods. Police dogs barked. To his right, the chopper swooped down below the treetops, flying backward over the river, blinding Wyatt with its spotlight.

His lungs burned. There's no way out, Wyatt thought, slowing to a stop and putting his hands in the air.

"Hands behind your head," a voice thundered down at him.

Buffeted by rotor wash, Wyatt obeyed and waited, certain of only one thing: he would not be returning home that night to see his little brother.

CHAPTER 3

April 1984
Bahamas

Claudia Degas opened her eyes to see her reflection staring down at her from the mirrored ceiling above her bed. Arms and legs sprawled out, night mask pushed up on her forehead, makeup smeared. Some sort of snack ground into the pillow beside her face. Oh no, here it comes, she thought.

Her gut twisted. She rolled off the bed, crawled across the floor on hands and knees, and vomited in her husband's gold-plated toilet. Was it seasickness on day ten of their trip? Or was it just a raging hangover? She didn't recall drinking that much. Well, not more than usual. Maybe she was pregnant.

That thought blinded her with pain. She knelt beside the toilet and prayed. "God no, no more children. No more children with him. No más."

Where is he? she wondered, vaguely aware he wasn't snoring beside her. She looked back toward her bed. His greasy head and gaping mouth weren't there. Maybe he passed out on the couch, she thought. She crawled over to the door and peered down the length of the master bedroom suite.

Light poured in through the French doors that were open to the balcony over the water. She looked around. Not on the couch.

Could he be still gambling in the Game Room? It was possible, but even the Colonel got sick of playing against friends who let him win hand after hand. Maybe he was in another room with . . . one of his women of the night?

This was also possible. But appearances were important to the Colonel and it was not like him to flagrantly disrespect their marriage. No, work was the most likely culprit. Probably the Colonel had awoken early to attend to some important matter back home. After all, he'd practically started a civil war and they were now on a cruise. An odd interruption was to be expected, Claudia reasoned.

She rose to her feet and wobbled into the bedroom to use the gold-plated phone on her husband's desk to call Pablo, the Colonel's head of security, and see if he would track her husband down. As she crossed the room, something out of the corner of her eye drew her attention.

Her husband's slippers were out on the balcony, set side by side pointing out at the Caribbean Sea. His monogrammed terrycloth robe hung over the railing, and she could see his gold-plated pistol in the pocket. Victor really needed to dial back the use of gold plating, she thought. Toilet, phone, gun, toenail brush.

He must have gone for an early swim, she thought, walking to the balcony and looking out, expecting to see her husband splashing in the water. It was not unusual for the Colonel to dive off the balcony and take a dip—one of the prerogatives of owning your own yacht. In fact, it crossed Claudia's mind to join Victor. A swim would help clear her head, but looking over the railing, she saw only turquoise blue water, white sand, and a lone sea turtle paddling toward the hull.

"Victor!" she called her husband. "Vicki, where are you?"

No response.

She tried to stay calm. Clearly, her husband had returned from the Game Room, decided to take a little dip in the Caribbean, and had not yet returned to their room after the swim, which meant that he was either wandering the boat in his swimsuit or . . .

She quickly went back inside to the phone to call Pablo.

The head of security answered from the galley. "Yeah," he said, his mouth likely full of scrambled eggs and croissants.

"Good morning. Is my husband with you?" she asked.

"No."

"When did you last see him?"

"He was escorted to his room last night, after you both put Wilberforce to bed," Pablo said.

"He didn't gamble?" she asked, surprised. It was not like her husband to forgo a game of cards for an early bedtime. "Was he feeling okay?"

"Fine, as far as I could tell." He paused to chew. "Is he not with you?"

"No," she said, her voice hitting a panicked tone. "He's not in one of the common areas, or on the stern deck? Maybe he's on the top deck sleeping? You know how he likes his tan."

"One moment."

Claudia heard a rustling sound. She imagined the receiver buried in Pablo's perm-sized patch of chest hair. A radio crackled.

"He is not on the stern deck or in the common areas. But

ehhh . . ." Pablo breathed heavily, hesitating. "It is possible he
is somewhere on the boat, and I have not been made aware of
where he is . . . ehhh, quartered?"

Claudia knew exactly what Pablo was doing—covering for
her husband, if he was up to any funny business.

"Let me check with my team. We will search the boat and
we will get right back to you. No need to worry."

"I don't believe he's with another woman, Pablo," she said,
candidly. "I think he may have gone swimming last night. Or
early this morning. "

"Swimming?" There was another slight pause. "I am coming to you right now."

Click.

Claudia unlocked the door and waited. A couple minutes
later, Pablo exploded into the room, a walkie-talkie radio in one
hand and a gun in the other. Two armed guards followed him.
His face, his mustache, the patch of chest hair puffing from the
deep V-neck—all beaded with sweat. "Did you unlock the door
when you woke up or was it locked?" Pablo asked.

"Locked. Victor must have locked it when he came in.
Pablo"—Claudia's voice cracked—"I found this." She motioned
to the balcony.

Pablo brushed past her, immediately going to the Colonel's
robe. He tucked his own gun into his waistband and drew the
Colonel's gold-plated one from the robe's pocket and sniffed the
barrel. He checked the chamber, ejected the clip, and counted
the rounds.

"Full, save the round in the chamber," he said to himself.
He thought for a moment.

"What does that mean?" Claudia asked. "What are you
doing?"

"Be quiet," Pablo said. He stepped back and observed the

scene. Claudia watched his head swivel as he looked from the floor to the slippers to the robe to the table with the glass and the bottle and then out into the sea. Then his head swiveled back to her, then to the floor. He squinted, knelt down and ran his fingers through the thick luxurious carpet, back and forth. He picked something out of the fibers. Claudia couldn't tell what.

Pablo stood and lifted the radio to his lips. "Call the coast guard in Nassau and local fishermen. Tell them to initiate a search for the body of Colonel Degas. In the meantime, lock down the boat. Make all of the guests and the staff return to their quarters immediately. Search every room for the Colonel's ring. It will be missing a stone. Do not let *anyone* leave their rooms. If they try to leave the boat, shoot them."

One of the guards moved to the door, closed it, and stood in front, gun at the ready.

"Pablo . . ." Claudia said, thinking she might vomit once again. "What is happening?"

Pablo looked at her, but did not speak.

"I want to see my son," she said. "I want him with me."

Pablo raised his hand. Held between his thumb and his forefinger was a large pink diamond, glinting in the morning sun. "How did this get here?"

"I don't know." Claudia's voice quavered.

Pablo smirked, slipping the stone into his pocket. He removed his gun from his waistband and put it on the Colonel's desk. He then unbuckled his belt and slowly pulled it from his pants.

"Pablo, what are you doing?"

He stalked toward her and lashed the belt, the silver buckle cracking on the bare skin of her leg like a whip.

She screamed.

"Tell me what you did to him."

After a good twenty minutes of the belt and fists, Claudia had convinced Pablo she knew nothing of her husband's disappearance and that she had, in fact, been sleeping all night. Most likely, Claudia realized, she had snoozed through her husband's murder. Must have been the Dramamine, she kept saying.

A guard knocked at the door. "Sir, they found something."

Pablo spun on his heels. "What?"

The guard listened to the radio and relayed the information. "The ring, the one missing the stone . . . there is other jewelry as well."

Pablo swiveled his head back toward Claudia like a reptile.

"Stay here," he said. "I am not through with you." He wove his belt back through his pants, took his gun and radio, and nodded to the guard at the door.

As soon as he was gone, Claudia flopped onto the floor and sobbed. And she would have kept sobbing but she heard feet padding across the floor to the balcony, then back to her. She saw the flash of a gun and looked up, expecting Pablo.

"Mrs. Degas?" Her son's friend, Chris appeared, holding her husband's gun out to her.

"You need to take this," he said in a quiet and polite voice. "And we need to get your son."

The landslide moment in the life of Wilberforce Degas, aka the Glowworm, began that morning he awoke aboard his father's mega-yacht, face down on the floor, aware of muffled chaos.

Wil tried to push himself off the floor and discovered his face stuck to the carpet, bonded by blood. His blood. He bore

a giant gash on his cheek where his father had clocked him the
night before, a deep cut made by the Colonel's pinky ring.
Overnight, Wil's blood and flesh had intermingled with the
carpet fibers of his stateroom to form a large scab that now
acted as an adhesive, pinning Wil's face to the ground. Every
time Wil tried to move, he felt searing pain, humiliation, and
an unquenchable desire to harm his father. To kill him even.

Riding a rush of anger, he pushed himself off the floor. His
face jerked back. Blood spurted anew. He grabbed a monogrammed hand towel from the bathroom and held it to his face.
He heard more screaming outside his room. What in god's name
was going on? Footsteps thudded up and down the hallway.
He went to open the door, but it was locked from the outside,
so he put his ear to it and listened. His mother was sobbing. He
heard a man's voice, followed by the sounds of a slap. "Woman,
speak!" the man said. Wil assumed it was his father—no one
else could dare lay a hand on her.

"Please believe me, Pablo!" his mother cried. "I know
nothing!"

Pablo. Wil's mind spun. Could it be? His father's most trusted
lieutenant beating his mother?

Then Wil heard something like the crack of a belt. His
mother screamed again.

"Let me out!" Wil pounded on the door. "Get away from
her!"

More chaotic sounds filtered down to Wil, then something
shifted. Footfalls pounded down the hallway away from the
family staterooms to guest quarters. Wil pressed his ear to the
door. The voices were farther way, but he could hear Pablo
yelling.

"How do you have the Colonel's ring? What do you know?
Speak or I will kill you!"

A man's voice pleaded in return, "Pablo, someone planted that in my room. I have no knowledge of how it got here."

"Liar!" Pablo screamed again. "Where is he? What did you do to him?"

"I don't know, por Dios," the voice cried out in response. "I swear I don't know what happened to him!"

Then there were gunshots, a lot of them. Wil ducked and cowered at the bottom of the door. Silence.

"Keep searching," Pablo shouted. "Someone will know something."

Wil listened now as footsteps approached his stateroom and stopped outside the door.

BAM! The door rattled. BAM! Someone was trying to kick it in. Wilberforce scrambled across the room, looking for a way out. He climbed into a sleeping berth as the door burst from the hinges.

"Ahh!" Wil covered himself with a blanket, shrieking. But instead of seeing Pablo in his doorway, he saw Chris and his mother, holding his father's pistol.

"Bud, we need to leave now. Right now." Chris wore a backpack and looked oddly cool-headed. "Off the boat. Let's go."

"What is happening?" Wil said. "Where is Father?"

"Your father is missing," his mother said softly.

"What do you mean missing?" Wil asked. "We're on a boat."

"It doesn't matter, we must go." As she spoke, Wil noticed her face was covered in bruises.

"Did Father do that to you? I'll kill him!"

"Pablo," his mother whispered. "I don't know what's gotten into him. He is interrogating everyone on the ship. He just killed Raul."

Wil struggled to grasp what was happening. His father's closest lieutenant had beaten his mother and killed one of his father's best friends. Granted, Raul was a total creep, but he was one of his dad's favorites. A word came into Wil's head—coup. Was this a coup? Had Pablo harmed his father? Where was his father? For the first time in a long, long while, Wil actually wanted to see his dad.

"We must leave now. Now!" Wil's mother yelled, flailing her arms and snapping him out of his trance.

"Okay," he said. Wil could hear Pablo and his thugs searching room to room on the lower decks. "Just let me grab something first."

Claudia and the two boys slipped past the staterooms to the main deck and raced down the stairs to the lower deck. *Little Mule,* *La Crema*'s tender—the small but fast Donzi that they dragged behind the mega-yacht—had been pulled up to the stern by one of Claudia's loyal guards. They climbed aboard and Chris fired up the motor, but as they did, Pablo's goons caught up with them on the stern deck, aiming their weapons and shouting threats.

"Señora Degas," one of the goons called out. "We will not harm you in front of your boy. You can stay, but if you try to leave, we must shoot!"

Claudia pulled the Colonel's gun from her blouse. "You better not. The Colonel is not dead. Pablo is trying to trick you. He will be coming back. And know what will happen when he does?"

"Your husband is dead," one of the goons said.

"Are you sure? Are you absolutely certain? Because if you are wrong . . . well, you know what will happen."

She could tell this got the goons thinking. Anyone who knew her husband knew his signature recipe for torture—he would have men flayed alive and fed to sharks and seagulls.

The pause was long enough for Chris to cut the line and slam the throttle, engaging over three thousand pounds of horsepower.

The goons opened fire, but it was too late. The Donzi practically jumped out of the water and raced toward Miami. "Mrs. Degas, take the wheel," Chris called, clearly a little uncertain how to drive a boat. The boy switched with her, and she brought the Donzi up to full speed. The only way they were getting caught was by aircraft or a U.S. Coast Guard cutter, which was exactly what Claudia wanted. She was never going home. From this point in her young life forward, Claudia Degas and her son would be adrift. She knew she would be the only anchor her son would ever have.

The two boys sat in the cockpit behind Claudia as the boat tore along the surface of the Caribbean at ninety miles per hour, the blades of the propeller chewing waves, literally pushing the boat out of the water. Chris looked at Wil. It seemed he had aged enormously in the last few minutes. His skin looked pale and tight. His hair, which had previously shown signs of premature baldness, now seemed especially thin and greasy as it whipped in the wind blowing across the Donzi's bow. The item Wil saved from his stateroom before leaving the mega-yacht was clutched to his chest, snuggled like a teddy bear—his Nintendo, the Donkey Kong cassette halfway ejected from the mouth of the machine.

CHAPTER 4

June 2017
Millersville Courthouse

Bushy red clown hair. Suit splattered with mustard. Star Trek Voyager pin on a maroon tie. A snowy layer of fresh-fallen dandruff on his shoulder. Wyatt thought his court-appointed lawyer man looked like someone Aunt Narcy would meet online . . . and then reject. Worse, if a guy can't keep a quarter inch of dead skin off the lapels of his cheap suit, how was he going to keep Wyatt out of jail?

Wyatt really began to sweat when he saw the prosecutor they'd be up against. Young. Patient. Professional. Looked like she spent a lot of time at CrossFit. And knew how to strut. Then she spoke. "Age can be deceptive. The boy you see before you is not quite fifteen years old. But he is capable of tremendous violence and cunning. Do not be deceived by youth . . ." When she began arguing why bail should be denied, all hope Wyatt would walk free vanished.

The state's case was strong. Thanks to the camera mounted to the belly of the helicopter that chased Wyatt, the Millersville Police Department had video of Wyatt heaving Derrick's fanny pack into the Cachoobie River. When recovered, the bag contained cash and a bloody revolver. Preliminary ballistic tests of the shell casings from the gas station matched the barrel of the gun from the bag, which had Wyatt's fingerprints on it. Wyatt's hands and forearms tested positive for gunshot residue, thanks to the gun accidentally discharging in Narcy's car. And DNA testing revealed that traces of the blood found on the money and the bag had smeared onto Wyatt's shirt while he was running to throw it in the river. All the bloodstains matched the victim, who was now in a coma.

Not only did heaps of physical evidence tie Wyatt directly to the crime, so did digital evidence. Detectives determined that the gun used in the crime had been purchased online, using Bitcoin, from Wyatt's computer bay in the high school. The same lab where Wyatt tutored Derrick.

The only person who could testify in Wyatt's defense was the attendant, and he wasn't talking to anyone anytime soon. And since Derrick was still at large, and there was no other suspect, Wyatt became the primary suspect in the shooting. As it often happens, because the case was so good against Wyatt, the prosecutor didn't really want to find Derrick to pursue that angle.

The prosecutor addressed the judge, and Wyatt could feel everyone in the room stare, from the clerks to the judges to the press in the gallery. All were enthralled by the prosecutor, including Wyatt.

"Your honor," she said. "Given the preponderance of evidence linking the defendant to the crime, his history of criminality, the seriousness of this crime, and the fact that the defendant led police on a chase that is estimated to cost taxpayers in excess of one quarter of a million dollars, we, the people, ask your honor that he, Wyatt Jennings Brewer, be denied bail."

No ruling had ever been granted so swiftly.

"Bail denied." Bam. Down came the gavel.

Wyatt was remanded to the notorious County Youth Detention Center (CYDC) to await trail. After the decision, Wyatt's brother, watching from across the courtroom, dropped his head into his hands and sobbed. Cody's long blond hair shook as he cried. Narcy, for her part, looked encouraged. Vindicated. She wobbled to her feet, gripping the rail, her legs buckling as she shrieked, "Wyatt, you killed my car, and you are killin' your mother. I hope this judge locks your smart butt up and teaches you about respect. Startin' with respectin' me."

The gavel came down again, and the judge ordered Narcy to leave, which she did, dragging a bawling Cody with her from the courtroom. Wyatt's mother was even more inconsolable than Cody. First a husband, then a son. It was too much.

As Wyatt was led out of the courthouse by guards, his lawyer waddled over, making one more attempt to get Wyatt to negotiate a plea deal.

"Son, plead guilty to attempted manslaughter in exchange for fifteen to twenty years. Best deal you're gonna get."

CHAPTER 5

June 2017

Millersville County Youth Detention Center

For a few days, Wyatt was left alone. His arrest had gained him enough notoriety that his reputation as a badass kept most of the other inmates away. Then a boy called the Spider Kid knifed a mall security guard and was placed in Wyatt's cell to await his trial.

He was around seventeen years old and the scariest person Wyatt had seen in his life. Bar none. Even in movies. The Spider Kid's mouth contained two rows of rotted-out teeth that had been filed down to sharp points. His black, empty eyes bulged from his pale, cadaverously thin face. A giant black spider had been tattooed on his stomach to appear as if it were eating the boy's belly button, which protruded unnaturally from his abdomen as a result of a birth defect. Emanating out and across his body from his belly button—eating spider tattoo were many more tattoos, covering his chest, legs, neck, and face.

Wyatt's cellmates said the tattoos signaled membership in

a splinter group of the notorious Central American gang MS-13. Wyatt just thought they were hella freaky.

Wyatt lay in his bunk a couple hours after lights out, thinking about his case and upcoming trial, wondering if he could find a new lawyer and sad that his mother had not come to see him, until his thoughts were interrupted by an eerie feeling. Like someone was watching him.

He scanned the bunks and across the cell saw a pair of black, empty eyes staring back at him. The Spider Kid hadn't breathed a syllable or moved a nanometer. He hadn't even blinked, but instinctively Wyatt knew something was about to go down. Like when two dogs encounter each other on the same patch of sidewalk. Either one or the other was going to get mauled. His adrenaline spiked and heart raced.

The Spider Kid shot up off his bunk and came straight for Wyatt, taking a giant swing while remaining almost totally silent. Wyatt balled up, covered his face and prepared to absorb a blow.

He heard a big BONNNGGGG but felt nothing. Wyatt glanced up and saw the Spider Kid reeling back, reaching for his forehead where a trickle of blood oozed toward his eyes. He was dazed. Wyatt realized the Spider Kid had banged his head on the top bunk. Pure luck. Wyatt hadn't even thrown a punch and the Spider Kid was already tottering.

Wyatt tried to exploit the advantage. He rolled out of bed and scrambled for the emergency call button on the door. But the Spider Kid blocked Wyatt with a forearm and, lightning fast, kneed Wyatt in the face, knocking him back onto the bottom bunk. The Spider Kid grabbed the top rail and, like a monkey, started kicking Wyatt, stomping on him. The nearby kids, having been awoken by the tousle, watched, cheering and egging the Spider Kid on.

"Yeah, boy! Yeah, kick 'em in da face!"

Wyatt balled up and rolled out at the Spider Kid. This knocked the Spider Kid back off the bunk, and when Wyatt spilled out onto the floor, he landed on his back. Their eyes met again. The Spider Kid was in a trance, completely unhinged.

As fast as he could, Wyatt flipped onto his stomach and tried to get his legs and arms under him, but the Spider Kid kicked him right in the mouth. Wyatt's head rocked up and he felt the pain in his mouth and neck. He was momentarily unable to move, and the Spider Kid stomped straight down on his ear. Wyatt's head bounced off the concrete floor. His ears rang, he lost his equilibrium, and the room got all wobbly.

Wyatt lunged for the Spider Kid's ankles, thinking if he could get the Spider Kid to the ground, he'd have a chance. But the Spider Kid was faster than Wyatt, hopping like an insect, alternately dodging blows and dealing them out.

Fist. Jump. Kick. Fist. Fist. Jump. Kick. Knee to face. Wyatt's head yo-yo'ed back and forth from the Spider Kid's hands, feet, and knees. The ringing in Wyatt's ears drowned out all other sounds. The Spider Kid kicked Wyatt so hard he flipped on his back, prone, flat on the cell floor. He pounced and sat on Wyatt's chest, holding him down with his weight, pinning Wyatt's arms to his sides with his knees. The Spider Kid unloaded on Wyatt's face, fist after fist. And Wyatt could do nothing about it.

Soon Wyatt lay limp, completely whipped. The Spider Kid rose and took hold of the top rail of the top bunk. Standing over Wyatt, he raised his foot and held it in the air. Wyatt stared up at the bottom of the cheap prison-issue sandal, looking at grit and hair and blood. The Spider Kid yelled to the room, "Should I do it? Should I crush his face? I can kill him right now."

"Do it!" The cell voted unanimously. "Do it!"

The Spider Kid leaned back, closed his eyes and luxuriated

in the cheers from the crowd. Wyatt saw his chance. He felt energy surge. As the Spider Kid hitched his leg back one more time to build up for a lethal kick, Wyatt rolled to his left, right up against the Spider Kid's sandaled foot and pulled the Spider Kid's ankle tight to his chin. He pushed his forehead into the Spider Kid's shinbone, and the Spider Kid's right leg locked straight out. Wyatt then levered the Spider Kid's leg and knee and, twisting his ankle, Wyatt rammed his head as hard as he could into the Spider Kid's shin. The Spider Kid's ankle popped, and he gave a thin scream as he toppled backward, hitting his head on the metal rail of the bottom bunk on the way down.

Wyatt's cellmates cheered, oohing and ahhing in the joy and horror of the fight.

Wyatt held the Spider Kid's leg until he felt the muscles slacken. He instinctually knew the boy was unconscious, but he didn't look up or let go. He just held on tight and twisted like he was trying to tear the Spider Kid's foot off until he felt tendons snap. The Spider Kid roared to life, wailing in pain. Wyatt ripped the Spider Kid's prison sandal from his foot and began lashing him with it. He put his fingers through the toe holes of the sandal, making a bloody glove to protect his hand and knuckles and crawled on top of the Spider Kid's chest, raining blows down onto his face. The Spider Kid's eyes rolled into the back of his head and Wyatt hammered harder, feeling blood splashing.

Wyatt had no idea how many times he hit the boy. Three. Five. Fifty times? He had completely lost control. All the anger that Wyatt felt came pouring out. Anger he wasn't even really aware of—toward his father for leaving, toward his mother for being weak, toward Narcy for being a burden, toward Derrick for tricking him, toward himself for letting it happen, and toward this Spider Kid and anyone who'd ever tried to take advantage of him—all came flooding out of Wyatt and found a home in his fists. And the scariest part was that he liked it.

Wyatt was vaguely aware of his cellmates scattering and the cell door rattling open. Boots rushed in. Hands tore Wyatt off the boy and twisted him into a WRAP, a straightjacket for the entire body, including head and neck. WRAPs were meant to calm an out-of-control detainee, but it usually had the opposite effect, inducing panic, claustrophobia, and hyperventilation. It was like strapping someone into a heart attack. Or a seizure. Like a moth with its wings ripped off, Wyatt bucked and thrashed and beat his arms until he passed out.

CHAPTER 6

June 2017
Millersville County Youth Detention Center, Isolation Unit

The bolt slid, a door wheezed, rubber-soled shoes squeaked across the metal floor. They stopped and turned to face Wyatt. He clamped his eyes shut and curled up on the metal cot, thinking about his home, the bunk bed he shared with his brother, and wishing he could just be there. Even with Narcy.

"Get up." The guard kicked his cot.

"I'm not going to the infirmary. I'll wait until the surgeon is here to fix my tooth."

"Ain't here to take you to the infirmary. You got a visitor."

Wyatt perked. "Is my mom here?"

"Don't know nothin' 'bout that. They don't tell me whose name's on the sheet—just to come get you." She adjusted her hips. "Better move, son. Or I'm movin' on."

"Hang on," Wyatt peeled himself off the bunk and stood, pants sagging more than usual. The food served in isolation—

rancid bologna on rubberized bread—was so disgusting he hadn't eaten in days. He followed the deputy down a hallway that blazed under fluorescent lights.

Instead of going to the family visiting room, the guard guided Wyatt to a private meeting room reserved for conferences between inmates and the lawyers trying to get them out, or police officers trying to keep them in. He had no idea if a lawyer or a cop was waiting on the other side of the door.

"Stand there." The guard pointed to a yellow line, across from a small round window about shoulder high. "When you're done," she said and slid her ID card through a reader. "Come to the window and I'll let you out."

The door whined open.

"You can go in now," she said and disappeared back down the hallway.

Wyatt entered the room to find a single visitor, a large man, around forty years old, with weathered skin, sunglasses, and a thick beard, sitting at the small metal table in the center of the room. The guy was jacked. He looked like a gorilla squeezed into a dark, shiny suit, which strained against him. Sleeves of tattoos peeked out from under his shirt cuffs. He shifted around, trying to find a position to fit his bulk. He reminded Wyatt of a biker posing as a security guard, or a mixed martial arts fighter dressed for an arraignment. Wyatt had no doubt the man was a cop. His instincts told him he needed to be on edge, leery of the man, so Wyatt jumped a little as the heavy cell door clattered shut.

The man pointed to the chair bolted to the floor across the table. "Pull up a chair. If you can manage to squeeze in."

Was he joking? Wyatt sat, finding plenty of room.

The guy didn't take off his dark glasses. Just stared at Wyatt for a while, and Wyatt noticed his face was badly scarred.

The wounds looked fresh, the stripes across his cheeks on the left side of his face still pink.

"Wyatt, I just came from the hospital where they put that kid who got shot up. Little Ronnie, I think his name is. Doctors told me he had a rough night. They think he'll die."

The chair grew cold under Wyatt. He felt weak.

"And the kid you beat in your cell," the man went on. "That kid with all the tats. He ain't doing much better. Only difference is, that banger's got a lot of buddies from his MS-13 just itching for you to get out of solitary so they can get at you."

"If I had anything else to tell police, I would," Wyatt said. "But if I confessed, I'd be lying. I didn't shoot anyone. And the kid with the tattoos deserved it."

"Personally, I think you're getting a raw deal. Might have a better one for you." He said this quietly, matter-of-factly.

"Why would I trust the police to make a fair deal?"

"Who said I was a police officer?" The big man leaned back, crossing his arms. Wyatt thought he could hear fabric stretching.

"So are you a . . . lawyer?" Wyatt asked weakly.

The man let out a slow breath. "Why does it matter to you what I am? You should only care about what I can do for you . . . and what I want you to do for me."

Wyatt's mind sharpened as he grew suspicious.

"Then what do you want?"

"Three months." The man held up three thick fingers.

"For what?" Wyatt said, baffled. "Sorry, man. I don't understand. What do you want?"

"Three months. I want three months of your time. Here's a waiver." The big man pulled a thin legal document from the bag and placed it on the table in front of Wyatt. It looked like a menu from a fancy restaurant—bone white paper with a fancy seal embossed at the top. The letters "CV" were painted in gold in the center and an inscription read: *United States of America * Department of Defense.*

The man angled a pen at Wyatt. "Sign that and we can get out of here."

> I, Wyatt Jennings Brewer, being of sound mind and body, have agreed to commit myself to three months' internment at Camp Valor. I swear to keep the existence of the camp and all activities therein confidential. Any mention of the camp and its programs will result in imprisonment. I understand my sole compensation will be the experience itself and the liberty to return to society after a ninety-day period of service. I hereby waive any right to hold the U.S. government, Camp Valor, or its staff or any participants accountable for any injury, physical or mental trauma, death, or dismemberment during my internment.
>
> Wyatt J. Brewer

"Who are you?" Wyatt asked when he'd finished reading the waiver.

"My name is Sergeant Hallsy."

"And . . . what is Camp Valor?"

"It's a summer work program for at-risk youths."

Wyatt looked up. "Run by the Department of Defense?" He pointed to the inscription.

"They don't run us, per se. Just fund us. The DOD has big budgets." The man grinned, revealing his surprisingly white teeth. "You should be psyched about that."

"What's all the stuff in there about death and dismemberment?" Wyatt jabbed at the paper with his finger.

"It's a waiver." The big man shrugged. "Like when you rent a bicycle or ride a roller coaster at Disneyland."

"Disneyland?" Wyatt scoffed. "This sounds like an experiment, a place where you're tortured . . . or given an orange jumpsuit and forced to pick up trash."

"Buddy, you're already in an orange jumpsuit," he said, motioning to Wyatt's chest. "And wouldn't you rather be outside picking up trash on the side of the road, where you can smell the breeze, and get a tan?" The man leaned back and waited. "But do you really think I'd waste my time grabbing a kid outta jail to come collect cigarette butts and pop cans?"

"So what kind of work would I do at Camp Valor?"

"Love the curiosity. But that's not how it works. You wanna find out, you gotta do it."

"But I can't jump into something blindly," Wyatt said. "At least here, I know where I stand. I have a trial coming up. I don't know anything about the program. I don't know anything about you. I mean, you told me your name, but it could be a lie. You showed me this piece of paper, but—"

"Stop. And listen. It doesn't make a bit of difference if you know me or not. Or what my name is. Or what the paper says. Or what you'll do at Camp Valor. You are facing life in prison— some of that is of your making, some of it not. *None* of it matters. The path you chose has led to this spot. It is a deep, dark pit that you cannot escape from. Now . . ." He leaned in toward Wyatt and looked up over his glasses. Wyatt could finally see his eyes. "I am your bridge. I am offering you a way to walk out of this hole and cross over into freedom." He swung his hand over the table and walked two fingers across it, leaving a trail of prints in the metal finish. "Do you want to take the first step, or not." He wiped the prints with the sleeve of his jacket.

"Three months," Wyatt said, thinking three months any-where would be better than in the CYDC. "And I'm free? I get to go home?"

"What it says in the waiver," he said, pointing to the pa-per. "You'll be back in school by the end of summer, eating mac 'n' cheese and chicken fingers in the lunch line."

Wyatt took the pen, drew a breath, and considered what to do. It's just a piece of paper. I can always run . . . and what is this Hallsy guy going to do? Chase me? Good luck, Wyatt thought, and scribbled his name.

Hallsy grinned, slipped the document back in his bag, and stood up without saying a word. He fished an ID card out of his pocket, swiped it through the reader on the door. Once again, it whined open. He looked back over at Wyatt, face crinkled. "You waiting for someone?"

"The guards," Wyatt said.

"Why," Hallsy asked flatly.

"Don't I need to be processed out? See a judge? Get some kind of permission? At least get my things?"

Hallsy arched an eyebrow. "A judge? They can't help you now." With that, Hallsy stepped out and passed from sight.

The door remained open. After a few moments, Wyatt got up and looked around, afraid he was being lured into a trap. He peered through the window to the door Hallsy had just ex-ited. The guard who'd walked him down the hall was gone. No one was there. No one was watching.

Wyatt looked again beyond the doorway. It lay open and dark and shadowy. It called to him.

CHAPTER 7

April 1984
Miami, Florida

The last time Wil Degas saw Chris Gibbs was at the Biltmore Hotel in the Miami suburb of Coral Gables. In the hours and days since fleeing *La Crema,* Claudia Degas and her lawyers had been petitioning the U.S. State Department for political asylum and scrambling to protect the Degas family assets, a fruitless endeavor. Meanwhile, Wil and Chris had been holed up in Wil's room at the Biltmore, curtains drawn, living off the mini-bar, room service, and endless rounds of Kong, Duck Hunt, Tetris, and Hogan's Alley.

Wil shut out the maids. Trays, dirty dishware, napkins, and wrappers piled up around the room. As did the daily newspapers that the boys scanned for news of Wil's father. The Colonel had been presumed dead, his body believed to be bobbing somewhere in the Caribbean, but so far no corpse had been recovered.

Three broad theories emerged regarding the Colonel's disappearance. One theory, proffered mostly by U.S. and Bahamian authorities, had the Colonel accidentally drowning while drunk. An alternative theory, often offered up by news sources from Central and South America, described assassination by a foreign power like the U.S. or a betrayer like Pablo Gutierrez, the Colonel's head of security and number two. This made some sense, since after icing his rivals aboard *La Crema* Pablo quickly replaced the Colonel as Central America's resident paramilitary thug.

The third theory, which was widely touted in tabloid media, suggested that Claudia Degas drugged her husband and pitched him overboard. Some tabloids even went so far as to speculate that Wil helped Claudia do the shoving. Wil's personal theory was that one of his father's men, likely Pablo, had murdered his father in an attempt to seize power.

For three days the boys spoke little. Mostly they played video games, read the papers, and waited—waited for news and for the dreaded moment when Chris's parents would arrive from New Hampshire to take him home. For fifteen-year-old Wil, losing Chris was by far the darkest cloud looming on the horizon, vastly darker than learning the details of his father's death, darker than losing his family fortune, darker than never returning to his country. Starting in boarding school, Wil had come to rely on Chris as his only source of light and happiness. To Wil they had become more than best friends, they were fellow survivors. Blood brothers. And now, in a curtained and smelly hotel room, Chris once again provided Wil with his only source of light. A source that was dimming fast.

When the day finally came, both Wil and Chris stared at the boxy room phone, an orange call light blinking as it rang and rang.

"Might be room service," Chris said hopefully, glancing at the piles of plates, forks, knives, and trays in the corner. "We do have half the hotel's silverware in here."

"I wish," Wil said somberly. "I did the calculation. From your parents' house to the Biltmore is fifteen hundred fifty-five miles—that's approximately twenty-four hours of road time. Assuming they were able to drive six hours the first day, twelve the second, and six this morning after breakfast with a stop for lunch, that would put them here at 3:00 p.m. It's 3:30. I'm betting they had a long lunch. Or your dad kept hitting snooze this morning."

"Then I won't answer it," Chris said, letting the call click over to answering service. The phone was silent for a few seconds. Then it rang again.

Wil sighed. "Might as well pick up. They'll just come to get you if you don't. And I don't want to see anyone, if that's okay with you."

"You sure?"

Wil nodded. Chris picked up the receiver, said hello. Wil could hear Chris's parents on the other end—his mother excited, teary and relieved. Chris's parents asked if they should come up to the room to get Chris. He said no, he'd be down in a minute, and hung up.

Wil leveled up in Kong, his fingers clacking the remote. Chris gathered his things and stepped into the bluish light beside the TV, but Wil would not look up from his game.

"I'll see you back at school in a couple weeks," Chris said.

Wil's eyes grew glassy tears, his pupils following Kong. "I hope. I don't know. I don't know what's next."

"Doesn't matter," Chris said. "Wherever you go, we'll be in touch. I promise. I'll come see you."

"Where? You don't know where I'll be. I don't know. My mom doesn't even know."

"Wherever it is, I'll come see you. I'll always be your friend, Wil, I promise."

Wil finally looked up from the TV screen. "Okay. Wish me luck, Chris. I'm going to need it."

Chris kneeled beside his friend and extended a hand.

Wil shook it weakly. "Wait," he said. "Before you go I want to do something." He fished a steak knife from the pile of silverware in his room. "We're going to be brothers"—he dangled the dirty blade— "gaming brothers." Wil etched his initials into the top of his Nintendo and added the date: *4-14-84*. "Let's never forget this."

"Never." Chris took the knife and etched his own initials— CMG.

Wil returned to his game play.

Chris picked up his bag. "Wil, promise me you'll get outside. Don't stay locked up in here. You need fresh air. You need the sun. It'll make you feel better."

Wil rolled his eyes.

Chris's voice grew serious. "No, dude, that's not good enough. I need a promise. I made a promise to you, now I want one back. Or I'll drag you out of this room right now, I'll take you down the elevator on my shoulder and throw you in the pool."

Wil laughed. "Okay, okay. I promise," he said. "Might not be today. Might not be tomorrow. But I'll get out. I swear I will."

Wil hit pause and the two embraced for a short, backslapping, mini–dude hug and then Chris walked out into the hallway.

Wil watched Chris walk down the hall until a maid peeked out of a room and saw Wil's door open. She came hurrying over. "Excuse me, sir, can I—"

Wil shut the door, chain-locked it. He flopped back down in front of the TV with his remote.

Wil sat in the darkness for a few minutes, then got up and moved to the window. He pulled back the drapes and recoiled from the blinding South Florida light. Squinting, he looked toward the roundabout. An aggrieved valet waited by a rusty station wagon with New Hampshire plates. Wil could tell the valet was pretty sure he wasn't getting a tip.

Chris's dad came first, tossing Chris's bag in the back seat and walking around the front of the wagon. Mr. Gibbs's outfit matched the car in its lameness: shorts hiked over his belly button, a too-tight imitation Polo shirt and comb-over. He moved like a fighter—fists balled, steps wide, chin tucked, and eyes up. To Wil and the valet's surprise, Mr. Gibbs passed the valet a couple bills. Not a total cheapskate, Wil thought.

Chris's mom looked like June Cleaver, a pretty-enough lady with a rigorously groomed hairdo and a polka-dot dress. Wil smirked, thinking about how scared and out of place this proper lady must have felt being in Miami. Chris opened the door for his mother. A nice move, Wil thought. Genteel. They all piled in at once. He was hoping Chris might look up, to wave at Wil before he left, or better yet, to invite Wil to join them. Instead, with a puff of bluish exhaust, they drove off. Wil let the curtains fall into place and returned to his gaming setup.

A few days later, Wil was telling himself, you have to get outside. Go visit the pool. Get out in the sun. You promised Chris. You promised you would do that.

He continued to lecture himself until a knock came at the door. He was sure it was his mother. He would tell her he was going to the pool and she didn't need to pester him. She'd complain about the scent filtering out the door and beg him to let the maids clean.

But when he opened the door, his mother just stood there, tears in her eyes. "I have sad news," she said.

Wil assumed it was about his father, but what she had to tell him was far more crushing than anything he had expected. There had been an accident. The Gibbs's crappy station wagon made it all the way to Virginia and got caught in a storm. Mr. Gibbs decided to push through and lost control while crossing a bridge in a flash flood. Skid marks were left on the blacktop. The wagon went into the river.

"No one survived," his mother whispered.

Wil's reaction was worse than even his mother expected. He began frothing at the mouth. He dropped, he seized, flopped to the ground, and went limp, writhing like a worm. . . .

PART TWO

CHAPTER 8

June 2017

North American Wilderness, Location Unknown

Wyatt awoke on cold hard steel, confused. Why was he back in his cell?
But the air smelled different—fresh, and cooler than he was used
to, and he felt it moving, blowing against his skin. The steel floor
canted.

Wyatt opened his eyes but saw nothing—just black. Something covered his face, smothering him. He tore it away. A sleeping bag. Light blinded him. He saw only a gray-green blur and
a white cube. The floor swayed back.

He braced himself. Tense. Blinking until his eyes focused
on—What was he seeing? The cube was a pallet of grocery
items—canned food, toilet paper, Wheaties boxes stacked six
feet high. All wrapped in plastic and lashed down on the pallet
under a slate-gray sky. A sliver of yellowing morning light
etched its way past a ridge line of tall pine trees poking out of

a low-hanging mist that spilled like gas from evaporating dry ice onto a silver sheet of water. He saw waves.

He was on a boat, a dim memory now coming to Wyatt of Hallsy heaving him out of a car and laying him on a sleeping bag. An engine hummed and a sharp laugh punched through the morning calm. Wyatt arched up onto his elbows, craning around to see a pilothouse. He pushed himself up off the deck, his body brittle and sore but at the same time deeply refreshed. He had not slept so long and soundly in months. Maybe ever.

He limped slowly across the flat deck to the pilothouse. Inside, Hallsy leaned against the single bench seat, drinking coffee, grinning.

Next to Hallsy stood a tall, heavyset Native American man wearing a red flannel shirt. A Toronto Blue Jays baseball hat rested on his horse's mane of jet-black hair.

"Where are we?" Wyatt asked.

"He wakes," said Hallsy, ignoring the question. He motioned to the Indian beside him. "Wyatt, meet Mackenzie."

"A pleasure," said Mackenzie, squinting over the edge of his mug. "You gotta get that looked at."

"Huh?" Wyatt muttered, still groggy.

"You have blood trickling out of your mouth." Mackenzie lowered his mug toward Wyatt's chest. Wyatt looked down to see bloody drool pooling on a fold in the jumpsuit below his neck. Wyatt probed his tooth with his tongue. It wobbled in his gums and felt even looser than before.

Hallsy patted Wyatt on the back. "There'll be a medic around later. Maybe he can save it. If not, yank it out."

"Nah, that tooth is done, eh." Mackenzie groped around the pile of maps and notes behind the steering wheel. "Take this." He came up with a dirty piece of fishing line. "You can pull it yourself. String. Doorknob. Pop."

"I like that option," Hallsy said.

Wyatt felt woozy. He steadied himself. "I'll wait for the medic."

"Suit yourself."

Mackenzie drove on for a while and then turned his face upward, squinting. "Haze is about to clear." His long black hair began to riffle and a strong breeze gusted. The mist hanging over the boat seemed to peel back, revealing a tall island.

Mackenzie motioned with his coffee cup. "That's us."

The island was heavily forested; looming pines and spidery cedars jutted out from the shore and curled upward. A line of smoke rose from behind the high and distant ridge. Or was it mist? It was hard to tell.

They rounded a rocky peninsula and entered a crescent bay with a sandy beach and a wide, concrete dock. A short distance uphill past the beach sat a white-and-red lodge and a series of white cabins. An American flag snapped in the breeze, fairly glowing in the sunlight now tearing through the overcast skies.

T-shirts and towels hung on clotheslines, canoes sat upside down on the beach. Footprints pockmarked the sand, and a simple sign hammered into the post at the end of the dock read, CAMP VALOR. But, strangely, Wyatt saw no people.

He could smell cooking. Breakfast—bacon and maple syrup. Must be chow time. The last food to cross Wyatt's lips had been slopped onto a tray and slid into his cell through a slot along the bottom of the door. Wyatt's body seemed to cave in at the smell of a proper breakfast, and his stomach didn't just growl, it screamed.

Mackenzie arched an eyebrow at the boy. "Hungry, eh?" he said and reversed the motors. The boat eased up to the dock. Mackenzie looped a bowline around a post and held the boat fast. "Welcome to Camp Valor, Wyatt. I wish you luck."

"He'll need it." Hallsy brushed past Wyatt, slung a large backpack onto his back, and stepped up onto the dock. Wyatt followed, wobbling as his body adjusted from the swaying boat to firm land.

Hallsy strode briskly up the little hill toward the lodge. Wyatt hurried behind, sweat dripping down his back as the day suddenly transitioned from cool to hot. They reached a porch at the top of the stairs and pushed through a screen door.

The lodge was divided into three main areas. A simple Mess Hall with long wooden tables was immediately to Wyatt's left. Beyond the Mess Hall was a large den with a massive fireplace and a meeting area, decked out in bearskin rugs and memorabilia—snowshoes, flint knives, canoe paddles, and college pennants. Straight ahead was the kitchen and maintenance area with saloon doors—one marked "In," the other "Out." And directly to his right was a wall lined with photographs.

Wyatt scanned the lodge and noticed it was completely empty, the tables cleared and cleaned. Only the smell of breakfast and Pine-Sol hung in the air.

Hallsy checked his watch. "Damn. Just missed breakfast. Guess we wait for lunch."

Wyatt inadvertently groaned.

Hallsy gave him a sympathetic look. "Never mind. This way." He headed for the kitchen. Wyatt followed, casually glancing at the photographs that hung on the wall to his right: individual portraits of teenage boys and girls and, at the bottom of each portrait, a plaque.

No names were inscribed in the plaques, just a year and a short phrase. A photo per year going all the way back to 1941. Wyatt read an inscription.

1987

DEMONSTRATED REMARKABLE BRAVERY, COOL-HEADEDNESS, AND CARE FOR HER FELLOW CAMPERS UNDER EXTREME DURESS.

"Who are these people?" Wyatt asked, pointing to the portraits.

"Valor Wall. The Top Camper from each summer gets a plaque."

Wyatt noticed that translucent black fabric had been hung over several of the portraits like veils. "Why are some photos covered?"

"If the photo is covered, it means they are gone."

"You mean dead?" Wyatt asked.

Hallsy pushed through the "In" door. "C'mon. Food is this way."

As soon as his nose entered the kitchen, Wyatt smelled new scents: garlic and fish and sourdough bread. And finally he saw people, but not campers. In the back, an old punk rocker in a tank top and an apron chopped garlic and filleted fish, head-phones on, Sex Pistols—"God Save the Queen"—blasting in his ears. He had a short Mohawk and an ear full of rings and looked Indian. Needless to say, with the music shrieking, he didn't hear Wyatt and Hallsy enter. Nearer to them, an older woman hov-ered over a wooden cutting board, rolling dough.

"Excuse me, Mum," said Hallsy with more politeness than Wyatt had seen to date. "Is there any breakfast left that we might have?"

"Just tossed the last of it into the compost bin." Without looking up, the old woman jutted her chin toward a giant trash can, the last bits of a magnificent brunch mixed in with eggshells, bacon grease, and dirt. Worse, the remains of industrial coffee filters had been dumped on top of it all, creating a small mountain of coffee over everything.

"Eric," the old lady said without looking up. "With the start of the summer, it's all we can do to keep up with the regular scheduled meals. You know better than to ask."

"You're right. Sorry, Mum." Hallsy wandered over the trash can. "Mind if we scrounge on this?"

"The garbage? Go ahead."

Hallsy poked through the food pile. "C'mon. You'll want to dig in. Got a little hike ahead of us." He brushed coffee grounds off the top of the heap.

"I'll wait 'til lunch."

"Suit yourself, Wyatt."

The woman stopped rolling. She glanced back, blowing the strands of gray hair falling in her eyes. "So you're *Wyatt*?" she said.

Hallsy fished a half-eaten biscuit out of the can. "In the flesh." He blew off some flecks of egg and took a bite.

The old lady dusted her hands off on her apron. "I was wondering when you'd join us." She stepped to the counter and extended a bony hand. "You can call me Mum."

Wyatt reached out, took her hand, and felt thin skin around swollen, arthritic knuckles.

"I'm the director's wife," she said. "My job is to see that everyone here—at least while in camp—is fed and reasonably well taken care of."

Her large, wet, blue-turning-gray eyes looked Wyatt over, holding on Wyatt's prison jumpsuit, the trickle of blood seeping down his chest and his bruised face. "And it looks like you are in need of some taking care of. Tell you what. If you give me a few minutes, I'll throw something together."

Hallsy tossed his biscuit into the pile and spat out his mouthful. "Now you tell us!"

The "something" Mum threw together turned out to be a breakfast feast: fluffy eggs, bacon, fresh buttermilk biscuits with gravy and jam. Wyatt just scooped, chewed, and swallowed blissfully, not saying a word. Hallsy did the same.

Neither seemed to notice that Mum had left the kitchen and returned to the table with an armful of clothing. "Campers over the years tend to leave things," Mum said, setting the pile down on the table next to Wyatt. A pair of cargo shorts, belt, what looked like an original Tony Hawk T-shirt—a thick reddish plaid wool shirt like the one Mackenzie wore—underwear, socks, and a pair of L.L.Bean duck boots.

The clothes were clean and neatly folded but looked old and smelled musty. Gauging by the Tony Hawk T-shirt, they were maybe thirty years old.

"This shirt is totally vintage," Wyatt said. "Are you sure you want me wearing it?"

Mum scowled. "I'm sorry they aren't the latest fashion."

"No, I didn't mean it that way," Wyatt said, realizing he had offended the woman. "It's a super-cool shirt. Tony Hawk is a legend. What I mean is the shirt is vintage. I know guys who collect this stuff—or try to anyway. This is worth . . . two hundred bucks on eBay. Maybe more. I could sell it for you."

"You won't have time for that," she said, smiling. "So long as it fits you should wear it. Go ahead, try it on."

"Okay." Wyatt unzipped his prison jumpsuit, glad to get out of it. He put the shirt on, and it fit just the way he liked it. A little roomy. But just fine. "Perfect," he said. "But if you change your mind, let me know."

"Sure." Mum nodded and turned toward the kitchen. Then

she swiveled back to the table, hesitating a bit. "You might also want this." She drew a fixed-blade knife, in a leather sheath, out of her apron. It was an old Buck knife with a pearl grip. Someone had taken good care of it. The leather was soft, the blade razor sharp.

"Mum, you can't do that," Hallsy protested. "He hasn't even qualified yet!"

"He will," she said. "I am certain of that."

Hallsy shook his head. "Not even through the morning and you're already spoiling him."

Hallsy stepped out from the kitchen onto a dirt path, heading toward the imposing hill in the center of the island. Wyatt tailed him, eyeing the cabins off to the right where he saw more signs of camper life—clothes hanging from porch railings, ruck-sacks leaning in cabin doorways, tents spread out to dry on a patchy, athletic field, a faintly smoldering fire pit—but still, no campers.

The sun was hot and the sky completely cloudless, robin's-egg blue. Wyatt was relieved when the path cut up into the shaded forest, lush with waist-high ferns, giant outcroppings of bedrock, and tall pine trees. A thick mat of fallen needles car-peted the forest floor.

Even though the air was cooler in the forest, they were mov-ing quickly and Wyatt took off his new long-sleeved shirt and tied it around his waist. He felt the gentle swing and tap of the sheathed knife against his side as he walked. The sheath, which hung from the belt Mum gave him, was leather. And when Wy-att slipped it onto the belt, he noticed a faded patch, a thick notch in the belt where a knife had hung before and worn into the leather. It was possible that this notch could have been from another knife, but Wyatt did not think so. Both the clothes and the knife had come from the same camper, Wyatt was pretty sure of that.

The ground they covered gradually became steeper. The rock outcroppings grew more prevalent, transforming into cliffs. As they hiked toward such a cliff, a girl came out from behind it, running down the narrow path toward them. Finally, a camper, Wyatt thought. And a cute camper at that—tall, dark hair, about seventeen years old. She wore skimpy track shorts and a tank top and carried something slung over her shoulder. It looked like a yoga mat or a bedroll.

"Morning, Dolly," said Hallsy.

"Morning, Sergeant Hallsy." The girl nodded to the thing slung on her shoulder. "Equipment malfunction. Be right back."

"Roger."

Dolly jogged toward Wyatt, watching him warily. As she got closer, Wyatt could see her face more clearly. He could now see she was *very* pretty, strikingly so, which he didn't expect to find at a work camp for juvenile delinquents.

"Mind giving me a little room?" she asked, nodding to the path where Wyatt stood blocking her way. Wyatt blushed, realizing he'd been standing and staring at her dumbly.

He stepped aside, and as she darted past Wyatt saw that the thing on her shoulder was a . . . rocket launcher.

Wait, Wyatt thought. What did I see? She can't be carrying a rocket launcher.

He looked back at Dolly hurrying down the path. Perched on her shoulder was a green-and-black four-foot tube with an eyesight, handgrip, trigger, and shoulder strap. He'd seen many like it in news stories from Afghanistan and Iraq and in the war movies he'd watched with his dad. And yes, this *Dolly*, who looked like she'd trotted out of the pages of a Reebok catalogue, had a weapon that could down a plane jangling off her shoulder just like a yoga mat.

"Put your tongue back in your mouth," Hallsy called back from the far side of the cliff. "We need to hurry."

"But, was that a *bazooka*?" Wyatt's jaw hung open.

"Stinger missile."

Before Wyatt could get words out Hallsy cut him off. "Save your questions . . . you'll have more soon. Trust me."

Keeping pace with Hallsy's long stride had Wyatt gushing sweat, and he welcomed the fresh breeze that kicked up near the top of the hill. It cooled his skin and his lungs, which burned, as did his eyes. Behind them lay an endless spread of green islands and blue water. They were in the middle of a vast and largely uninhabited archipelago. When he had signed the waiver, he thought that if things went bad, he could run away. Looking out at this wilderness, Wyatt now knew that escape was impossible. There was no turning back; whatever awaited Wyatt at Valor he'd have to meet, head on.

Ahead rose the final ridge leading to the peak. Hiking it, Wyatt crested the rise with his head down, putting one foot in front of another and—in this way—he almost tumbled straight off the sheer rock face to his death.

The ridge simply dropped straight down into a deep, vast chasm. Wyatt staggered back.

"Whoa there," said Hallsy, grabbing onto Wyatt's Tony Hawk T-shirt. "Easy, brother."

Wyatt could see the cliff face was in fact part of a long, jagged edge forming the circumference of a giant crater sunk deep into the center of the island, two miles in diameter and several hundred feet deep.

Outside of Millersville, where he grew up, Wyatt had seen his fair share of open-pit mining operations.

"Is that a strip mine? Or a quarry?" Wyatt asked.

"Caldera." Hallsy crouched over his backpack, drinking water from a bottle. "The island that we are on is an ancient volcano, long extinct. Or so we hope." He winked and passed Wyatt his water bottle.

Wyatt drank and peered down into the crater. The rocky sides of the caldera dropped steeply into the basin, which was thickly blanketed in lush plant life and dotted with natural pools of crystal-clear water. Woven into the greenery was an obstacle course, shooting range, pool, soccer field, climbing wall, airstrip, landing pad, hangar, a hodgepodge of military vehicles (tank, jet, drone, dune-buggies, etc.), and—yes—campers. They roved across the compound like ants.

"What is this place?" Wyatt asked.

"Told you. It's the Caldera. Some of us call it the Sugar Bowl."

"I mean, what goes on here?"

Hallsy made a calming gesture. "Just wait. Get it all at once."

They heard a buzzing sound, quiet at first, then swiftly growing louder. A large hovercraft-style drone shot up out of the Caldera.

Hallsy groaned, "Security drone, hold still."

The drone whizzed right up to Wyatt, which was unnerving enough, but what really freaked Wyatt out was that suspended from its belly was a small cannon, consisting of a large-caliber rifle with a pan of ammunition—like a flying tommy-gun aimed directly at Wyatt's face.

"Halt. You are trespassing on U.S. government property," said a voice from the drone, tinged with an odd accent.

A round of ammunition rotated out of the pan and into the firing chamber.

"Hallsy," Wyatt said, panicking. "What is happening?"

The drone continued, "Put your hands behind your head and lie face down immediately."

Wyatt dropped the bottle, and the water glugged out. He raised his hands and began to put himself on the ground. Hallsy stepped between Wyatt and the drone.

"Avi," Hallsy said in an exasperated tone. "He's a new camper. He's starting late, so he hasn't been through indoc. Take it easy."

"I do not have any biometric data on this individual."

"I know. I told you, he just got here."

"This is not standard protocol. We need to resolve this as soon as you reach base camp or I will revoke your security clearance."

"Fine. Take it to the Old Man."

The drone backed away, then buzzed toward Hallsy. "Remove your glasses," said the strangely accented voice.

"Avi, you're going to scan me?" Hallsy half-laughed, backing away. "Dude, you can see it's just me." Hallsy put on a phony smile. "Your good ole buddy, Hallsy."

"I don't care how long I know you. I have no buddies. It's how I keep us safe and secret. Don't move." The craft simply swooped and then hovered inches from Hallsy's face. Hallsy's beard ruffled in the wind from the drone's rotors.

Hallsy removed his sunglasses, and a green light from the drone passed over his right eye.

"Hallsy, next time you violate protocol, I will have no choice but to commence with security measures."

"Yeah, thanks a lot, pal."

"It's not my fault you are sloppy. And you know better than anyone what sloppiness can do."

Hallsy suddenly looked angry, for-real angry. "Say that to my face when you're not hiding behind a drone."

"Yeah, right," the drone said before banking sharply and racing back into the Sugar Bowl.

"Camp security is not my favorite department." Hallsy kicked at the dirt. "One day I might take one of those drones and make Avi eat it."

"Avi? Avi sounded like he had an accent," said Wyatt.

"Good ear. Former Mossad." Hallsy picked the bottle off the ground, wiped off the dirt, and screwed the top back on. "Israeli intelligence. He's our new head of security."

"New? Sounds like you've known each other for a long time," Wyatt said.

"I worked a bit with Avi's brother. Didn't go well." Hallsy looked off. "Anyway, don't let Avi's lack of charm get to you. He's very skilled and disciplined. But by nature, he's paranoid, deadly, and meticulous. Not a fun combo. Come on. There are people waiting to see you." Hallsy slung his pack onto his shoulders and headed downhill.

The further Wyatt descended into the Caldera, the more surreal it became. On the soccer field, he saw a slight, eleven-year-old girl in intense hand-to-hand combat with a bear of a man. He must have been two hundred and fifty pounds, and he was trying to club her with a baseball bat. As hard as he could. A group of children watched and Wyatt was pretty sure—or at least he hoped—that the man was her instructor, because he was swinging at her with all his might, trying to take her head off. And if he connected on a swing, with the size of her head, it might just work. And yet this girl was dodging the blows, lashing out at him with incredible speed, and handily beating him.

On the shooting range, a teenage boy looked on as an instructor showed him how to use a flame-thrower to incinerate a car. A couple rows over, a young girl launched grenades at a mud hut, like one you'd see in the middle of Afghanistan.

Wyatt now realized that what he had seen from the boat—the stuff he thought was mist or smoke rising above the ridgeline—was a mix of burning car and hand grenades.

As Wyatt and Hallsy approached a picnic area, they came upon a girl about Wyatt's age, with short hair and soft features. She was hovering over a rough-hewn wooden table. Sweat poured from her face and ran into her eyes as she focused on something that sat right in front of her; Wyatt imagined it was a knot or some kind of puzzle, but he couldn't see it.

"What's that girl doing?" he asked Hallsy.

"Let's take a look." Hallsy walked closer, motioning for him to follow. As they approached, a female came out from a shady spot. At first, Wyatt thought it was Dolly, she looked so similar. Then he realized this girl was older and clearly an instructor. Like Dolly, she was very pretty and in exceptional shape, but there was something harder about her. She walked directly toward the table, holding a stopwatch in her left hand, and did not turn to acknowledge Hallsy or Wyatt.

Hallsy motioned Wyatt to stop. "Can we approach?" he asked the instructor.

"Just be quiet," she said and motioned them forward. As she did this, Wyatt noticed that her right hand and part of her forearm were missing and the entire right side of her body was laced in fine scars. She wore wraparound sunglasses, and Wyatt was pretty sure her right eye was fake. Something about the way it didn't move.

"Rory," the instructor said to the girl intensely sweating at the table, "you have one minute left. How are you doing?"

Rory rubbed her temples and stared down, shaking her head. "Not good."

The instructor glanced at her watch, "You are getting close. Time to act. Or run."

"I know." The girl cradled her head, pouring sweat. "I'm thinking."

As they came closer, Wyatt could see that on the table in front of the girl sat a bomb. Yes, a bomb.

Wyatt didn't know anything about bombs, but even to his untrained eye, this one looked like it could do some serious damage. There were at least eight sticks of dynamite wrapped in cellophane, all duct-taped together, forming a tight bundle with blasting caps on the ends. Attached to the dynamite by a web of wires was an old cell phone that the girl had opened and the phone's guts hung out, but Wyatt could see the LED screen was working—forty seconds on the clock ticking down.

The instructor began to pace, visibly uncomfortable, and Wyatt could not help but look at her missing hand and her scarred face and the bomb sitting on the table and think that somehow one of her students had messed up this exact exercise before.

"Rory, you have thirty-five seconds to figure this out or we are dead." The instructor counted down, "Thirty-four . . . thirty-three . . thirty-two . . ."

Instinctively, Wyatt backed up. Hallsy put his hands on Wyatt's shoulders and stopped him. He didn't speak but gave Wyatt a look that said stay still.

Wyatt wanted to run. The instructor continued the countdown, "Fifteen . . . fourteen . . . C'mon, Rory. Figure it out or we are all dead."

The girl, Rory, was blinking hard, her eyes red and nervous, moving skittishly in her sockets.

"Seven . . . six . . ."

Wyatt strained against Hallsy's hands, pressing back. But Hallsy's resistance was firm.

"Hallsy, we gotta run," Wyatt pleaded.

"Shhh," hissed the instructor, as Rory angled a set of snips toward a mess of wires coming from the cell phone.

"Three . . . two . . ."

Rory turned her face away from the bomb.

"BAM!" A loud crack rattled the Caldera. A spurt of flame raced from the phone to the blasting caps. Wyatt wriggled away from Hallsy and threw himself onto the grass, burying his head and face in his arms, but the blast did not come.

"You're good," Hallsy said. "We put a little flash in it to make the deactivation drill a little more realistic. Nice dive, anyway."

Wyatt peaked out to see Rory trembling and crying weirdly without sound. The instructor stood behind the girl, slapping the table. "You're dead, Rory. Dead. You're not even lucky enough to have this—" She stuck the stub of her right forearm under her face for Rory to see. "You gotta put it together or you wind up in the dirt." She pitched the stopwatch into the ground.

Then the instructor glared at Wyatt, the skin on the left side of her face pink and fresh, the other side scarred like bark of a twisted oak. "You," she said to Wyatt. "Distract one of my girls again, and you're going to wish to god you had no mouth to speak from."

Her furious scowl shifted to Hallsy. "And you—"

Hallsy's hands went up. "I know. I know. My fault, Cass. Don't blame the new kid."

The hard scar tissue lacing her face softened slightly. A long stare and she nodded. She bent down, picked up the watch, and checked the time. "Rory, you can cry and jog, can't you? We're due at the obstacle course. Now."

Rory wiped her eyes and the two jogged away.

Wyatt pushed himself up from the grass, brushing dirt from his new old clothes, now stained green. "Who was that?"

Hallsy stepped over. "Remember Dolly, the girl on the hill?"

"The one with the rocket launcher?" Wyatt said. "How could I forget?"

"Cass is her sister—older sister. She'll be all right after a while. But for now, you might want to keep your distance. Let her cool down."

Wyatt sighed. He'd already made an enemy and he'd only been there a day.

Wyatt heard another buzzing sound approaching. "Is that drone back?"

"No, that one's a helicopter." Hallsy turned his head to the sky.

The buzzing turned into thudding, and Wyatt also detected a distinctly different kind of sound. "Is that music?"

"My bad," said Hallsy with a shake of his head. "Never should have told them to watch *Apocalypse Now*. Show-offs."

Just then, a helicopter rocketed out over the edge of the Caldera, gunmetal gray, speakers mounted to the landing struts, the gold-and-black Camp Valor logo painted on its doors and belly. It banked hard, descending toward the landing pad, kicking up dust and shaking trees. The music echoed through the Caldera. Wyatt finally placed it. Metallica. "Enter Sandman."

It was too loud to speak above the rotor wash, so Hallsy signaled for Wyatt to follow him to the landing pad. Campers from around the Caldera left their drills, instructors looking irked. Landing pad crowded, the airship descended. Rotors cut out. Touchdown.

The doors opened and six passengers emerged. Wyatt's first thought—did the pilot sit on a phone book or a booster seat?

She couldn't have been more than thirteen, blond hair spilling down when she took off her helmet, pink lip gloss, mouth blowing bubbles with pink chewing gum. Four of the five others were also teenagers, dressed like they'd just left a skate park—cutoffs, running shoes, tank tops, sunglasses, baseball hats turned backward, but they also wore tactical helmets with mounted night vision goggles (NVGs), vests webbed with ammunition, and sidearms. Over their shoulders, they carried AR-15s. Two girls and three boys. Wyatt guessed that most of them were only a few years older than him, but they emanated an air of coiled-up power and confidence. Wyatt had rarely seen this kind of cool self-assurance in adults, let alone teenagers. Given their movement and formation, Wyatt could see that they were guarding the sixth passenger, who emerged last.

The man was old. Late seventies. Tall, lean, craggy-faced, intense. He was dressed like a gym teacher in an '80s movie—golf shirt, too-tight shorts, running shoes, and socks hiked up to his knees. Wyatt might've snickered at him, but the old guy was no joke. He moved smoothly and deliberately, like he was stalking prey, no motion wasted. And his pale blue eyes settled on Wyatt, and instantly the teenagers seemed to draw bull's-eyes on Wyatt's forehead.

"Stand down." The Old Man nodded to his escorts. "Get some food while the bird refuels. You're going back out before it gets dark." The Old Man strode away from the helicopter and headed for Wyatt, his lips curling into a cowboy's smile as he approached. "Welcome."

CHAPTER 9

1984–2010
Miami, Florida

Upon hearing the news of the death of his friend, Wilberforce Degas's fragile psyche didn't just break, it imploded. The sheer volume of tragedies that occurred in his short life—and there would be more to come—would have felled almost anyone. But for a boy as complex and yet as delicate as Wilberforce, the string of tragedies didn't just crush him or knock him down, or set him back a few years, it rewired him.

Wil changed from the inside out. His entire thinking short-circuited, his history had become hardcoded, and his brain rewrote itself. The father he despised, the one who beat and humiliated him, became his hero, his mentor, his idol. Wil blamed all his sadness in life not on his father's actions but on the death of his father, which caused his separation from Chris Gibbs, from boarding school, from the outside world, from friendship of any kind. Wilberforce became obsessed with finding his father's murderer. Wil's instincts told him Pablo had been the killer, though he had no real proof. Still, Wil did his best to track Pablo's movements in Latin America in the press and an emerging network called the Internet. Only a few years after his father had been killed, it seemed as though Pablo had deserted Latin America and gone into hiding. Wil suspected in Eastern Europe.

Claudia Degas, once the toast of Central American society, became something like his nurse, servant, and only companion. Once Wil had sworn off the outdoors, his mother would venture out for him. Her doting, his only lifeline to the outside world. She brought him food, fresh clothing (which he rarely changed into), and, of course, video games.

"Something scary has happened to Wil," he heard his mother whispering to a girlfriend on the phone one afternoon. "It's like . . . his DNA has changed."

It was true that the boy was biologically different. He had always been inclined to stay indoors, but now he had developed a physical allergy to the sun. Never outwardly social, he lost all interest in friends whatsoever. He lost his sense of taste and smell. What he put in his mouth was nearly the same to him as what came out the other end. He got no real satisfaction or pleasure from eating or drinking, but he felt the compulsion to feed. And to consume.

Wil's favorite means of consumption was through the phone lines. From the increasingly dingy hotels he would occupy with his mother, Wil struggled to earn back his family's dwindling fortune and power, finding ways to leverage his particular skills and talents to make a buck and win some influence. He became a phone phreak, using tones to hack long-distance carriers and resell their services. But unlike other earlier phreaks like Steve Jobs and Steve Wozniak, Wil would place calls and then listen in. As a phone phreak and obsessive electronic gamer, Wil made a natural hacker. From the first time he hacked into a network, Wil figured out how to extract valuable information. And how to make money from it.

Wil would design video games that he released for free, planting malware that would act as a Trojan horse, granting him access to a player's hard drive and to the hardware itself. Wil would syphon funds, amass data, and blackmail. Wil loved to blackmail his victims. Among hacking circles and even the small group of hackers and game designers he began to employ to help him, he became known as the Glowworm. He never went outdoors, and like the glowworms that lived deep in the pitch-black recesses of caves in Mexico and South America, he used glittery things on the web—money, power, access—to trick his victims into wandering into a snare.

Eventually, the Glowworm's criminal activities required him to leave the United States and move his organization to Panama, where he ran his elicit gaming empire from a windowless skyscraper overlooking the beach. He had told the realtor who found the building he wanted the best views of the ocean, and right before he moved in, he blacked the windows out, cutting off all light and anything resembling a view. Behind the tower of glass and darkened windows, the Glowworm amassed an army of engineers, hackers . . . and, of course, some shady fellows with guns and masks. It was a veritable geek death squad. The goal of raising this dark horde was twofold: protection from the law and to exact revenge when he figured out who had killed his father.

If there was one element that seemed to keep the Glowworm human, it was the memory of Chris Gibbs and the understanding that even if human friendships were no longer interesting to him, they were at least possible. To remind himself of this, the Glowworm kept the 8-bit Nintendo video console etched with their initials with him everywhere he went.

Around 2010, Wil's long-suffering mother suddenly died. Wil had mentioned that he wanted fresh ground meat, so she had gone out to find him a suckling pig. His mother had found a pig and was chasing it to butcher when she fell over with a heart attack. This loss severed any real contact he had with humanity. With the death of his mother, the last tiny fragment of the little human boy inside Wil died too, and all of the cares and desires of a normal boy ceased to exist for him.

He was now beyond emotional pain or sadness, and his only desire was to inflict pain and sadness on others. He was also a practical creature, and the death of his mother presented the Glowworm with a problem. He still needed to eat. Or rather, to consume. And he needed something else. The Glowworm realized that if he were to remain in the darkness while inflicting true pain on the outside world, he needed something light and glittery that he could use to lure prey to him.

He needed a beautiful, shiny thing that, on the inside, concealed a sharp, barbed hook.

CHAPTER 10

June 2017
Camp Valor

The ancient mining shafts were damp, dark, musty, and lit by a string of old Edison lightbulbs. Drones buzzed past, weaving around Wyatt, Hallsy, and the Old Man like electric bats. They wound past myriad corridors, and storerooms for food and weapons. Wyatt noticed a recharging station within a hangar for the drones in one of the more cavernous rooms. The charging station consisted of a series of copper plates, upon which the drones would land and draw a charge.

They arrived at a large cellarlike room guarded by an old Newfoundland sound asleep on a large Persian rug, mouth open, drool oozing out. Along the far wall stood a long bookshelf, carefully crammed with many volumes of books, *National Geographic* magazines, and files. A dehumidifier bubbled in the corner. In the center of the room sat a large desk, covered in maps and papers and a laptop that had been pushed to the side.

"Those look familiar?" said the Old Man, motioning to the desk, where an antique brass lamp cast a puddle of warm light onto an open manila file stuffed with a copy of Wyatt's arrest report and other documentation about his life. His most recent mug shots sat on top of the stack of papers.

Wyatt had never seen this set of mug shots before—there were others he had seen, but this set taken after his last arrest was new to him. In the photos (two in total—one facing forward, one profile), he looked deranged, his long, tangled hair hanging around his sweaty face, framing a screw-you grin. Wyatt felt a tinge of embarrassment to think the Old Man had just been perusing his file and staring at Wyatt's douchey mug.

"Not my best day," Wyatt said.

"I agree," said the Old Man. "But that failure was not entirely your fault. We aren't born great drivers. You were born with great reflexes, but must be taught skills." The Old Man fished a pair of glasses off the desk and crossed to the far side of the room. "If you knew what you were doing, you might've gotten away."

Wyatt wasn't quite sure what to make of this.

"I'm sorry," he said. "Can you repeat that?"

"You're not much of a getaway driver," the Old Man said, smiling. He propped his glasses on his nose and scanned spines of the books on the shelf, evidently looking for a certain title. "And you weren't much better on foot. But we can help with that, too. Here we are."

The Old Man found the book he wanted. *Lord of the Flies.*

Wyatt looked to Hallsy. Was this old guy for real?

Hallsy shrugged. "For a kid who doesn't even have a driver's license, I was actually kind of impressed with how Wyatt drove."

"Good point, Sergeant." The Old Man opened the book and

thumbed through pages. "Shows promise." He stopped thumbing, licked his finger, and carefully turned a page, which looked exactly identical to every other page from the side, except on its surface there was a digital readout and a number pad. The Old Man keyed in a code. "Ruger, move!"

The Newfoundland rose and lumbered aside, just as the desk rotated to the side, revealing a hidden staircase.

The Old Man's knees creaked as he took the first step. "Down we go."

Down they went. Almost immediately, Wyatt could feel the air change. The staircase became drier the deeper they walked. There must have been an AC system somewhere. At the bottom of the stairs, a heavy metal bomb-proof door swooshed open. A head poked out with spiky dark hair with dyed tips. A pair of virtual reality goggles covered the man's eyes. He pushed them down to his neck and craned up at the threesome coming down the stairs.

The man didn't speak, he yelled, pointing directly at Wyatt. "He does not have clearance for this area." It was the voice from the drone, the voice of the Mossad agent with its distinctive accent. "I do not have his biometric data. This is a code 7.2 violation. Why do we have protocols if we do not keep them?" His pointer finger shifted to Hallsy. "And I told you this. You know better, you're—"

"Avi," the Old Man said calmly, "What do you need from the boy?"

"What do I need? I need c-o-m-p-l-i-a-n-c-e from the boy and . . ." His eyes grew wild. "From my so-called colleague." He glared again at Hallsy.

Hallsy held his hands up. "Guilty as charged, brother. Not a rules guy."

Avi shook his head in disgust, then turned back to Wyatt. "But since the boy is here." Avi tapped his lip, thinking. "Why don't I get his blood now? And his iris."

"Sure," said the Old Man. And without waiting, Avi removed an EpiPen-like device and stabbed Wyatt in the shoulder. Wyatt felt the pen grab a chunk of his flesh and retract.

"Djyayyyyy!"

"Done," said Avi, pressing gauze against the wound. "Now I have blood and a tissue sample." He reached for his pocket again. "Hold still, I need to get your eye."

"Don't touch my eyes!" Wyatt drew back, just as Avi removed something from his back pocket.

"Sorry, I mean your iris," said Avi. "Just need a photo. We can do it with a smartphone." And indeed he held an iPhone. "Hold still."

Wyatt forced himself to hold still. Avi held the smartphone camera in front of his eyes and scanned the iris. "Okay." He pocketed his phone and pointed to a door marked "S7." "If you need something, you can find me in there. But if you are going to disturb me, I ask that you know what you want before you come. I am very busy. I do not like to have my concentration broken. So you are welcome, but be prepared. No funny business."

Wyatt was thinking, Yeah, I'll visit you—uh—never.

Avi disappeared behind a door, shifting his virtual reality goggles from his neck to his face.

"He's an excellent chief of security. But there's a reason we keep him in a cave," the Old Man said. "Come on."

Wyatt followed him into an adjacent room, the "hot" room. It was like the "control room" out of a war movie—computer screens on the walls, the screens showing data flows, maps, and camera feeds.

The Old Man turned. "Wyatt, as you have no doubt surmised by now, Camp Valor is not your average summer camp."

"Campers running around with bazookas and flame throwers cleared that up for me," Wyatt said with a smug grin. "I get the feeling we won't be learning many arts and crafts." Wyatt laughed at his own joke and immediately regretted speaking.

"On the contrary." The Old Man leveled a serious look at Wyatt. "You will be learning arts and crafts. Martial arts mainly, and tradecraft. The only difference is the stakes for not learning here are absolutely catastrophic to you and to our country." The Old Man's look softened. "Would you like to know why?"

"Yes, sir," Wyatt said, feeling the "sir" come naturally.

"Good." The Old Man nodded to Hallsy, who clicked a remote at the screens. "Here is a little teaser we put together, to help you get a sense of what to expect here." Pump-up music played while the screens showed a video: a plane barrels across the sky, a teenage girl back-flips out of the plane with a knife in her teeth wearing a winged suit, a motorcycle is chased through a city, a boy—he must have been eleven—covered in blood, butchers and eats a sea lion on the edge of an ice floe while his mates scuba dive beneath the ice.

The Old Man paced. "Camp Valor is a top-secret training facility. You will not find it on a map, and no aircraft—except our own—will even fly overhead. Outside of our ranks, our existence is known only to the president of the United States, the director of the CIA, the SecDef—or secretary of defense—and a few partners of ours in the special forces community."

"Why the secrecy?" Wyatt asked. "What's the training for?"

"Good question," the Old Man said. "At Valor we identify at-risk youths who have the right mix of intelligence, talents, taste for danger, grit, and"—the Old Man paused and chose his next word carefully—"motivation . . ."

Hallsy chimed in, "Meaning, what Valor offers you is a chance to get out of jail free. We want young boys and girls here who understand that failure is not an option. That's what he means by motivation."

"Thank you, Hallsy," said the Old Man. "Yes. We find people with the right mix of skills and motivation to become assets for the U.S. government. And then we train them to do that."

"Excuse me." Wyatt suddenly felt timid. "Can I ask a question?"

"Sure."

"Isn't an asset like a"—Wyatt paused to think back to a hazy discussion of economics in middle-school Government class—"couch or your house or a financial instrument . . . or a bull-dozer, isn't that an asset?"

"Yes, those are assets. But in our business, so is a spy, or an assassin, or an operator capable of carrying out varied assignments. Someone who, when trained and supported properly, can be of vital use to his or her country."

"An assassin?" Wyatt asked, involuntarily stepping back, heart rate rising. "You mean I'll have to kill people?"

"We didn't say that." The Old Man held up his hands in a mollifying gesture. "Not now."

"Then what will I be asked to do?" Wyatt could feel himself panicking, taking another step back.

"You'll do whatever we ask." Hallsy leaned in and blocked the door.

"Let's not get ahead of ourselves," the Old Man said. "Either of you." He gave Wyatt and Hallsy pointed glances. "Sergeant Hallsy, why don't you describe the summer program to Wyatt, to give him a little more idea of what to expect?"

"Sure. The summer will be divided into three phases: Indoctrination, Live Learning, and Reality-Based Instruction and Practice, or RIP.

"Phase One, Indoctrination, is exactly what it sounds like. It means we get you processed and indoctrinated into camp life. Because you were in solitary confinement, you missed Indoctrination." Hallsy nodded in the direction of Avi's lair. "Which is why Avi had his knickers in a twist."

"Yes, and you will have some catching up to do, but," the Old Man said, "if you're capable of learning at the rate we expect, that should not be a problem. We'll get you indoctrinated while you are engaged in Phase Two. . . ."

"Phase Two, or Live Learning," Hallsy continued, "is when we begin to prepare you mentally and physically to operate while providing basic weapons and combat training along the way. It's similar to basic training in the military but deeply accelerated, and we emphasize the learning component. We are not just 'training' you tactically but teaching you how to think like an operator." Hallsy paused for emphasis. "We can teach you how to complete almost any task, but we want you to understand why and be able to solve problems on your own. Does that make sense?"

"I think so," Wyatt said. "It's kind of like what my dad used to say, like the difference between teaching someone how to fish, not just how to eat."

Hallsy grinned. "Exactly. So that's the Learning component. The 'Live' component refers to environment. First, we train you within the confines of the island and then we put you out in live environments where we begin to remove the safety nets. All the while, we will work hard to make this training safe, but make no mistake . . . we have lost campers." Hallsy paused to let this sink in. "Live Learning starts tomorrow. Let me ask you a question. Wyatt, are you familiar with the SEAL BUD/S program? And the activities conducted during their Hell Week?"

"I'm not even sure what BUD/S stands for," Wyatt said, a little embarrassed. "Should I?"

"BUD/S stands for Basic Underwater Demolition Training/SEAL," the Old Man said. "And it's better you don't have a reference point. Suffice to say, our program is equally as challenging, perhaps more so. During our Hell Week, it's likely your class will be reduced by half at least."

Wyatt shrugged, nonplussed. "No offense, sir. I just came from hell. It's hard to imagine anything worse than what I just experienced."

Wyatt noticed the Old Man and Hallsy share a smirk. "Well," Hallsy said. "Should be no problem for a tough guy like you."

"I'm sorry, sir, if I gave the wrong impression," Wyatt said as his mind flashed back to solitary confinement. "I didn't mean to say I am tough. It's just hard to imagine something more, well, hellish than what I just experienced. I'm never going back."

"Fair enough," the Old Man nodded. "And if you perform, we'll do everything we can to make sure you don't go back. At Valor, we will challenge you, push you, and shape you. You will grow in infinitely more ways than you did in the CYDC. Or locked in a hole." The Old Man went on, "Those experiences are meaningless. The suffering at Valor has purpose. Should you make it past Hell Week, you will be both stronger and more capable than you ever thought possible. And you will begin to form unbreakable bonds with your fellow Valorians."

Wyatt raised a hand. "What do you mean 'make it'?"

The Old Man looked at Hallsy. "Did you tell Wyatt about quitting?"

"No," Hallsy said. "Technically, you are only a candidate

until you pass the Hell Week. As such, you are free to quit at any time. To quit, all you have to do is sound a horn and camp will end for you. You can do it anytime, even after Hell Week, though once campers make it through that, they rarely drop out. Like Navy SEALs, or any elite military training program, we only want people who want to be here—and want it as badly as we did.

"Wait," Wyatt said, "you were campers once? Both of you?"

"Of course." The Old Man smiled mischievously. "All of the instructors were."

Wyatt blurted out the question burning in his mind, "Does that mean both of you have been to jail?" Seeing their surprised reactions, he rephrased, "I mean, were ever arrested or . . . in trouble?"

Hallsy and the Old Man looked at each other. "The details of how we came to Valor are not relevant," the Old Man said. "And they're confidential. If you want to learn about us, the only way you can do so is by getting the proper security clearance that gives you access to that information. But for now, what's critical to know is that we will never ask you to do something we haven't done ourselves. Remember that, Wyatt. Because you will be asked to do some scary things."

Wyatt nodded.

"And it all has a purpose," the Old Man said. "All of your training ladders up to Phase Three: Reality-Based Instruction and Practice. Or RIP. This is when we teach you how to become an operator. We will give you high-level skills and tradecraft training and work to put it to action. You'll learn key skills known only to members of Navy SEALs, DELTA, and the CIA. Should you be invited back next year, you would attend Group-B, learn higher skills, and the following summer, you'd move into Group-A."

"Group-A?" Wyatt said. "What is that?"

"Group-A is where you want to be," Hallsy said. "The As are almost entirely operational for the duration of the summer and the school year, meaning they run missions repeatedly and only return to Valor for brief rest, equipment fixes, and any training augmentation that can occur."

The Old Man added, "You may have noticed them with me earlier—the group that flew me in on the helicopter. Those were all members of Group-A, the most elite warriors we have here."

Wyatt recalled the bubble gum–chewing pilot who looked like she needed a stack of phone books to sit on to fly the chopper. The Old Man continued, "This summer, there are five As in total—three boys and two girls—and they are in constant rotation, usually deployed in small teams, almost always in RIP phase. As Hallsy mentioned, the goal of every camper here, and our goal as instructors, is to make sure you make it to Group-A. And we will show you why." The Old Man nodded and Hallsy clicked the remote again.

The screens in the Hot Room showed a map of the world becoming increasingly studded with red dots. Hallsy pointed to the screens. "The U.S. government and our allies track tens of thousands of potential plots daily: from terrorist cells to gangs to cyber-criminals to rogue nations. Occasionally, we identify a threat, or a target, or a questionable group."

The screen flashed to a shot of a high school with grainy surveillance footage showing two shadowy teenagers. One, a nerdy kid with a bag, meeting another student wearing a University of Michigan sweatshirt outside the school.

"The kid with the bag is part of a cell we had tried to infiltrate. The kid with the University of Michigan shirt was from last year's Group-A." And then he added cryptically, "A very high performer."

The video was grainy security footage to begin with, but to Wyatt it seemed like a digital blur had been placed over the face of the boy with the U of M shirt. "Is the boy's face intentionally blurred?" Wyatt asked.

"Good observation," the Old Man said. "Yes, that young man has moved on from Valor and is now fully operational with another three-letter agency. Once again, until you get clearance, we can't show you his identity."

Wyatt nodded and kept watching. In the video, the halls are filled with students. The nerdy kid carrying the bag makes a move to remove something from it, and the other student strikes him lightning fast. So fast that no one sees. The nerdy kid appears to pass out and falls directly into the arms of the boy in the U of M sweatshirt, the boy who hit him, the boy from Group-A. Another student, a girl, comes up quickly and takes the bag. Her face wasn't blurred and Wyatt immediately recognized her as the pilot. "She's the pilot from earlier."

"Yes," Hallsy said. "She was an A last year but did not graduate, so she's back again.

The girl sprints out of the school with the bag. The nerdy kid who had the bag originally is dragged toward an office, where Hallsy steps out, dressed like a teacher, and ushers them into a room, presumably for medical help. The door closes, and the screen cuts to a shot of the bag in a safe room. The camera angles into the bag. It's filled with automatic weapons and hand grenades.

"Notice the flawless execution. The teamwork," Hallsy said. "None of the bystanders noticed the action. The three operators had removed the threat in a matter of seconds."

Wyatt marveled at the swiftness. It was true—no one in the crowded hallway was aware of what happened.

The screen cut to black. "That was a simple mission," Hallsy said, "but that event, had it continued," Hallsy paused, "could have resulted in the death of dozens, maybe hundreds of students. But we stopped it, broke up the cell. And no one knows about it." Hallsy looked straight at Wyatt. "Missions like those are why we are here."

"You see, Wyatt," the Old Man joined in. "Some threats are simply better dealt with by one or a handful of teenagers, like the ones you see here, who are better suited than even well-trained adult operators or the police or the FBI. The techniques Valor uses are varied but extremely potent and, when executed seamlessly, effective. Sometimes, there are plots carried out by children and teenagers who operate under the radar in schools and colleges here and abroad, and the only way to get close to those kinds of targets is to become one of them. Other times, a cell or threat is comprised of adults, and the best way to infiltrate it is with a child who will not draw attention."

"And sometimes we're just better," Hallsy added. "Sometimes the best person for a job—period, regardless of age—is right here on this island."

The Old Man nodded. "Often the right solution is pairing resources with the proper attitude. Wyatt . . . we like rule breakers, people who, at an early age, think differently. The crazy ones who do things their own way. The ones who bend the world to them. That's what we have here at Valor. That's who we want."

"Sounds like criminals," Wyatt blurted out.

"Yes," the Old Man smiled, "just like you, and perhaps most of us at Valor. Isn't that right, Sergeant Hallsy?"

Hallsy crossed his massive tattooed arms. "I'd say there's an outlaw gene that runs in all of us."

Before leaving the cave complex, Wyatt had been issued a rucksack, sleeping bag, emergency thermal blanket, wool sweater, tin plate, topographical map, fork, flashlight, matches, compass, basic toiletries, and water bottle. He slung the pack on his back and followed Hallsy out of the Caldera back toward base camp.

Once again, they missed a meal, but Mum had been warned ahead of time, so she left foot-long submarine sandwiches with turkey, gravy, stuffing, and cranberry sauce all jammed into hero rolls. Hallsy slipped his sandwich into his own rucksack and when Wyatt did the same, Hallsy stopped him. "I can wait to eat. You can't."

"I'm okay to wait," Wyatt said.

"No. It's already lights out. You and the rest of the candidates are supposed to be in bed."

Wyatt unwrapped his dinner, and as quickly as he could without hurting his tooth, he ate the giant sandwich.

"Hallsy," Wyatt said as they headed toward the cabins. "Does my mother know I'm all right?"

"She thinks you're still in jail. . . . So you tell me, does she think you're all right?"

Wyatt didn't answer. As they neared the cabins, he saw Dolly and Cass standing in the middle of the field with another boy, conferring. The boy looked to be about sixteen or seventeen, with jet-black hair and pale skin, and he watched Wyatt carefully as he and Hallsy made their way toward the cabins marked "C Boys" and "C Girls."

"Sergeant Hallsy, is that the last Group-C candidate?" the boy called out.

"Yes. Why don't you come get him settled," Hallsy said, and the boy started jogging their way.

Wyatt nodded at the boy and said to Hallsy, "I thought it was lights out."

"Dolly and Hud are the 'Blues' for Group C."

"What's a 'Blue'?"

"A Blue is like a team captain or an officer. Dolly is the Blue for the girls, and Hud—short for Hudson—is the Blue for the boys. They are your contemporaries and are part of the same group, but they attended a more junior program at Valor last year. So they know the ropes more or less. And we give them some extra privileges and responsibilities, like role call, which is why they're still up. Most important, Blues are meant to help you—especially at first. When you start the summer, everyone needs help. Isn't that right, Hud?" Hallsy asked as Hud came jogging up. "You are here to help?"

"Yes, sir. Of course," Hud said. Wyatt now noticed Hud had one green eye and one blue eye. They were wolf eyes and they narrowed in on Wyatt. "Follow me," Hud said and set off toward the cabin. Wyatt walked next to Hud. Beyond him in the distance, he could see Dolly walking back to her cabin. She looked too beautiful for Valor.

"Do you know what she did to get here?" Wyatt asked Hud when they were out of Hallsy's earshot.

Hud's two-tone wolf eyes flashed at Wyatt. "That's not something you ask. Not day one." Hud's eyes shifted down to the knife on Wyatt's belt. "And it's too early for that, too. You don't deserve that until you make it through Hell Week and qualify."

"I didn't ask for this. It was given to me."

"Exactly." Hud strode up onto the porch and pushed the door open. The cabin had looked quiet from the outside but now Wyatt saw it was packed with bunks and teeming with activity. Only a quarter of the boys in the cabin were in their sleeping bags. The rest were hanging about.

A big Middle Eastern kid was playing dice with a wiry, backwoods boy. The pale kid was shirtless, had white-blond hair, and had a tattoo of Kentucky on his right pec. A black kid, who looked like he could squat the entire cabin, was doing push-ups. And almost everyone was talking. Wyatt did not see an open bunk.

"Where do I sleep?"

"Floor," Hud said and then shouted, "Listen up!" Hud walked toward the middle of the room and everyone quieted down, everyone except an Asian boy who appeared to be bragging to a pair of slack-jawed, scrawny twins.

"So they came up on me, but I was in my Honda, the one I had set up to drift. I got my Gat low in my seat like this . . ." The Asian kid signaled like he had a gun held low, telling his story.

Hud walked up behind him. "Conrad, I said listen up."

"Yeah, when I'm done." Conrad motioned him away and kept on with his story. "So I had like the choice to run or—"

Hud put his hand on the boy's shoulder. Conrad shot up to his feet and spun around. "Why you up in my grill, man?" Conrad raised his fist to punch, but Hud's move was fast. A punch to the neck, and the kid just dropped, unconscious at first, but then choking trying to breathe.

Hud placed a foot on him to pin him to the floor but did not look down. Hud spoke quietly, "Half of you won't be here tomorrow, so I don't care if you stay up all night, ruining yourself. But I want my sleep. 'Cause I'm going to need it. We all will, if we want to make it to day two, let alone the end of the summer. Or to make Top Camper, which I will have you all know now is my prize to lose. So you've been warned."

Hud glanced around the cabin as the candidates hurried back into their beds. "Thank you." Hud reached down and yanked the sleeping bag from Conrad's bed and threw it on the floor. "There you go, Wyatt. You have a bunk."

CHAPTER 11

Spring 2010
Beirut, Lebanon

Raquel liked her kibbeh raw—ground lamb, spices, bulgur, a drizzle of oil over top, a couple shakes of salt, served with slices of raw onion and pickled turnip. She was only nine, but it was her favorite dish. Relatives would kid her about it. "Raquel looks like a doll. And she loves raw meat!" And she did look like a doll, except cuter. She was a true Lebanese blonde, though only Lebanese on her father's side. On her mother's, she was Syrian.

In the afternoons her great-uncle Samir, who had raised her after her parents died, would instruct a waiter to set up a table for her on the sidewalk outside of his restaurant, Phoenicia, one of the culinary gems in Beirut. Raquel would eat alone, enjoying a partial view of the Mediterranean, the quiet street, and fading sun. Perfect.

And that is where she was one afternoon when the tourists rounded the corner. Japanese? Raquel thought. No, Korean. Two men, one woman. The men carried big cameras. All were old, a little gray, and chattering away like schoolchildren. Or ducks. Raquel thought they sounded like ducks. She smiled, imagining them as ducks in a poultry yard, and a little girl lurking behind them with a cleaver.

They saw her smile and melted. They approached. In highly broken English smattered with some Arabic, which they rapidly Googled on their phones, the three attempted to explain themselves. The old lady took the lead as ambassador, explaining that she was a grandmother and she had granddaughters back in Korea that were just like her. Likely not just like her, Raquel might have pointed out if she'd cared to.

The old lady took one of the men by the arm and said that he was her husband and the other guy was her brother-in-law and explained that they were food bloggers back in Korea.

"Not profession," her brother-in-law pointed out with a chuckle. "Hobby. Passion hobby. We foodie."

The little girl batted eyelashes at them. And the old lady finally got around to asking what they wanted from her. With exceeding politeness, she asked if they could photograph Raquel eating kibbeh for their blog. She promised they'd write about it, and people in Korea would be very interested in seeing her eating kibbeh.

As the old woman spoke, the little girl imagined a duck with graying eyebrows quacking and quacking until it gets its head lopped clean off. Fewapppp! A spurt of blood and the duck head does a circle in the air, mouth still quacking. Raquel smiled slyly and giggled, and the brothers with the cameras and the old lady all took this to mean it was okay to go ahead and snap a few pictures.

Cameras came up and trigger fingers came down. Repeatedly. Raquel felt every shutter click as a bullet tearing through her. Gunned down. Strafed. Shot to pieces. Worse with those giant lenses, she imagined eyeballs telescoping through the air to touch her and roll around on her skin, like slimy marbles. She wanted to scream, to attack, to pick up her fork and jam it in the old lady's ear. Her hand trembled, itching to strike, but the smile on Raquel's face stayed sweet as a bowl of rice pudding.

The photo shoot only lasted seventy seconds, and the cameras stopped. The trio bowed many times, gave many-many thanks, and then made their biggest mistake yet. The capper. The coup de grâce. The old lady's brother-in-law drew out a wad of Lebanese pounds from his pocket and dropped a couple bills on the table. A tip. The girl scowled.

More bows. Polite apologies. "Many thank." The three then entered the restaurant and proceeded to order up a feast— hummus, kafta, frog legs, makdous, sujuk, and, of course, raw kibbeh. They photographed every dish. Up close. *Many time*. A beautiful night. No doubt about it.

When the Koreans left, the sun had just set and none of them noticed the kibbeh sitting untouched at the table where the girl had been earlier. Only a couple flies buzzed around the untouched meat. The fork was still speared through the onion. But the knife was missing.

The following morning three Korean tourists, a husband and wife and the brother-in-law, were found murdered in their hotel suite, their throats slit while they slept. All of their money, their computers, their phones, and expensive camera equipment had been taken. This initially led investigators to conclude that robbery was the motive behind the killing; however, one curious detail confused the case. The two male victims had been stabbed in the eyes as they died.

The murders made international headlines and the case drew

attention from Korean politicians who placed considerable pressure on the Lebanese police and intelligence community to solve the murders and bring justice. This shouldn't have been too difficult a thing to do. The killer or killers had entered the hotel room using a stolen keycard. The hotel had cameras in every hallway, in the lobby and on the grounds, but when investigators reviewed the video on the hotel's server, they saw it had been hacked. Within an hour of the first reports of the murders, someone had hacked into the hotel's network and deleted twenty-four hours of digital surveillance. All signs pointed to a state actor or terrorist group.

Raquel once again sat in the fading sunlight outside her great-uncle's restaurant, calmly eating her raw kibbeh with onions and pickled turnips. This afternoon was little different than others except she had a brand new Korean-made computer and was shopping online when the screen to the computer no longer responded to her commands. A message box appeared: *Glow-worm12 wants to be your friend and has sent you a message. Click to see.*

She clicked. A video file opened, one she had never seen and one she hoped she'd never see. It was security footage from the hotel that revealed a nine-year-old killer, footage Raquel had learned from the news shows had been mysteriously deleted. She saw herself in the hotel hallway, then entering the Koreans' room. Fear prickled through her; she grabbed the laptop and prepared to throw it in the sea. Then she saw a new message: *Don't be scared. I deleted the files to protect you.*

Raquel: *Who are you?*
Glowworm12: *Your biggest fan . . . I have been looking for someone like you my entire life.*

Raquel: *Where are you?*

A pause.

Glowworm12: *Want to see?*
Raquel: *Yes.*

The camera on her computer activated, a chat window opened on her screen and she found herself looking into darkness, and then a figure approached the screen.

CHAPTER 12

June 2017
Camp Valor

Wyatt glanced down at his wrist: 5:25 a.m. Still damp, not quite light, and painfully cold. Wyatt shivered on the beach with twenty-five other camper candidates, all part of Group-C, all wearing bathing suits. All recently yanked from dreams of summers back home—Sunday-morning cartoons, pickup baseball, video games, lazy days avoiding a summer-reading list. Now they stared at icy water, calm in the breaking dawn.

Hallsy paced out on the dock in the swirling fog, a long carbon-fiber paddle in his hand. "All you have to do is focus on what you are doing right now and you will make it through this program and have a chance to make history. It's that simple. Stay focused on the now. If you think about what will happen ten hours from now, you'll fail. If you're thinking an hour ahead, you'll fail. Don't even think ten minutes or even ten seconds ahead. Just give me a hundred percent of now, and I'll tell you when you can let up. Do that and you'll do great. If you start to question why you are here and if you can make it—if you think about the road ahead at all—you will be fighting two battles: one now and one later. Let the other battle wait. You'll get there soon enough. This is a mental game first and foremost. Lead with the mind, and the body will follow."

Hallsy turned to face the cove. Staff floated in canoes, bundled up, breath steaming, waiting for the swim to begin.

"Before we start, I want you to hear an admonition about reputation," Hallsy said. "Reputation is everything. It is built starting today. 'But this is a secret place,' you may be saying to yourself, 'so why does reputation matter? No one back home will know if I quit or cheat or don't give that one hundred percent.' The truth is, you will know, and I will know, and your fellow Group-Cs and the Bs and the As will know. Reputation always matters. What you do here in the next three months will follow you for the rest of your life. Whether you go on to join the SEAL teams, DELTA, or the CIA, or enter the private sector, how you behaved at Valor—among those who know you—will define you. This is when our reputations are created. Legends are made here. Remember that."

The boys and girls lined up on the beach, seeming to mull over the sentiment and the idea of reputation and then spit the whole concept back out.

"How 'bout his ass takes a swim," the big Arab-looking kid who had been playing craps said under his breath. Snickers followed. Wyatt noticed the kid with the Kentucky tattoo was so thin he almost looked skeletal in the morning chill, already shivering, his bones rattling under his skin. But he was smiling.

Hallsy didn't hear. "All right." He glanced at his watch. "Enough talk. Time to get to work. We are going to start the day with a dip in the water—a two-mile swim to Flint Rock to start the morning."

"Two miles?" Wyatt heard another camper say. "That's like . . . far, man."

"Got a problem with that? If so, you can go back to jail right now." Hallsy stared back. "You don't like this, you're welcome to go chill in your cell. Who wants that?"

No one spoke. "Okay, then. Those of you who have not qualified, this will serve as your swim test. Later, we will assign swim buddies. For now, you are not allowed to assist fellow campers. Okay, let's get wet." Hallsy stepped from the dock onto a paddleboard, a massive gorilla of a man seeming to glide out onto a cloud of smoke.

The frozen campers shared awkward glances. Was this really starting now? In this icy water?

"How about I make it easy for you," Hallsy said, dipping his paddle and shooting the board out toward the open water. "Last one to the rock has to do the swim twice."

Campers surged. Arms, legs, bodies crashed through the steely surface. Wyatt's skin stung as if it were being jabbed with needles. His heart hammered.

It was hard at first for Wyatt not to think about how far two miles really was. Had he ever swum that far? He was freezing. Would the water get warmer? Would every day be like this? Would every morning start with water so cold he wanted to scream?

Stop it, Wyatt told himself. Stop thinking.

Just reach, pull, kick, breathe, and repeat. Reach, pull, kick, breathe, reach, pull, kick, breathe. Swim. One stroke at a time.

It was working. Focus on the now, he reminded himself. *Don't think a stroke further ahead.*

Two of the campers decided they'd rather go back to jail

before they reached Flint Rock. One of the first two to quit was Conrad, the big talker from the night before. He and another boy were pulled dripping out of the cold water, plopped into canoes, draped with towels, and given a large pill and warm liquids to drink. Then their hands were cuffed and they were whisked back to the island.

Wyatt tried not to look at the quitters. He wasn't sure he wanted to stay, but he sure as heck didn't want to go back to the CYDC. Reach, pull, kick, breathe. Repeat. Until the shore materialized, and he pulled himself up onto a large, forty-foot stretch of bedrock, the beach at Flint Rock. The beach faced the rising sun and was now warmer. He lay chest down on the rock, letting the heat rise up into him. He was too cold and tired to do anything but catch his breath and shiver.

"You swim better than you drive."

Wyatt glanced up at Hallsy, peering down from his paddle-board. "You swim almost as good as the Blues." Hallsy nodded to Hud and Dolly, the only other two candidates to beat Wyatt to the island. Hud was by far the strongest candidate in the group and, not surprisingly, he had been the first to reach the rock, followed by Dolly. "Keep up the hard work," Hallsy said, padd-ling back out toward the incoming swimmers, "and you just might make it through the rest of the day."

When Wyatt's teeth finally stopped chattering and his mus-cles loosened, he sat upright to watch campers arriving at the island. Once again, another candidate quit. She was pulled out not far from shore, given a blanket, the liquids, and the pill to take before the cuffs were clapped on.

Wyatt turned to the tall athletic girl sitting next to him. "What's that pill they gave her?" he asked.

"It's to make us forget."

"Forget?" The voice came from the large black boy who

had been doing push-ups the night before. "How do they do that?"

"I don't know. A drug. They make you take it so that when you get back to your life, this place is only a dim memory. Like a dream."

"Damn." The black kid shook his head. "That ain't gonna be me."

"Me either," said the girl.

"I'm Ebbie." The black kid stuck out his hand.

"Annika," said the athletic girl.

The kid with the Kentucky tattoo raised a finger. "Sanders. And I don't know how y'all got here, but I'm here 'cause I got a taste for driving nice cars that other people pay for."

"Your name is Sanders? And if I got it right you are from Kentucky?" Ebbie asked incredulously. "Like Colonel Sanders?"

The kid nodded. "KFC all the way, baby."

"And who are you?" Ebbie said, turning to Wyatt. "Everybody's been wondering about the boy who got the personal escort from the Old Man and Hallsy."

"Name is Wyatt. And I'm no one. I don't know why I'm here."

"Lemme solve that for you," Ebbie said. "You here 'cause you're bad. And expendable . . . now lemme ask a question. After all these fools have quit, who is gonna be the poor sucker to come in last and have to swim back?"

Turns out, it wasn't even close. The last waterlogged swimmer crawled up on the rock long after the second to last. The boy was very tall, maybe six-four, Arab or Afghani. He had a huge hooked nose and large hands.

He lay on the rock gasping. Hallsy walked over. Everyone was thinking the same thing. Would he have to swim back? Or would they cut him a break? Clearly, he had lost the race to

Flint Rock not because of effort, but because he could barely swim.

Hallsy let him catch his breath before he got down on his haunches and said, "How you doing, Samy? Didn't think you'd make it. You all right?"

The big Arab squinted, frowning a little, face plastered on the rock. "Yeah. Perfect, boss. Good to go," the kid said in a mingled accent of Far East and American ghetto slang.

"Good, 'cause you got another two-miler." Hallsy rose, looking back in the direction of base camp, hidden behind islands in the archipelago. "I'll give you fifteen minutes to rest up and get warm. Then it's back in."

Samy sniffed, seemed to taste something in his mouth. He stood, his skin blue and his joints creaking, clearly in pain. He shot a snot rocket from his nose and then looked back toward base camp. "Why rest?"

"I'm sorry?" said Hallsy.

"Sir, camels don't need no rest." Samy pounded his chest.

"Camel, huh?" Hallsy said. "You don't mind being called a camel?"

"I don't mind callin' myself a camel. They badass animals. Watch." Samy splashed into the water. A slow breath and a slow stroke, and he started back again.

Hallsy clapped his hands. "All right. No rest for the camel."

While Samy swam, the remainder of Group-C paddled in canoes, nice and easy, cruising back. "Slow it down, guys," the staff coached them. "You'll want to conserve your energy."

Wyatt couldn't take his eyes off Samy, floundering behind, straining to stay afloat, sloppily moving forward. Back at the beach by base camp, Group-C squeezed out push-ups and sit-ups and up-downs while Samy half-drowned in the water somewhere between the shore and Flint Rock. Minutes passed. Arms numbed. Legs stiffened. The sand calisthenics were worse than the cold water, or so the campers imagined. They moaned and groaned, their willpower ground down with the sand and sun like milled wheat.

The sun inched across the sky. No Samy. Grumbling rippled among the campers. "If he can't swim, what is he doing here?"

"What are we waiting for?"

"Where is he?"

Squinting up from a push-up, Wyatt saw Hallsy slide into the cove, drifting on the surface of the water. A body splashed alongside Hallsy's board. The kid had made it. Or he had almost made it.

Less than two hundred yards from shore, the big kid began to sink. Arms slipped under. His head disappeared. Hallsy leaned over and peered into the calm surface. Samy bobbed up again. And sunk and bobbed again. This motion worried Wyatt.

Wyatt's father had taught Wyatt how to swim at an early age. And not just how to stay afloat, but proper technique. It was one of the things they did together. His father would be gone for months at a time driving his rig, but when his father was home for short periods during the summer, he would take Wyatt hunting and fishing back home. Wyatt took to the muddy rivers and warm reservoirs of Millersville County like a river rat. It was hard to peel him out of the water. Wyatt's father had also taught him some basic lifeguarding techniques; likely he was worried about Cody and wanted Wyatt to know what to do if someone was drowning. Watching Samy now, and observing the way he struggled in the water, Wyatt thought it looked like Samy had a cramp. But he wouldn't quit.

Wyatt could hear Hallsy tempting him to give in, "Brother,

just grab the board and you're done. Make it easy on your-self. . . ."

But the kid wouldn't.

The seriousness of the situation attracted even the attention of the Old Man, who came down from the porch of the Mess Hall and walked out on the beach to join the rest of Group-C.

"Okay. Listen up," he said. "We have not yet assigned swim buddies, but that boy is having trouble. He's already swum four miles, nearly, at his point. He's passed his swim test. If you want this boy to continue in Group-C, I'm going to let you help him to shore."

Wyatt scrambled up to his feet. A hand grabbed his arm, holding him back.

"Wait," Hud said. "He can barely swim. He should be cut. He's a liability to all of us. He'll slow us down."

Wyatt looked to the Old Man for help.

"Your Blue has a point," the Old Man said. "You both need to figure out what it means if you help."

Hud held firm to Wyatt's arm. "It sucks, but let him wash out now. It's the hard choice but the right choice."

Wyatt glanced out. Out in the water, Samy thrashed like a fish on a line.

Wyatt nodded. "You're right. He'll slow us down."

Hud released his grip.

Wyatt waited a beat. "But so will I at times." He sprinted down the length of the dock and dove in, swimming as hard and fast as he could.

He reached Hallsy's board but could not see Samy. Wyatt dove down and groped for Samy, who was hovering under the surface, gripping his cramped leg, trying to straighten it. He looped his arms under Samy's chest and pulled him up. They breached the surface.

"Let go of me! I ain't done."

"He's a camper," Hallsy called down from his board. "He can help you. It's okay."

Samy seemed to process, nod, and sink again. Wyatt kicked and tugged, and dragged the big frozen boy, who was stiff and still cramping, back to the beach. Wyatt felt another body beside him in the water, helping to pull Samy in to shore. Dolly.

Others joined, including Hud. They carried Samy up the beach and plopped him in the sand. Mackenzie brought him a warming blanket and helped straighten his leg and stretch out the cramp. The boy's body had turned blue, his lips a deep shade of purple.

"You have five minutes to rest," Hallsy said as he walked down the length of the dock carrying the paddleboard.

The Group-C members congregated in the sand. Wyatt nodded at Dolly. "Thanks."

"Hud was right. Next time you want to play hero, think of the group first." Dolly's reaction surprised Wyatt.

She scowled. "Failure like that on a mission will get us all killed. He needed to get himself there."

"He just needed a little push at the end," Wyatt said.

"This is day one. If he can't do it now, you think he'll be ready for day ninety, when things really get hard? You think you're helping, but you just bought that kid more hurt. And us too." Dolly turned and walked down the beach to where Hud was waiting. They shared a water bottle.

"Who cares?" Wyatt heard Hud say to Dolly, still glaring at him. "They'll both be gone soon."

"Your swim buddy is also your land buddy and your air buddy and your everything buddy. Your swim buddy is not just your friend, not just your family, your swim buddy is far more important to you," the Old Man said. "Your swim buddy is you in another body. You are responsible for each other and you will look out for each other. If your swim buddy screws up, that means you screwed up. If they get lost, you get lost. You don't have to like who you are paired with, you have to love them like your life depends on it. Because it does."

Hud raised his hand. "What if your swim buddy quits?"

"No one likes to see that happen, but it does and will. If your swim buddy quits, one of the staff will pair you with someone else."

The Old Man ended his speech by assigning everyone a buddy. And as he could have guessed, Wyatt was paired with Samy.

Hud was right about Samy slowing him down. After five minutes of rest, Samy was still shaking from the cold and unable to jog. So Wyatt had to help the big kid up to the top of the Caldera and back. They came in last and exhausted. The punishment this time was fifteen up-downs before lunch. Wyatt checked the clock as they filed into the Mess Hall. At the start of the morning, twenty-five Group-C candidates had splashed into the water. It wasn't quite noon, and only eighteen were left.

Mum's warm lunch was supposed to offer reprieve—fried fish, cornbread, soup, and salad. Some kids just stared at the plates, zombified. Faces in a hover, jaws moving, forks shoveling, mouths slurping and gobbling, but no one speaking . . . lunch at Valor.

Wyatt found himself at a table with Ebbie, Sanders, and Annika. Not that he was paying attention. He was facedown in his soup when he heard a chair pull up beside him. Samy plopped down across from Wyatt. His skin had returned from bluish to light brown. Samy didn't say anything, just held up a fist for a bump. It hovered. A big-ass fist, brown and scaly.

Wyatt's eyes shifted over to Dolly, who sat across the room with her sister, Cass, and Hud and Rory. Rory had been part of Group-B, but after the bomb fiasco was sent back to Group-C. She'd have to complete the summer with them if she wanted to progress. She'd, of course, known Dolly and Hud from the previous summer and glommed on to them. Wyatt could feel alliances forming that went beyond swim buddies. So be it, he thought, and reached out to tap Samy's fist. Ebbie and Annika followed suit.

The big kid smiled. "Damn, boy," he said. "These people should know camels can't swim. But they can eat. Watch." He picked up a fish fillet the size of the sole of a shoe. He held it up between his two huge fingers and dropped it into his mouth. The entire thing. He pounded his chest as he chewed. "That's how a camel do," he said in his strange ghetto patois. And then Samy laughed, clapping at the table, yelling, "Yeah, baby. This gonna be fun!"

Lunch was too short. A quick thirty minutes and they were back out in the water. Swimming and running. Calisthenics. Swimming and running. Calisthenics. And repeat.

The last exercise of the first day was an hour of treading water. Wyatt was sure Samy would not pass this test. But as they were now swim buddies, Wyatt's fear was that Samy would take him down too.

As before, they stepped off the dock into the deep water. The big Arab kid said, "Don't worry, boy, I gotchu." Wyatt found himself cracking a smile.

In they went, Samy immediately struggling for the surface, kicking like he was running to stay afloat, frantically moving his hands, working very hard to keep his face above water.

"Relax," Wyatt said. "You can't swim when you're tight.

Don't try to kick so hard. Slow your arms and legs down, less motion, go easy and you'll do better."

Samy tried this and at first he sank faster, but after practice and some more pointers modifying his movement, he caught the hang of it. Samy kept his lips above the surface, trying to control his dog-paddling. "Guess camels can learn to swim."

The hour passed slowly. The challenge for everyone was not the swimming but the cold. Every camper was shivering violently when they climbed up onto the dock.

"Who wants a fire?" asked Cass.

Teeth chattering, everyone nodded.

"Okay, then, follow me." Cass lead the wet campers into the woods to a giant spruce, half-fallen. It had died some years ago and been blown over in a storm but lay on its side, sun bleached and silver. Cass lopped the limbs and the campers dragged them back to the fire pit. She sawed the massive tree into billets, splitting the logs into firewood that lit easily with a little kindling and a match. Crackling flames licked up into the dried wood and roared to life.

Dinner was served by the fire, bread and a hearty stew. When all had eaten, the Old Man addressed the campers, "Congratulations to all of you for having endured day one of physical training. I know that for many, this day comes as a shock and may be, by some measure, one of the hardest of your life. The days will only get more difficult. But you'll get better at difficult."

CHAPTER 13

October 2015

The Royal Panamanian Hotel and Casino, Monaco

At eighty, Pablo Gutierrez couldn't just drink, he could drrrrriiinnnnnk. Head down, little shot glass to his purple old-man lips, and knock it back. Again and again. He'd sit at the bar mid-morning 'til pre-dawn the next day, slinging back poison with the kind of stamina that would make even young men and women wilt. They'd wind up facedown, lips hanging on to the bar, while Pablo swiveled on his barstool like a kid at a soda fountain. Not that this ability to drink should have surprised, or impressed, anyone. Pablo had spent enough time in Russia, with real Soviets, to learn how to drink like one.

Pablo had fled Honduras for Russia, then part of the Soviet Union, in the late '80s. Like most Central American goons, Pablo was feeling the squeeze when the U.S. started cleaning house in the region. He got out just in time, a few months before his old buddy Manuel "Pineapple Face" Noriega was scooped up and brought to Miami to finish out his life taming cockroaches in a federal prison.

Man, that Ronald Reagan knew how to lay his whip down, Pablo thought and raised a glass in the Gipper's honor. Then he raised another glass to honor Lady Luck, who had helped him escape so many tight spots. Salud.

Yes, Pablo had lived a charmed life. In the years after the Colonel's disappearance—a mystery Pablo had spent a good amount of time and effort trying to solve—Pablo had been blessed with good times and even better fortune. He'd syphoned tens of millions of dollars from the pockets of impoverished peoples while carrying on the Colonel's legacy of laying waste, an activity Pablo enjoyed almost as much as the Colonel himself. But Pablo never really had an interest in politics or regional power, and if he was honest, he never even really liked Central America. It was too humid, and the guys were too macho, too temperamental, like Latin dance-fighters all dressed up and looking for a salsa brawl. And the women were brunettes. Pablo liked blondes, and not bottle-blondes—though they'd do in a pinch; he preferred real, live blondes. Yes, truth be told, Pablo was destined to leave the region and go north.

So when things got hot and Ronnie Reagan came a-knockin', Pablo skipped town and found work, protection, and happiness as a mercenary for elite members of the KGB. After the fall of the Soviet Union, those same guys would later form the core of Russia's oligarch class. When that happened, Pablo traded his fatigues for a slick suit and became the guy you didn't want to see if you ran afoul of a newly minted Russian billionaire. As his old KGB buddies grew preposterously wealthy and began collecting yachts, apartments in New York, and backyard zoos with zebras and gazelles, their attitude toward Pablo changed. He became their lackey, their errand boy. Plus, roughing guys up with fists and car batteries became less necessary when you could pummel them with bundles of rubles.

Pablo knew all this, but he didn't care. He was making loads of money, got to assassinate hombres here and there, and was surrounded by blond women. Only problem was, most of the women were a foot taller than he was. Guess you can't have it all.

By his early seventies, the former paramilitary thug was getting mildly arthritic and sick of craning his neck up at all the pretty young girls. So he looked for his next gig, and this time he decided to go legit . . . or something like legit. Pablo had socked away enough money and favors that he was able to leave Russia amicably and retire in style in Monaco, where he bought up a cozy little casino.

The Royal Panamanian Hotel and Casino catered almost exclusively to Russians and criminals, who were often one and the same. Pablo was in scumbag heaven. Rich and getting richer. Fat and getting fatter. Currently drunk and getting drunker. And, as a bonus, he even got to rough up a harmless tourist now and again. La buena vida, baby!

That night when Pablo peeked up from his shot glass, he saw the girl, a true blonde, and he felt like he was looking at a unicorn. He blinked to make sure the vision was accurate. Yes. It was. Across his bar, in the casino, at a poker table, sat the girl of his dreams. Dark eyes, olive skin, curvy build stuffed into a red dress that fit her like a rubber glove: so skin-tight it squeezed any extra flesh out the top of the dress. Height approximately five-six, meaning five-nine in stilettos, which meant Pablo would have to look up to her on the dance floor if he wasn't wearing his lifts, but otherwise they'd be even. She was eighteen, maybe younger. And of course, her hair was natural blond. Even her highlights looked real.

Unfortunately, she sat next to one of Pablo's most dangerous friends, Dimitrius Nabovuciomovich, or Dimmy, as he was
known in the Russian underworld. Pablo assumed the girl was
with Dimmy, which would have meant she was off-limits—the
guy was a straight-up psychopath.

But studying her across the bar, Pablo realized the girl was
plainly trying to escape the permanent cloud of cigarette smoke
spewing from Dimmy's brownish mouth and nostrils. And more
than that, she was stealing from him. Pablo watched as she laid
down hand after winning hand, Dimmy folding six times in a
row. Dimmy doesn't fold.

Who is this woman? Pablo thought as the girl grinned and
extended her pink-nail-polished hands and slowly pulled the
towers of candy-colored chips from the center of the table to her
seat. This winged pony could play a mean hand of poker. Pablo
had to make a move or he would regret it for the rest of his life.

Pablo sent her a bottle of 1942 Dom Perignon—there were
only thirty-seven bottles in existence, soon to be thirty-six. The
one Pablo owned cost the guy who'd actually paid for it a hundred grand. It had only cost Pablo the price of carrying it out
of the guy's house after electrocuting him for a few hours, but
Pablo's sentimental attachment to the bottle was great.

An elaborate ceremony was made as the casino's sommelier
walked the bottle over to the girl at the table. The high-stakes
game stopped with a lurch. Wine geeks gawked. The sommelier drew a small sword and lopped off the neck of the bottle.
Oohs and ahhhs and bubbles flowed. The girl smiled and waved
to Pablo, then indicated to share the bottle with the table. A
classy and expensive move, Pablo thought. He didn't see that
coming.

The players smiled and sniffed their glasses and then raised
them to the girl at the table and to Pablo. Everyone at the table

drank, and even Dimmy—who normally wouldn't touch anything carbonated because it gave him gas—slugged his champagne back in one fierce gulp.

Everyone drank except the girl, who put her glass down on
the table and, shooting Pablo eye daggers, reached back into the
cloud of smoke beside her, plucked the cigarette from Dimmy's
lips, and dropped it into her bubbly. Pablo couldn't hear the siz-
zle, but he felt it from across the casino. His heart seized. Not
only was this girl beautiful beyond belief, classy in a sleazy
way, and a natural blonde, she was also tough as hell. His Perfect Ten. Pablo swooned, madly in love. If Pablo lived to be
eighty-one, he vowed he would marry the girl. Even if she was
eighteen and she would likely look at him like a sagging grand-
father. Fortunately, Pablo thought that in Monaco you didn't
need to be handsome, or young or smart, or even cool. Sure,
those qualities helped. But money, well, money was magic.

The girl got up from the table, gathered her chips, flung a
few at the dealer and sommelier, and headed to the cashier. Pablo
staggered after her, finding his leg asleep from the many hours
of perching on the stool. He frantically sent his casino security
to slow her down and caught up to her in the line for the valet
outside the casino.

"Why are you stopping me?" she demanded.

"Little girl, it's not safe," Pablo said, working off his dead-
leg. "You have just won tens of thousands of euros. You can't
walk on the streets, not here. Criminals are everywhere. You
cannot be too safe. Let me lend you my personal car. My driver
will take you anywhere you want to go."

Pablo snapped his fingers—yes, a tacky move, but it kind
of fit the occasion. Tires chirped and a Maybach materialized at
the curb, doors opened, a bottle of champagne chilling in a
bucket on the seat.

"Since I noticed you did not enjoy my last selection, I thought you might try another vintage. This one is even rarer."

The girl glanced into the car, unimpressed but not quite offended. "The bottle you sent us at the table," she said.

"Sent to *you*," Pablo corrected.

"Was it expensive?"

"Very."

"Well, I'm sorry you wasted it on me. I don't drink, not alcohol."

"Perhaps, then, would you be kind enough to let me enjoy some of the bottle and your company. I would be honored to accompany you on your drive. For your safety, of course."

The girl pondered this for a moment. "Okay," she said. "But would you mind bringing me a Sprite?"

Another snap of the fingers and Pablo's bellhop raced back into the casino and returned with the beverage.

"Now, you must tell me," Pablo said. "Someone so lovely, what does she call herself?"

The girl stabbed the cherry in her Sprite with a cocktail sword and smiled. "Raquel."

Raquel told the driver to take her to the Hotel Hermitage, one of the fanciest hotels in all of Monaco. Pablo noted it quietly. This girl had to have some fortune of her own. As the car glided through the streets of Monaco, Pablo began to pry, asking where she was from and why she was in Monaco.

"I am Lebanese," Raquel said. "But I left several years ago. Now I live in Panama."

"Oh?" Pablo asked, curious. Panama was once a regular stop for Pablo.

"Yes, my guardian works in the tech industry. He owns a Panamanian gaming company. They make what's called 'massively multiplayer' video games. You know, like World of Tanks?"

Pablo shook his head. "I'm not following."

"Massively multiplayer means games that lots of people can play at once, for free. Like millions in one game."

"For free?" Pablo asked, as if insulted. "How does your guardian make any money?"

"Data . . . information," Raquel said. "He learns things about the people who play his games. And then he uses that information to . . . well . . . make them pay."

"Much of technology confuses me. But what you are talking about sounds like good old-fashioned blackmail. That I can understand," Pablo said, laughing.

She shrugged and smiled demurely.

"You said the company is from Panama, correct?"

"Yes."

"Though it has been many years, in my youth, I traveled to Central America quite a bit. I didn't know there were many start-ups in Panama." He threw the word "start-up" in there like he used it all the time; he was feeling cool and hip and current. "You are a long way from Panama. What brings you to Monaco?"

"I'm here with my guardian, who is here to settle an old business debt."

"Is your guardian from Panama?" Pablo asked.

"No. I think he was born in Honduras, but he was raised in the U.S."

"Makes sense," Pablo said, growing more curious. "How old is this guardian of yours? I did a little business myself in Honduras. I know it fairly well. And if I may flatter myself by saying, I was a pretty well-known businessman in the region." Pablo straightened up, puffing his chest. "Perhaps I know him."

"Oh, I doubt that," Raquel smiled. "You are so clearly a great

man. And my guardian was a nobody. Here we are," she said
as the Maybach pulled up to the grand entrance of one of Monaco's grandest hotels. A white-gloved bellman opened the door
for Raquel. Pablo's mind raced for an excuse to join her, to spend
just a little more time with her, but then to Pablo's surprise, the
girl gave him an opening.

"You seem very curious about my guardian. If you would
like to meet him, you can come up into the hotel with me." She
stepped out of the car, teasing Pablo with her long, tan legs.
"Maybe we can all have a bite to eat later."

"I would be honored," Pablo said, grinning deeply, dentures
gleaming as he strained to pull himself from the car.

They took a private elevator to the third floor. On the short ride
up, Pablo stared at Raquel, crazily drawn to her. He could smell
her perfume and her shampoo, and he imagined he could taste
her lipstick, red and freshly applied. He could also smell the stale
cigarette smoke Dimmy had breathed all over her. That mildly
dampened the mood, but still Pablo salivated. Had there not been
an elevator attendant—a zitty eighteen-year-old smirking in a
starchy tuxedo and white gloves—Pablo might've hit the emergency stop button and attacked her right there.

The doors opened to nearly complete darkness. Raquel
stepped from the elevator, but Pablo hesitated. "Why so dark?"

"My guardian is sensitive to light, so we blocked out all windows. And dimmed all other light."

"But what about the other guests on the floor?" Pablo peeked
out. "Don't they complain?"

"We have booked the entire floor. So we can work. My
guardian never stops working, and he brings a coterie of employees wherever he goes. And, like all game designers, the
workers here stare at screens all day long, so they work in dark-

ness. It's very common. It makes it easier for them to see what is on screen."

Pablo blinked and he now could see faintly glowing screens dotting the cavelike hallway. "Not the job for me," Pablo joked.

Raquel laughed, and slipped her hand into Pablo's. "Come with me. Don't worry, your eyes will adjust."

They stepped off the elevator into darkness, which became even darker as the elevator doors closed. Pablo's eyes strained to see but were slow to adjust. Temporarily blinded, he felt a twinge of fear, perhaps for the first time since he was a young child. He pulled back on the girl's hand, legs wobbling slightly.

"Are you okay?" Raquel asked.

Suddenly Pablo felt old, very old. "Yes, but I cannot see."

"How about now?" A light cut through the darkness. The girl's cell phone. She took his hand again and they moved deeper into the space. Doors to the suites on each side of the hallway were open. Thick black plastic was taped over the windows, and cheap cubicles were set up like honeycombs inside the luxurious suites. Hundreds of people seemed to occupy the floor, typing. The rhythmic clacking of keys sounded like chewing, like thousands of creatures feeding in the darkness.

The employees were not the kind of people Pablo was accustomed to in Monaco. Gone were expensive suits and skimpy dresses and the occasional Hawaiian shirt donned by some boneheaded tourist. All around Pablo were pale boys and girls, covered in tattoos and piercings, sporting hairstyles that looked like they belonged on insane vagrants, not on the heads of young men and women. The rooms and hallways smelled sour, like the floor, and everyone on it, could use a power washing. All the employees wore the same black hoodie with GLOWWORM GAMING INC written on the back in glow-in-the-dark lettering.

"There are more people in here than I expected," Pablo said. "You said all of these people are in your guardian's employ?"

"Yes. But you should see the headquarters back in Panama," Raquel said. "We have an entire building, like a skyscraper."

"It must be very difficult for your guardian to travel."

"It is. He has a 747 to transport him, and getting to and from airports without exposing him to light is a challenge. So he rarely leaves Panama. He will only do it if he feels he must."

"You said he was here for a business debt. Must be a big one."

"Yes, a very big one. An old debt. One of his earliest."

Raquel led Pablo to the largest suite on the floor—the double doors leading into it were tented in red velvet to provide extra protection from light. As they pushed through the velvet curtains Pablo identified the source of the sour, rotting stench. The suite was hot and reeked like a cross between an armpit and a butcher shop. Pablo felt like he was being swallowed by a dying creature.

As they entered, something in the back shuddered and scurried.

"My eyes! Cut off the light!" a voice rasped with a hint of a Honduran accent and a strange slurp.

Raquel retracted the curtains and shut off her phone. Nearly complete darkness subsumed them.

Pablo blinked. Straining again to see large computer screens across the room, their luminescence set so low they looked like blocks of ash against charcoal. The luxurious bed and other furniture had been pushed to the side of the suite to make room for the computer gear. Black garbage bags had been stapled to the windows and then covered again by velvet.

"Better," the voice said from behind a high-backed office chair that was silhouetted by the dim light of the screens. "Is that you, Raquel? You should know better."

"I'm sorry," she said. "But I have someone who'd like to meet you. He lives here in Monaco but he knows Honduras well."

"Oh, how nice," the slurping voice said. "I wonder if I know him."

"Actually," Pablo coughed. "I don't think it's likely."

"Well, let me be the judge of that," the voice said as an ergonomic chair began to turn. "Let's have a look at you."

CHAPTER 14

July 2017
Camp Valor

After completing the obstacle course, the twelve remaining Group-C candidates ran up the steep bank of the Caldera on a jog that would leave the Sugar Bowl and continue down to the dock, followed by a swim to Flint Rock and back.

They'd just eaten lunch an hour prior. The sun hung high and hot. Wyatt and Dolly jockeyed for the second and third spots near the front of the pack, Samy kept pace not far behind, and Hud, naturally, had the lead. Coming in second or third was getting old for Wyatt. He had just logged his best time on the obstacle course and was damn proud of it. But he was still seven seconds slower than Hud that day, and it wasn't even Hud's best time. First on a swim, first on a run, first to pop up from the endless up-downs. Hud took to the shooting range like Chris Kyle, the legendary Navy SEAL sniper. When they wrestled, Hud dominated. He even chopped wood better than anyone else, banging out clean, crisp billets. Wyatt had to grudgingly admit, the bastard was good. Surly and arrogant. But good. Damn good.

Even though he was the Group-C Blue, Hud was not entirely Machiavellian in his quest for survival at Valor. Sure, he'd wanted Samy to wash out early to make it easier for the group, but now, almost a month later, Wyatt had seen enough kindness in Hud to at least leave him confused. Sometimes he was a total jerk and other times he was, well, a hero. Witness the Log Challenge.

Each member of Group-C was supposed to drag a 150-pound log from the beach to the rim of the Caldera. For many, to complete this feat alone was not just hard but simply impossible. After all, the log outweighed over half of those in Group-C, including all the girls. But that was the point. The instructors at Valor wanted to make it impossible for most candidates to complete the challenge alone.

The twelve lined up, staring down at the logs, each of which had a name carved into the trunk.

Hallsy paced along the sandy beach. "The first candidate to reach the top of the Caldera will be given a full day of rest, the second will be given the afternoon off, and the third will be given an ax during Hell Week. The rest of you will spend the remainder of the day in PT. The last person to carry their log across the line will do an additional three hours of PT after lights out."

No one groaned, but all twelve candidates slumped a little. Not an easy day ahead for eleven of them, and for the twelfth, it would be a day and a night of hell. And to earn rest would require an exertion that only the strongest could push out. The prospect of rest was vastly more appealing than anything that Valor could have offered the Group-C candidates. A day or even a half day to recuperate was akin to collecting health tokens in a video game—a chance to fight longer.

And then Hallsy stuck the knife in deep and twisted it. "There will be one final challenge. This event will be timed. Anyone who fails to complete the challenge in under three and a half hours will be washed out. The event begins now." Hallsy drew his pistol from its hostler and unloosed a round into the air.

The strongest candidates in terms of pure brute strength—Samy, Ebbie, and Hud—sprinted forward, tipping up the logs so they could get partially underneath them, and began dragging them uphill.

"Hud," Dolly said as she tried to drag the log. "I'm not going to make it. I need your help."

Hud, who was already fifty yards along, called back, "Soon as I get to the top, I'll come back for you."

Wyatt considered this. If there ever was a Group-C candidate who'd want to get all the benefit for himself it was Hud. Still, for Hud, Dolly mattered, perhaps more than himself. Even though dating was not allowed at Valor, Wyatt had heard that Hud and Dolly had had a relationship the previous summer. Dolly had cut it off, but Hud, clearly, was still in love. Hud now surged forward with renewed vigor.

Wyatt was able to get his log moving, but would be hard pressed to make the two-hour cutoff. To reach the top of the Caldera under normal circumstances took at least a half hour at a slow jog. With the log in tow, it would be close. And one look at Rory told Wyatt that the event would likely wipe out most of the class. And certainly most of the girls.

Rory, the smallest and lithest in the group, wrapped her arms around the truck and pulled with every ounce of pressure her sinewy frame could exert. The log didn't even shiver. She tried again and again. No dice. She put her hands on her hips and just stared at the impossibility of what had been asked of her. "There's no way. I'm done." It wasn't that she was too tired or weak or lacked will. It was just impossible.

Wyatt dropped his log and ran back to Rory. "If we are all going to make it, we've got to divide up." And then Wyatt realized something. "And the strongest need to be paired with the weakest. Dolly, you need to get Hud. He will only listen to you."

"He's going to come back for me," Dolly said, though Wyatt sensed a hair of doubt. "Not everyone is going to make it, Wyatt. That's the way it works here."

"No. It's not," Wyatt said. "You're missing it. Yes, Hud will be able to drop off his log and come back to save you—but that's not what the challenge is about. It's not about passing a few strong candidates on their own. Think about it—there are twelve of us. We have three and a half hours. If we break into groups of three, we can bring four logs up at a time. That's three trips—one and a half hours up and back for the first two, and one hour for the last run. They want us to make it, they just want us to do it together."

Dolly stared at Wyatt, processing, but she took no action. He urged her. "There's no time to waste. Get him now."

"Okay. I'll try to convince Hud. Meanwhile, the weakest should catch up with the strongest, who are already making progress. Rory, you come with me. We'll pair you with Hud. Kat, you go with Ebbie. Emmerson"—Dolly turned to a tall but soft California surfer—"you go with Samy. And Wyatt—"

Wyatt knew who was left, the Amazonian huntress, Annika, and scrawny Kentucky boy Sanders. "I got it." Wyatt nodded and moved to find the others.

And like that, they divided and raced into action.

Fortunately for the group, Hud not only saw the logic and listened to Dolly, but once they had divided up and decided everyone was going to make it under three and a half hours, he threw himself into the task with astonishing single-minded intensity.

Hud had already made it halfway up the Caldera on his own by the time Dolly and Rory caught up to him. He, Rory, and Dolly raced back so quickly that they were actually able to lap Wyatt's team on their second trek up the mountain. On the third run, Wyatt realized that his team was so far behind that unless they started jogging, there was no way the log was reaching the top. To make matters worse, the last log they carried had his name carved into it.

Sanders didn't mince words: "Wyatt, we're goin' as fast as we can, but I'm not sure if we're gonna get you there."

"Just keep moving," Wyatt said. "We'll get there."

By the time Wyatt, Sanders, and Annika were dragging his log toward the finish line, Wyatt could see he was the only one of the twelve campers who had not gotten his log to the top of the Caldera. He had five minutes to get the log up ten minutes of hill or he'd be washed out. And all three campers were completely wiped out. Nothing left in the tank.

"Run!" Hud came from out of nowhere and bounded back down the hill toward them. He took position at the rear of the log and Wyatt felt half the weight lift.

"Let's finish this," Hud said, and Wyatt, Sanders, and Annika pumped their legs and raced forward as fast as they could until they tumbled across the finish line with one minute to spare.

Wyatt, Sanders, Annika, and Hud lay on the ground, gasping. Hud pushed himself up, his arms and legs bleeding. Take a rest, show-off, Wyatt thought to himself.

"Good work, team." Hallsy came over, clapping. "There is only one log left. Only one of you might not make it."

"But I'm over the line!" Wyatt yelled. It was bad enough that he, who had just finished last, would have to do PT for three hours after dinner, but now he was being challenged on completing the event. He pointed to the end of his log, a good eighteen inches beyond the finish line marker. "My log is clearly beyond. Whatever—" Wyatt said, pulling himself up. "I'll pull it further."

"Not your log," Hallsy said.

Wyatt was confused. Then he saw Hud limping back down the hill. Wyatt's mind spun. He had counted eleven candidates on the top of the Caldera, including himself. Everyone was on the top. Who was Hud going after?

Then Wyatt put it together. To the side of the path, out of view of the rest of the candidates, was the last remaining log, the only one to not cross over the finish line—Hud's. Hud had not taken his log over the finish line, and Wyatt immediately knew why. He was the strongest. Of all twelve, he was the one who could handle the extra PT.

The group watched as a bloody, raw, dirty Hud dragged his 150-pound log alone, crossing the finish line with ten seconds to spare.

Looking back on this a couple weeks later while jogging next to Wyatt, Samy shrugged off Hud's heroic effort. "Don't fall for it. Guy is just brown-nosing. He's trying to un-douche himself. To wash off the taint for what he did to me. Plus, did you see how Dolly looked at him at the end of the log haul? He was just looking to impress."

Wyatt had in fact noticed Dolly staring admiringly at Hud after the log event, but he wasn't so sure Samy's read was right. Certainly Hud was trying to atone for prior ruthlessness and wanted to look good for Dolly, but who didn't? All the guys at

Valor secretly wanted to impress her. Wyatt included. She had that mix of beautiful and indifferent that guys always fell for. The beautiful part really being the key ingredient in the love potion. But still Wyatt thought he saw something else in the Log Challenge. Wyatt liked to believe that maybe Hud was changing.

They all were changing, and the skills and strengths they brought to Valor were becoming clearer. For example, Samy was not yet a "good" swimmer, for sure, but a few weeks in and he had become a rising star, one of the strongest candidates. For such a large, rangy dude, Samy performed well on the obstacle course and on jogs. Anything that required strength was a breeze for him. Swimming was still his weakest physical activity, but he had improved dramatically after he'd been taught how to swim. Samy consistently beat Wyatt when wrestling and grappling, but he also had Wyatt by about forty pounds. On the range, he wasn't a bad shot. And, of course, there were skills that would become valuable later on that didn't matter in PT. For example, Samy was the son of an Afghani interpreter and a Palestinian mother. He spoke English, Arabic, Pashtu, and Urdu, and claimed to speak Spanish, but there was no proof other than that he looked vaguely Latino.

Another all-star on the boys' side was Ebbie. Ebbie grew up in Detroit and had been recruited to play football for a fancy suburban boarding school. Ebbie brought a unique combination of street cred and high-end social polish to Valor, not to mention brute strength. He was fifteen years old, five-ten, and 250 pounds of muscle. His sports were football, where he was virtually unstoppable, and swimming, where he caused a wave across the lanes when he swam the butterfly.

Ebbie's brain was even more powerful than his body. He was an engineering genius with a liberal streak. Ebbie was sent to Valor after he was found guilty of misappropriating school funds—a lot of funds. When a wealthy parent at the school donated thirteen million dollars to build a state-of-the-art equestrian center for only five of four hundred students (two of which were the children of the donor), Ebbie hacked into the school's financial system and diverted the funds to purchase a tablet for every single one of the Detroit public school system's nearly 48,000 students. The tablets came preloaded with all of the courses taught at the prep school and a *My Little Pony* app. Ebbie would neither confirm nor deny the allegations.

And of course Rory was another star. Not physically. Not even mentally—though she was wicked smart. Simply by dint of determination, she was one of the best. And like a few of the younger campers, Rory kept a stuffed animal to comfort her. It was a blue elephant, made by Rory herself, using a blanket, pillow stuffing, suture thread, and buttons for eyes. She kept it in the bottom of her sleeping bag, nuzzling it at night after flying drones, playing war games, and "killing the enemy." Wyatt had to respect the little badass.

While the boys were, on average, faster and stronger, the girls at Valor were hardcore. And Dolly was by far the hardest of all, and the prettiest girl Wyatt had seen in real life. She was five seconds faster than Wyatt on the obstacle course, could beat him in long runs (but lost in sprints), and half the time she was faster in the water as well. Wyatt had yet to grapple with Dolly, who had trained in Brazilian-style jujitsu. Dolly had soundly beaten Samy in a wrestling match, and the beating had nothing to do with size or strength, but skill, pain points, and quickness. She actually made Samy tap out—screaming—simply by applying the right leverage to one of his fingers. Samy told Wyatt, "Brother, it was humiliating to lose to a girl . . . but man oh man, it was well worth it."

"What do you mean, 'worth it'?" Wyatt asked.

"Her hair. It smelled so good, my friend. It was worth losing to her to get to smell it. Just to get my beak inside her locks. Heaven."

The image of Samy's nose buried in Dolly's hair disturbed Wyatt. He tried to force it from his thoughts. Still, he had to ask, "What did it smell like?"

Samy scratched the thin teenage beard on his chin. "A little soapy. Little sweaty. And I think there was a spritz of perfume in there too."

"What kind of perfume?"

"Chanel No. 9," Samy said, poker-faced.

"What? What is Chanel No. 9? And how do you know what it smells like?"

Samy's face broke into a smile. "I have no idea, dude. I'm kidding. I seen Chanel No. 9 in commercials, you think I know what it smells like—"

"Never mind," Wyatt cut Samy off and jogged on, regretting that he'd opened his big mouth.

"Why you asking?" Samy called after Wyatt. "Hold up." Samy hustled after him. "Why you care what her hair smells like? What kind of perfume she got? Brother, you in *the big time*. Big time got you."

"What's the big time?"

"Love is what it is. Trouble is what it gets you," Samy said.

"No way. Dolly's with Hud . . . I think."

"You think? You mean you been thinking about that, too. You crackin' me up, man." Samy jogged on, half-doubled over in fits of laughter. "But in all seriousness here, man, you gotta get that sorted out in your head."

"I still don't know what you're talking about."

"You know exactly what I'm talking about." Samy eyed

Wyatt. "You fallin'. And Valor does not want that to happen. But I'll tell you what. If I learned anything in my life, and I'm not saying I have, it's that people are the only thing that matters in the end."

"Yeah," Wyatt said, teasing. "How'd you figure that out at all of fifteen years of age?"

"When you and your family are all refugees and those who are home are either killed or hiding, you learn pretty quick." Samy gritted his teeth and jogged ahead.

"Sorry . . ." Wyatt said, recalling that Samy's father was an interpreter who worked with U.S. special forces. "I shouldn't have asked. None of my business."

"I wouldn't have told you if I didn't want you to know."

Wyatt couldn't figure Dolly out. And it was driving him nuts. And it wasn't that Wyatt wondered—does she like me? He knew emphatically she didn't. What Wyatt wondered was—does she totally hate me?

His tooth was the perfect example of that. It hadn't healed very much since the first day. The gums were still soft and he was beginning to think he'd need to have it pulled. In fact, everyone in the group was telling him to pull it, including Dolly.

"Wyatt," Dolly said. "I'm sick of looking at you playing with your tooth, moving it around and blood seeping from your mouth. Go to Hallsy, or Mum if you want someone gentler, and have it taken care of."

"Yeah, Dolly. Thanks, but I think I'll keep it."

She shook her head. "You'll be happier without it. What are you worried about? How you'll look?"

In fact, Wyatt was a little worried about how he'd look with a huge missing front tooth. He'd look like the kind of cracker rednecks he grew up with and tried really hard to not totally become. Wyatt could only imagine how much Dolly would despise him if he sported the crazy, toothless redneck look.

One afternoon when they were in the Mess Hall eating lunch, covered in dirt, tired as heck, trying to keep their eyes open as they shoveled food into their mouths, the conversation at the table turned to Hell Week—when it would start and who would finish. At this point, the twelve remaining candidates felt they could handle whatever Valor threw at them, so long as it didn't change too drastically.

"Hell Week is the X-factor," Ebbie said. "It's the thing we just don't evaluate. It could be a factor of five times harder, or a hundred times. We don't know."

"All I know," Samy said, "is that I'm ready to learn some spy tricks. I'm getting tired of this routine."

"Be careful what you wish for," Rory joined in. She was sitting at the other table with Hud and Dolly. Wyatt listened to the rest of them, poking at his tooth.

"I was here last year," Rory went on. "And I saw the guys who are now Group-As come back from Hell Week. They were like . . . refugees. Or worse. They looked like roadkill that was not quite dead."

"Wyatt!" Dolly snapped from the other table.

Wyatt jerked up.

"Your mouth." Dolly stared at him.

Wyatt hadn't even realized it, but blood was trickling down his chin. Dolly rose, tossed down her napkin and walked around the table to him. "Watching you play with your tooth is making me squirm. Follow me."

"If it falls out it falls out. I'm not going to have my tooth pulled."

"Just follow me," she said, then, softening her voice a little: "Trust me."

Wyatt stood and followed Dolly out of the Mess Hall into the hot sun.

"Where are we going?"

"Mum's garden."

Wyatt stopped, "I'm not letting—"

"Trust me," she repeated. "I don't want to help you, but I am going to help you."

"Okay." Wyatt followed her around behind the lodge to the bluff where Mum had her garden and grew many of the vegetables they ate. The days were long and provided much sunlight, so the garden produced a bounty of fruits and vegetables. Mum had also built a tiny greenhouse for species that needed a more humid and hot climate. This is where Dolly took Hud.

Dolly opened the door. "Is it ready?" she said to Mum, who was inside tending plants.

"Hello, Dolly," Mum said. "I thought we were going to wait a little longer before sharing your surprise with Wyatt."

Surprise? Wyatt thought.

"I can't stand looking at his tooth anymore. Let's just try now."

"What's going on?" Wyatt asked. "What surprise?"

"Oh," said Mum. "You haven't told him?"

"Told me what?" asked Wyatt.

Dolly thought for a second. "I know how to help your tooth. Or I know how to try. As a Blue, I am able to request some special food. I didn't want to waste it on you, but to be honest, after your thinking helped us get past the Log Challenge, I decided to order you something." Dolly motioned to a succulent flower in the greenhouse.

"A plant? That's not food."

"The root is food. Well, technically it's a spice. Turmeric. If you put fresh turmeric on your gums, it'll help tighten them." Dolly dug up a root and, not asking for Wyatt's permission, grabbed his knife out of its sheath and cut off a slice. She held it out. "Try it."

"How do you know it'll work?"

"You don't have to trust me," Dolly said, putting down the slice of root. "Don't try it." She stepped past Wyatt and headed back to the Mess Hall. "Go toothless."

Wyatt watched her go, picked up the slice of root, and turned to Mum. "Does it really work?"

Mum smiled. "I have no idea. Dolly ordered it for you. Not me."

Wyatt slipped the root into his mouth. It tasted sour and bitter and made his mouth pucker.

Two days later, the students attended a class Cass was teaching on how to use gasoline as an accelerant. A gallon of gas, Wyatt had learned, was as powerful as a stick of dynamite. Cass taught them how to make two types of bombs—a car bomb booby trap and a SoBe bomb. The car bomb was simple: Cass rigged a grenade inside the gas tank door.

"Tigger the grenade, you also trigger twenty gallons of gas. It'll kill anyone inside or within ten feet of the car."

The SoBe bomb was more interesting, though harder to figure out how to use. "Fill a SoBe bottle with gas, screw on the top, and place it in a fire. What do you expect will happen? It'll explode, right?"

Wrong. Wyatt and the candidates watched as the lid burnt off the bottle and the boiling gas inside the glass exploded out and ignited, creating a blowtorch effect. "The SoBe bomb," Cass said, "is kind of like a Molotov cocktail with style."

The class was on the range in the Caldera. On the way to the next event, Wyatt tried to catch up to Dolly, speed walking next to her on the narrow path. It had only been two days, but his gums had firmed up and he wanted to thank her.

"Hey, Dolly, that was a cool class your sister taught. I'd like to talk to her about how to try to deploy the SoBe bomb. I had a few ideas just now."

Dolly didn't look back, just spoke over her shoulder. "Why don't you tell her and not me?"

Okay. This was not going as planned, Wyatt thought. "Sure. I will. Listen, I just wanted to tell you, the turmeric. It worked. Thank you. I know there was a sacrifice from you and everyone else to get the root. I appreciate it."

She glanced back and nodded.

As much time as Group-C spent together, they still didn't open up personally. They didn't share much about their respective histories. They knew a little about where each person was from, a few scant details about how each got to Valor, but not much beyond that. Part of the reason for this lack of information sharing was simply that they were so busy they didn't have time for the kinds of conversations in which guarded people open up. On the other hand, if they wanted to talk about their personal lives, they would have found the time. There were other factors, aside from practical ones, that kept them tight-lipped.

The twelve Group-C candidates who remained from the original twenty-five were by nature guarded and secretive. Even a big talker like Samy was slow to share anything meaningful or private. In fact, Wyatt was not sure if most of what Samy said—and he said a lot—was true or not or just made up on the spot to keep him and the rest of Group-C entertained.

In those spare moments, they almost dared each other to talk about their personal lives. No one wanted to. Least of all Wyatt. "C'mon, Wy," Ebbie said on a long paddle back from a trip, canoes lined up side by side. "Tell us about your family. Where you from? You gotta girl out there waitin' for you to come home?"

"Next," Wyatt said.

"No, man, I'm serious," Ebbie pressed. "I've told y'all where I'm from and how I got here. Why not just start with hometown . . . Where is that?"

Wyatt deflected. "What I want to know is not where are we from, but where are we now?"

"Like where is the camp?"

"Yeah. Where are we?"

"That you don't need to know," Hud said, cutting into the conversation. "They don't tell us where we are to keep us safe. End of the summer or maybe during Phase Three, the RIP phase, we're operating live. Until then, all you need to know is we're far north. We're far from everywhere."

"I think we're in Montana," Annika said, pulling against icy blue water with her paddle. "Or Alaska."

"Nice dodge, Wyatt," Ebbie said. "Way to steer the conversation from real life to geography."

"I just don't want to talk about my life. I don't think anyone here does."

They all nodded. "Right," said Samy. "Everyone but me and Ebbie!" Laughter echoed across the bay.

"Know what's the craziest thing?" Rory said solemnly from the bow of Hud's boat. "We're twelve now. And we're all close. But we're still like strangers. It's like you guys are the closest strangers I've ever known."

"After Hell Week," Hud said, "half of us will be total strangers again . . ."

"Yeah, man," Ebbie said. "Take pill, shut your eyes. And forget. Ain't gonna be me."

Close strangers. Wyatt understood how you could be close to a total stranger. As time wore on the closest stranger Wyatt encountered at Valor was the one reflected back at him as he dove off the end of the dock and in the tinted lenses of the staff's wraparound sunglasses. In his own reflection, Wyatt saw a boy he didn't recognize: face chiseled, eyes very blue, crisp, and serious, with muscles . . . real muscles. Before arriving at Valor, Wyatt had what might be generously described as a comfortable physique. Now he had ribs, abs, and biceps. And his long hair was now short, crudely chopped, and dyed by the sun.

Wyatt surprised everyone when he agreed to the haircut. His mane of mangy blond hair had grown completely unruly and wild.

"I can't stand looking at that anymore," Dolly said one day as they crowded around the fire.

"What?" said Wyatt.

"Your hair. When you're on the obstacle course, it gets in your face. It's driving me nuts. And it smells." Dolly nodded. "Sorry to be the one to tell you, but it's true."

Wyatt grabbed the locks by his shoulder and sniffed. He made a face. "You're right."

"I know I am," Dolly said. "Question is . . ." She grinned. "Are you ready?"

"For what?"

"Pass me your knife, and I'll show you."

Wyatt looked down at the heel of his buck knife, sticking out of the sheath.

"No, dog!" Samy said. "You can't really be thinking about letting Dolly cut your hair with a knife!"

Wyatt drew it out and felt the blade. Razor sharp. Wyatt thought of his dad. The balding trucker with a scruffy goatee and hatred of authority. His dad had always encouraged Wyatt to grow his hair long, to be a rebel, to not be a *suit*.

"Have at it," Wyatt said. He handed the knife to Dolly.

The Group-C candidates around the fire exploded in cheers and hoots. Dolly lopped Wyatt's hair off in long sections, tossing fistfuls into the fire, causing flare-ups that smoked and smelled horrible. "Incoming," Dolly said as a few campers scattered, pinching their noses. Samy doubled over laughing so hard he shook. Hud sulked at the flickering edge of the circle.

As the smell of Wyatt's burning hair dissipated and the fire returned to its regular pleasant crackle, Wyatt's thoughts tripped back to his father. Wyatt had become a rebel and now here he was, being transformed into a weapon for the U.S. government. Wyatt wondered what his dad, the free-lovin' deadbeat, would think of him now.

The Old Man and Hallsy had come down to watch. They snickered and joked about the "shearing," but in their humor, Wyatt sensed sadness. Something was amiss. Their smiles were phony, hiding their inner thoughts. And Wyatt knew this because of some eavesdropping.

Earlier that day, Wyatt left the Cave Complex and passed the Old Man's office. The door was open and Wyatt heard arguing.

"I was there for the intercept . . . this group is not playing around. If the DOD comes in at forty-five million, they're going to be too low. You gotta get your contacts to press for more money. We'll lose him. Outbid."

"You think I don't know that! He's like a son to me," the

Old Man shouted back. "I'm pressing as hard as I can, but you know damn well upfront you're going in without a leash." The Old Man's voice stopped, and Wyatt heard footsteps approaching the door. He tried to hustle away but the door swung open and the Old Man didn't exactly catch Wyatt snooping but something close to it. He turned back to Hallsy. "Let's talk about this downstairs." And then shut the door.

Now fireside, Wyatt watched the Old Man and Hallsy, both hunched over in a warlike crouch, smiling, but weighed down. Neither had looked him in the eye that night. Wyatt did not know if he was being paranoid but he felt they had been arguing about something related to him.

"Line up!" Hallsy called out one afternoon. Wyatt hoped this would be their last swim before dinner. Wyatt kicked off his boots and took off his thinning (and foul smelling) Tony Hawk T-shirt, padded across the sand, and got into formation for the swim.

It was a week or so after the summer solstice, the longest day of the year, and the days at Valor were looooonggg. It was close to 6 p.m., but given the sun's position in the sky, it felt earlier. Sunset would come around 10:30 p.m.

Wyatt had just run four miles, over very steep terrain, but he didn't feel winded. Just a thin glaze of sweat and an expectation that the day would get a little harder with the swim to Flint Rock and back, but that would be it. Wyatt was unaware, or perhaps mildly aware, that he had become comfortable with the challenge.

Hallsy, the Old Man, Mum, Cass, Avi, and the other key staff came down to the dock. As the Group-C candidates waited on the beach for staff to give them instructions, Wyatt smelled a familiar scent wafting over the water. He almost couldn't place the smell. It came on the breeze from over the water. Then he heard the *Sea Goat* and saw Mackenzie at the helm, steering the boat into the cove. Sitting on the *Sea Goat*'s bow, placed up on a riser so they wouldn't get wet, were thin boxes—perhaps twenty or so—stacked in two neat columns. Wyatt instantly recognized the boxes and felt his stomach spasm at what was inside. Pizza.

"At ease," the Old Man said. "This evening there has been a change of plan. The staff and I need to head into town for an emergency meeting."

He tried to read the staff on the dock to see a clue. But their faces were inscrutable.

The Old Man went on, "It'll take us about two hours to get there, an hour to conduct our business, and two hours to get back. You will be left alone on the island with no supervision during that time. We have ordered pizza for you. A projector has been set up by the fire pit." The Old Man motioned toward the outdoor meeting area. "A small selection of some of the staff's favorite movies has been set out. If you can figure out how to hang a sheet, you can watch some movies. You might also find some pops and ice cream in coolers as well."

Wyatt glanced from face to face of his fellow Valorians. Could it be that they were really having pizza and movies and ice cream and sodas and no staff? Everyone tried to hide their smiles.

Everyone but Hud, who looked uncomfortable with a night left to be just a kid. Wyatt felt that Hud was one of those people who couldn't just hang out. He always had to be proving himself, always surly and on edge.

"Since we are letting you off early tonight, tomorrow might be a little more challenging, so we recommend you get to bed early. And since Avi will be gone, you may want to organize a security detail, but that's up to you. You've proven yourselves to be responsible with supervision, so we want to test you without it. Enjoy yourselves and relax. You guys earned a night off."

A cheer rose up at these words, and the pizzas were placed on the dock.

"Word to the wise, campers," Hallsy said over his shoulder on his way down the dock. "Don't forget you're trying to earn your way out of prison. Slip up, and you just might go back."

The staff boarded the *Sea Goat,* and as the boat and supervision left the island, Wyatt had an irresistible tingling in his stomach—something he had not felt since the night he'd stolen Narcy's car. He was buzzing with freedom.

CHAPTER 15

October 2015

Third Floor, Hotel Hermitage, Monaco

Pablo had seen some weird and scary stuff in his life. Lots of it. Like the old lady who came back from the dead. It was in the early days with the Colonel. They'd put down a bunch of the villagers and the old lady lay in a ditch, shot in the lung, half-burnt, not breathing. Pablo shoveled a spade full of dirt on her face and she popped up, moaning, and came at him, hair scorched, half her scalp bleeding.

"MAAAHHHHHHH!" she had screamed. Pablo saw, at the last second, that she held a high-heeled shoe in her hand and was going to slam it into his face.

Pablo covered up, maybe even shrieked a little. The Colonel casually shouldered his rifle and double tapped the lady. She tumbled back into the ditch, a couple ounces of lead in her brain. Pablo stood on the edge of the ditch looking down, chest heavy, mind just catching up.

By god, the scorched old lady with the high heel had given his heart a jolt. But she had nothing on what he saw now, as the ergonomically designed office chair swiveled around and Pablo beheld a human transformed.

It was vaguely male. The body had iridescent skin and black eyes, and was naked, except for what might have been a pair of gym shorts, or an adult diaper covering his crotch. He was completely covered in a jelly, like Vaseline, the scant patches of head and body hair matted down in clumps. Pablo could not tell if his skin actually glowed or if it was the jelly on the skin that glowed, but a greenish iridescence glimmered and twinkled across the man's body, like someone had put a handful of fireflies in a blender, hit "frappe," and injected the glowing emulsion into his veins to be pumped through his vascular system.

Even as an old man, Pablo's mind still worked like a detective's. He recalled the writing on the back of the hoodies—Glowworm Gaming.

And here it is, he thought. The Glowworm.

The Glowworm's feet were long, bony, and sported six-inch-long toenails. Jesus, Pablo thought, feeling bile rise up in his throat. Oddly, Pablo noticed, the Glowworm's fingernails were manicured. Must be so he could type. A computer thing.

The Glowworm's mouth was sunken and black, and his tongue moved around his lips nervously. The slurping sound Pablo had heard before, he now realized, was caused by the absence of teeth. Pablo hardly could have guessed that the Glowworm had elected to have his teeth removed. Just as he'd elected to have a feeding tube implanted into his stomach, a clear tube that snaked from his abdomen to a machine that pumped food into the man. The pump sat on his desk, next to an old Nintendo gaming console and a Vitamix blender. Arrayed around the blender were protein powders, limp vegetables, and heaps of raw ground meat. What kind of meat, Pablo was scared to guess.

But weirdest of all was the series of diodes that had been placed across the Glowworm's body. They pulsed electricity into his muscles, which twitched and sputtered, so that he could get a workout without having to leave the chair. And it appeared the workout was getting results. The Glowworm was *ripped*, but not in a natural, human way. He was cut like the men in El Greco paintings. He was skinny-fat with selective, unnatural bulging muscles that spasmodically clenched and unclenched while his eyes and face remained completely calm.

"Come closer," the Glowworm said after some silence. "I can see you well from where I am. But in this light, I'm not sure if you can see me."

Pablo stepped closer, the smell of the Glowworm making him nauseous, like the BO of a horde of zombies. "Don't you recognize me?" the Glowworm asked pleasantly.

Despite the missing teeth and the green, shiny stuff smeared on him and the smell and the diodes and all the other distracting changes that had been made over the years, when Pablo got closer, he saw it. The face of the reclusive fifteen-year-old boy he had known almost thirty years before.

"Wilberforce," Pablo said.

"Good, you recognize me," the Glowworm said, then switched to Spanish. "I am Wilberforce no more. I am the Glowworm. Oh, what memories we had," he chuckled. "I used to call you tío, Pablo, before you killed my father and tried to kill me and my mother. I have looked forward to this day for many years. And I can promise you"—the Glowworm eyed the blender on the desk—"I plan to savor my revenge for a long time."

Pablo did not even bother to run or defend himself. There was absolutely nothing he could do. The suite, which he thought was empty save the Glowworm, was not. It was filled with guards who, at that moment, were emerging from the darkness, dressed completely in black, heavily armed and wearing night vision goggles. Far more troubling than guns pointed at him was what Raquel held in her hand—a six-inch, razor-sharp Japanese boning knife. And perhaps even more troubling than the knife was the smile on Raquel's face. Luminescent, eerie, and beautiful. It was a hungry smile.

But Pablo had one card left to play. "Wilberforce," he said, then corrected himself. "I mean, Glowworm, I know you will kill me, which I deserve. Yes, I roughed up your mother a little."

"A little!" The Glowworm opened his mouth and strands of saliva stretched across the open black hole. It looked like he was going to speak. Instead, he coughed like a cat puking up a fur ball. "A little? I heard you beat her. I saw the bruises and the blood."

"You're right. Maybe a *little* more than a little." Pablo nodded in agreement. "And if I had my way, I might have killed her. But I didn't. And I did not kill your father."

"Mentiras!" The Glowworm's legs twitched and quaked, and the creature began to rise up out of its seat. Raquel moved closer and held her blade to Pablo's neck.

"You speak lies!" the Glowworm said.

"Your father was an evil, terrible, cruel man." Pablo's voice was shaking. "And I would not have had it any other way. He was my hero and my mentor. And I have made it one of my life's goals to unlock the mystery of who killed him. I am almost one hundred percent certain I have solved it, and that the killer is still alive. You can always kill me, but before you do it, why don't you listen to me first and maybe discover who truly deserves your wrath?"

"So far, I have listened to nothing. To air, to baseless denials.

Boring. Now it's time for you to listen." The Glowworm nodded to Raquel.

Raquel's movement was so fast, Pablo hardly could track her hand and the boning knife. He saw a blur and then felt searing pain on the side of his head.

Pablo screamed and reached up to feel his left ear, but it was gone, only a tuft of raw cartilage and seeping blood.

The demonic girl picked up the ear. It looked pale and hairy in her hand. She bit into it, tore off a piece of gristle. And chewed it like gum and then spat it out. "Tastes disgusting."

"I don't care about taste," said the Glowworm. "I want some."

The girl dropped Pablo's ear into the Vitamix blender, blended it, and pumped the slurry into the Glowworm's stomach.

"Yum," the Glowworm cackled and shifted his eyes to Pablo. "I mean this in the strongest, most literal way possible. My hunger for revenge is all-consuming. My only interest is to watch the person who deprived me of my childhood suffer and to feed off of that suffering. Again, I mean literally." He enunciated the word clearly. "If you have anything to say, cut to the chase. Otherwise, I'd prefer we begin dissembling you."

"Fair enough." Pablo bowed, trying to play it cool as sweat beaded on his face and neck. He pulled the neatly folded silk pocket square from the front of his suit and pressed it to the side of his head. "But killing me would deprive you of that satisfaction. Did you ever consider that the killer of your father may have been an agent of the United States, a state actor? Wouldn't that make sense?"

The Glowworm shrugged. "Sure. That is possible. It was a competing theory at the time. One theory was you killed my father, the other was someone did it on behalf of the Americans. Of course, you could have been acting both for yourself and as an agent of the United States."

"Come now," Pablo said, an edge to his voice. "You insult me. You can't be serious. I have been called a lot of things in my life—scumbag, thug, murderer—but a friend of the Americans is one I've never heard."

"Anything is possible, Pablo."

"Good point." Pablo raised a finger, damp with blood from his ear, or the flap of skin where his ear should have been. "Remember that. Anything is possible. So let me ask you another question. Was there anyone on the boat who had an unusual amount of access to your father?"

"Just me and my mother . . ." The Glowworm leaned in. "And you."

"Yes, but you are forgetting. Was there anyone else who might have been allowed in your staterooms? To perhaps plant evidence or steal information . . . Was there anyone who was with you almost the entire time?"

"You, of course, are referring to my friend, Chris Gibbs." The Glowworm swiveled in his chair and reached for the gaming console on his desk. He pulled it into his lap and seemed to pet it, like a cat.

"Do you know how many people aboard the boat were not interrogated by me?" Pablo held up two bloody fingers. "Dos."

"Sure. I wasn't. Chris wasn't. But that was only because you ran out of time."

Pablo nodded and glanced into his handkerchief, now sopped with blood. "I did run out of time. Someone helped your mother escape from her room. Do you know who helped her?"

"My mother saved us."

"Not exactly," Pablo said. "Who came to her first? Who helped her out of her room? Can you recall that detail?"

The Glowworm's mind turned back to the day his father was killed. He lay on the floor of his stateroom. Face stuck to the carpet. There was gunfire in the hallway. Pablo had killed his father's friend Raul. Then Pablo's men moved on to another room and there were new footsteps and then the door to his room was kicked open . . . by Chris. His mother stood behind him, holding his father's gold-plated gun. The moment Chris and his mother had rescued him had been a ray of light during the darkest time, and now he began to feel the ground under his feet shift.

"You are right. I had always thought she'd gotten him. But it is possible that Chris had gone to my mother's room. And he led her to mine." The Glowworm's fingers absentmindedly clicked the power and eject buttons on the console's face.

"And how many Americans were on that boat?"

The Glowworm looked lost in thought and oddly hurt, oddly human. "But he was my best friend."

"Yes, I'm sorry to tell you this now. Chris was an agent of the United States."

"But he was just a boy. We were just boys."

Pablo shook his head. "He was not just any boy. I have every reason to believe that he was part of an elite American program to train young agents and assassins."

"But how could he have gotten to my father's stateroom? He was locked in his berth on the other side of the boat."

"Excellent question," Pablo said, now feeling like he could see a possible way to survive this encounter and even live to brag about it. "And that is where I actually have proof. I have photographs that show exactly how your friend gained access to your parents' suite. And how he gained access to the suite of the rather unfortunate fellow who had jewels planted in his room. As you know, I put him to death after we found the jewels . . ." He then added, "Perhaps somewhat hastily."

"Where is the evidence?"

"In my home, on my computer."

Pablo saw a flash of white as the Glowworm rolled his eyes in the darkness.

"We searched your computer. If there was evidence on it, my people would have found it."

Pablo pushed back. "Then they missed it. Bring me my computer and I will show you."

"My people do not make mistakes . . . twice." The Glowworm settled back down in his chair, the slime that coated his body making a nasty squishing sound. He flicked his fingers, and someone left to fetch Pablo's computer.

"Just bear with me," Pablo said again, trying to find the proof he'd been promising for over an hour. But like most old people, he fumbled with anything digital.

The Glowworm, bored and doubtful, sat watching with the Nintendo console in his lap as the old thug opened and closed countless files in the mess of folders on his desktop.

"Ahh, I think this is it." Pablo clicked on a photo.

The Glowworm squinted, as if mildly appalled at the sight of Pablo on his seventy-fifth birthday aboard a Russian yacht off Ibiza, holding a fishing pole, drunken smile, beer gut spilling over a tiny banana hammock bathing suit, gold chains, man boobs, silver chest hairs so thick he looked like a bald silverback gorilla.

"Sorry. Wrong file again. Wait." Pablo scrolled down a list of folders. "Here it is." Pablo coughed and opened a folder labeled "Salt Stains on Hull," which contained a series of JPEGs. He opened the first two, each almost indistinguishable from the other. "These files are digital scans of photographs taken in 1994," said Pablo. "They are of the fiberglass hull of *La Crema*."

"I don't see anything," the Glowworm said.

"Let me zoom in. We need to look closer." Pablo increased the zoom until very faint, tennis ball–sized circular salt stains and smudge marks became visible. He pointed to the first photo. "These marks were found on the side of *La Crema* ascending and descending the hull below the master stateroom where your father and mother slept." He then referred to the second, almost identical, photo. "These other, matching marks were found on the hull on the opposite side of the boat where we discovered your father's ring and other jewelry. Which proves to me they had been planted." Pablo drew a finger along the edge of the stains. "See the circular shapes? These were left by a climbing apparatus that employed suction technology. Four suction cups—one for each hand and over the knees. The killer climbed like this." Pablo mimicked suction-crawling up the side of the boat. "Your friend Chris used the cups to scale the side of the boat to gain access to your father's room, kill him, and reach the other side of the boat to plant the evidence—the stone from your father's ring."

"Salt stains . . ." the Glowworm said, absorbing this information. "When did you find them?"

"The day after you left the boat."

The Glowworm looked skeptical. "And how do you know they were not used by the man who was found with the jewelry?"

"Very good question." Pablo patted the bandages covering his ear. "I did think that was possible, and initially these stains reinforced my belief that I had killed the right man. However, once we found this set of stains, we very carefully searched the rest of the boat and found these." Pablo opened another photo. This one was of the hull as well and depicted very faint salt smears like someone had tried to wipe away the suction marks. "These marks were made just above the waterline below Chris's room. You can see the salt trail seems to disappear the higher up the hull you go. We determined the boy used a sheet lowered from the window to try to wipe away the marks."

"And what action did you take once you discovered these findings?" the Glowworm asked.

"Well, first, you must remember, I feared whomever had killed your father might also kill me. And these marks were only one avenue of investigation. To be quite honest, I suspected those closest to me, long before your friend Chris Gibbs . . . and I killed a few of them." Pablo shrugged. "Some very close friends, by the way. Also, I had other problems back home. I was fighting for power and this investigation was not my only concern." Reading the Glowworm's reaction, Pablo added, "Though it was, of course, my top personal priority."

"As I would have expected it to be," the Glowworm said.

"Of course." Pablo coughed and plunged on. "In any case, when my investigation focused on your friend Chris as the primary suspect, I tried to find him at your boarding school. And that was when I learned he had supposedly died."

The Glowworm squirmed in his chair, his throat emitting a low rumble. "Supposedly? You think that was faked?"

"Without question." Pablo nodded emphatically. "And very carefully executed. There were newspaper reports of a car crash and a funeral service at your old boarding school, but I never found proof of an actual accident, and all of his records disappeared from the school. I concluded he was only enrolled at the school to befriend you."

Pablo watched the Glowworm's reaction. His face flushed a greenish-red hue.

Pablo went on, "Unfortunately, I had to flee Central America, so I was unable to complete my investigation or follow up on leads regarding Chris. But my conclusion is that the imposter known as Chris Gibbs was part of a special program designed to train young agents and assassins."

"You said that before," the Glowworm said, perking now. "What kind of a program? Would it still be active?"

"Hard to say exactly what kind or if it is still active . . . I suspect, yes. Someone had to have trained the boy. The Russians I worked with often suspected such a training program. Proof, well, that is another matter."

A low hiss came from the Glowworm. "If Chris Gibbs is alive and he is responsible . . . I want to find him. Where?" The Glowworm's body shook. "Where can I find him?"

"I can't tell you where at this time, but," Pablo added quickly, "I can tell you how I would go about finding him."

"Hurry up with it!"

"Well, knowing how security organizations operate, if Chris Gibbs is still alive, I must assume he would still be a valuable asset. An asset the United States would want to keep in its special operations fold. If he's alive, he would be nearly fifty years old. He'd either be director level in the CIA or SOCOM. Or, if he were still operational, Chris could probably be found posing as a civilian in one of the many theaters where the U.S. is at war. So, what I would do is begin looking for men who match those descriptions and then try to ID the older Gibbs with photos, and any DNA or fingerprints we could find."

"We?" the Glowworm said. "Does that mean you're interested in helping me? Perhaps joining the team at Glowworm Gaming?"

"I had not considered that. But in my retirement," Pablo said, "I have a lot of free time."

The Glowworm nodded. "Good, I think we may have an opening coming up." He ponderously tapped his lip with a slimy finger. He thought about something and said, "Bring me the person, or persons, at our company responsible for investigating Pablo and the death of my father."

A few moments later two young hackers, both in their mid-twenties, were led into the dark suite. One was tall, blond, and pasty with spiked hair. The other was dark-skinned and swarthy with a thick, scraggy beard and unwashed cargo pant shorts. Both hackers had on matching Glowworm Gaming hoodies and looked like they hadn't slept or bathed in days. A couple of scared techno-monkeys.

The Glowworm lifted his hand off the Nintendo and extended a pale slimy finger toward Pablo's laptop. "You thoroughly searched this man's computer, didn't you?"

The blond boy stepped forward. He had thick-gauge earrings, and his lower lip was pierced with a diamond stud. "Yes, we did. Fouad helped me hack in last month." The blond boy nodded to his darker counterpart. "Searching the computer, however, was my primary responsibility. I made a clone of his computer on my desktop. I have reviewed every piece of data on the computer. If you would like to review it?"

"You did not make a mistake?" the Glowworm asked.

"No, I am certain I did not." The diamond stud on the kid's lower lip began to tremble. "Is everything okay?"

"Yes. Just a routine performance review," the Glowworm said casually, glancing at Raquel, who took a step back. "Thank you for your transparency. But as you know, failure is not tolerated."

Without warning, the Glowworm shot up in his seat, hefted the Nintendo high up in his arms, and jumped at the hacker, slamming the gaming system down onto the boy's head.

The boy dropped instantly, but the Glowworm did not stop pounding him with the Nintendo. He just kept smashing and yelling, "Failure is not tolerated! Never, never fail me like that again!" He kept on, until the boy was almost faceless, twitching in a pool of his own blood on the floor of the Glowworm's luxury suite, surrounded by bits of plastic and metal. Raquel mercifully ended the hacker's life with a sling of her blade, nearly decapitating him, the knife was so sharp.

The Glowworm flopped back into his seat, his breathing returned to normal. The dark-skinned boy who had come in with the blond hacker lurched for a large porcelain vase and vomited into it.

The Glowworm turned his unnerving gaze to Pablo. "Welcome to Glowworm Gaming, Pablo. Fouad"—the Glowworm motioned to the young engineer puking into a vase—"will help you get settled in."

PART THREE

CHAPTER 16

July 2017
Camp Valor

Ropes were tied to the corners of a big white sheet. The sheet hauled up, pulled tight. A fire was lit, the projector plugged in. *Wet Hot American Summer,* a classic summer camp comedy, glowed on cotton. Campers gorged themselves, talking longingly of home. Dolly set a schedule for guard duty: everyone would have an hour, but no one was really listening.

Ebbie devoured two entire pizzas on his own, Samy "cameled" two and a half. Sugar flowed into bloodstreams. Laughter rose. Taut, half-starved bodies became sated. Sunburnt and chapped faces softened. Minds unfocused. Bliss. Finally able to act their ages for a moment. To let loose and forget Valor.

Wyatt lay down on the grass under the giant glowing bedsheet, watching Paul Rudd as a camp counselor when Dolly flopped down next to him and gave him a quick glance and a smile. "Mind if I sit here?"

"Sure," Wyatt said.

Dolly lay down beside him. Not so close that they were touching. But close enough that Wyatt felt his heart start to hammer in his chest. Had she asked him another question, he could not have answered. He couldn't speak. The movie and the glowing bedsheet, the other campers, were suddenly a thousand miles away. Pinholes against a black sky.

Wyatt felt himself pulled to Dolly in a way that almost scared him. Her face shone in the light from the projector. It looked like porcelain, her lips red. She glanced back and his instinct was to look away, but he did not. He kept his gaze on her. And she did not flinch. She grinned and turned her eyes back to the screen. Wyatt lost track of time and proximity and was the happiest he'd been in recent memory.

"Dolly," Hud's voice called out from the other side of the fire, breaking Wyatt's reverie. "Would you pass me a Coke?"

And everything shifted. The tilt of the planet that seemed to lean Wyatt into Dolly now tilted the other way.

Dolly's smile turned into a scowl, something uncertain. "Yeah, sure." Awkwardly she rose, walked to the cooler, fished out a can, and took it over to Hud.

She did not come back. She sat down beside Hud. Even closer than she had to Wyatt. Wyatt wanted to stick his hand in the fire. Maybe his head, too. He waited a few minutes, as the laughs rolled on, then he got up from the fire. He needed to put some distance between himself and Hud and Dolly.

"Where you goin', son?" Samy asked, craning his neck back.

"Bed." Wyatt retreated from the pool of light cast by the projector. "Wake me when it's my turn to be on lookout."

Wyatt pushed into the cabin. Empty. Dark. Musty. One look at his sleeping bag and bunk told him he wasn't ready to sleep. Too much sugar. Too much frustration. And he smelled bad. Really bad.

Wyatt found a dirty bar of soap and a stiff towel and instead of hiking into the Caldera where there were showers, he headed down to the water. The night was warm and dark.

At the beach, he stripped down to his underwear and waded in. The water was crisp, and he swam out to a pile of rocks. He took off his boxers and bathed slowly. Out in the black water, he remembered bathing in rivers on hunting trips with his father and Cody. Would his dad ever come back? Did Wyatt want him back?

Lathered, Wyatt dipped down, and, holding his breath, he hovered underwater. He rubbed the soap across his head and his face and stayed under the surface, embracing the cold, until he could take it no longer.

He stood—waist deep, arms crossed—and watched the sky. Stars stood out starkly. The Northern Lights swung, iridescent green on black. The movie and laughter that drifted down from base camp had died away.

"Thought you were going to bed."

Wyatt jumped and turned up to see Dolly on the shore.

"You have soap out there?"

"I'll bring it to you," Wyatt said. "I was just about to come in."

"That's okay. I'll come get it," she said and peeled off her shirt and shorts. She waded into the water in sports bra, undies. Then she dove into the dark water and swam out to the rock. She pulled herself out and sat next to him, shivering. "Soap." She held out her hand.

Wyatt passed her the bar. She took it and looked back at him. "I thought you said you were going back in."

"Right," Wyatt said and slipped back into the water, starting for shore.

"Hey," Dolly called after him. "What is your problem?"

"Problem?" Wyatt stopped in the water ten feet away.

"Yeah. You act like you can't stand me."

"I could say the same thing about you," Wyatt said, now confused. "You just told me to go back in."

"Well," Dolly said, "I don't want you to go back in."

"Then what the hell do you want?" Wyatt snapped, and took a few steps toward her. "You want me to wash out, so there's a little less competition around here for you and Hud?"

"What's that supposed to mean?"

"You know exactly what I mean. You two have been picking and choosing the team you want to qualify since day one." Wyatt studied Dolly's reaction. "It's true, isn't it?"

"It's not like there's a plot. We just want a solid team. We want the best in the field. And," she added, "we want you to make it."

"Both of you want me to make it?" Wyatt asked, still angry. Dolly started to respond, but Wyatt cut her off, "Forget it. I don't care what Hud wants. And you shouldn't either."

Dolly stared at Wyatt as she contemplated the words. The moonlight shining down on her seemed to soften her face. "You're right. I shouldn't care about what he thinks, because there's no room at Valor for any kind of feelings. For anyone . . . is that what you want, Wyatt?" She stared at him hard. "For me to feel nothing for anyone?"

Now Wyatt thought about his answer. "I want you to make up your own mind."

"Well, right now, while you're still here and I'm still here, I want you to stay. And wait for me."

"Fair enough." Wyatt said and waded back to her. He waited, waist deep, while she lathered herself with soap and slipped in, disappearing under the black surface. She came up near Wyatt, hair slicked back, eyes fixed on his face.

"You're freezing," she said. "You're shaking."

"I don't feel it," Wyatt said as she waded nearer.

"You don't feel cold?" she asked, her jaw clenching and body beginning to involuntarily shake.

"Not when I'm near you," Wyatt said, in disbelief that the words had actually left his mouth. She now was so close to Wyatt he could see the curve of her eyelashes. What was happening? Wyatt thought as she pressed her body next to his. Both felt each other's warmth. But neither moved. They just stared.

And then there was a flash of light and a sky-shattering boom as a bolt of lighting zigzagged out over the water. They backed away from each other, shy now. They could hear a low hissing sound in the distance as wind kicked up, the clouds blocking out the stars.

"Going to rain soon," Dolly said. "We should get back. And not together," she added.

Wyatt felt something electric and conspiratorial pulse through his body. "I don't want to leave," Wyatt heard himself saying, again shocked the words had left his mouth. "Not yet."

"Me either." She pulled him to her. The warmth returning. They just stared. And then the rain came, sweeping over the water, cold and stinging.

"Hey Dolly, where are you?" A voice called in the darkness.

Dolly's voice tightened and her face went pale. "Hud," she whispered.

"It's time anyway," Wyatt said. "You go first."

"But you're freezing."

"I'm fine," Wyatt said through chattering teeth.

"Okay. I'll see you tomorrow." She quickly kissed Wyatt on the cheek. Wyatt watched her wade back, the rain lashing his neck and shoulders. He dropped down into the dark cold water.

CHAPTER 17

June 2017
Camp Valor

3:30 a.m.

The rain helped disguise the water landing. Five heavily armed figures, clad in black and wearing NVGs crept up toward base camp. Off to their left, the remnants of a bonfire hissed and steamed, a blob of smoke, seemingly hovering above charred logs and pizza boxes. Errant soggy pizza crusts and soda cans dotted the ground.

The porch and lodge were empty of people and devoid of sentries other than Emmerson, the supposed guard, sleeping on the porch. A signal was given to proceed to the cabins occupied by the boys and girls of Group-C.

It felt like his bunk was hit with a baseball bat as the first explosion jarred Wyatt awake. The whole cabin concussed. The old wooden beams supporting the thin roof trembled. Dust and grit rained down on the seven waking boys.

More explosions followed—low-lying, on the floor of the cabin. Fully automatic gunfire erupted. Wyatt saw a figure in black wearing NVGs in the doorway to the cabin holding an AR-15, its barrel and breech barking red flames as ammunition tore through the weapon. Another figure clad in black, just outside the door, lobbed a flash-bang grenade into the cabin.

Wyatt tried to run but couldn't move. Arms and legs pinned down in his sleeping bag, his fingers fumbled for the zipper. Smoke filled the cabin, hot and acrid, blinding Wyatt and burning his eyes and lungs.

"Get out! Get out!" voices shouted. With the explosions and gunfire, Wyatt couldn't tell who was yelling. Sleeping bag off, Wyatt shot out of his bunk, barefoot, dodging the plumes of sparks crackling along the floor, ducking, covering his head.

Bodies plowed past him out of the cabin. Eyes wide, whites showing. Panicked. Shots hissed though the air. Explosions shook the walls. Wyatt checked to see that no one was left in the bunks. The cabin was clear. He tumbled out of the cabin past two hooded figures shooting into the air and tossing fireworks and smoke bombs into the cabin.

"In line!" one of them shouted and shoved Wyatt, leveling his barrel at the back of Wyatt's head. Rain came down in sheets. The rest of the boys huddled in the exercise yard, blinking, shivering, under the watch of another armed guard.

Wyatt ran over and joined the rest of the group, cowering in the mud. Hud whispered to him as he ran up, "Where's Emmerson?"

"Huh?"

"Was he in the cabin? We're missing Emmerson."

Wyatt looked around, not seeing him, and did a quick head count. Then he remembered. "He was on lookout."

Hud pounded the mud with his fist.

"Silence!" The two armed figures by the cabin approached and joined the third. They removed their hoods: Hallsy, Mackenzie, and the Old Man.

Wyatt instantly realized they'd been tricked. Lulled into a complacent stupor. A lesson to be learned and a mistake not to be repeated.

"Sir," Hud said, "we are missing Emmerson."

"He's headed home," Hallsy said, "and the rest of you might be joining him soon."

Cass brought the girls over and lined them up next to the boys. Wyatt and Dolly shared a nervous look. Both knew this would be the last time either would smile for a while. Things were about to get hard.

"We leave you for five hours. . . ." Hallsy marched up and down the line of campers assembled. "Give you a couple boxes of pizza and soda pops and not a single one of you is awake when we get back. Not a single candidate! You're like a bunch of little children. Babies. Actually, babies wake up if you so much as breathe on them. Not a person here so much as stirred. Had there been a security breach while we were gone, all of you would be dead and our enemies would have their hands on some pretty powerful toys in the Caldera." Hallsy shook his head. "Shameful. Damn shameful. And we're gonna make you pay handsomely." Hallsy grinned, lightning perforating the sky around him. "Boys and girls, we are now in hell."

The suffering devised by the sadistic geniuses at Valor was a training protocol smash-up consisting of PT, outdoor-survival training, war-gaming, and seven consecutive Spartan Games all rolled up into one week of hell. Each of the twelve candidates was issued a couple new pieces of gear to carry. These items included a dummy M4 rifle (plugged barrel), a black hockey helmet, five pounds of MREs (meals ready to eat), NVGs, and a Buck knife. That is, everyone but Wyatt was issued a Buck knife. He already had his—the pearl-handled Buck knife Mum had given him on his first day.

As Wyatt and the rest of the campers quickly assembled rucksacks for Hell Week, he now realized why Hallsy, and others, had taken issue with the gift. Receiving the knife was the honor granted to those who had made it to Hell Week. Being able to keep it, that was the reward for finishing Hell Week. Make it through hell, win a knife. In that moment Wyatt decided he would not give anyone reason to question Mum's confidence in him, her belief that he would make it through.

Seven days, Wyatt told himself, one day at a time, one hour, one minute. Just keep moving forward and you'll make it.

The day commenced with a simple command: "Crawl." Hallsy pointed to the top of the Caldera. "And stay down. Or you'll get your head blown off. We are in enemy territory."

All twelve fell to their knees. Rifles in ready position. They began the slow slog up the long, shale-strewn path. The pounding rain intensified. Fingers squished deep in mud. Knees were shredded. Wyatt's back screamed in pain. Twenty minutes up the path, Samy crawled next to Wyatt. "Hey, man, you know why they plug the barrels during Hell Week?"

"No," said Wyatt. "You?"

"Heard rumors. Weird to be carrying a gun that don't work."

"What kind of rumors?"

Hud looked back, shushing them.

Samy whispered, "I heard the staff plugged the barrels of the M4s during Hell Week to prevent campers from turning weapons on themselves."

•   •   •

Halfway to the top of the Caldera, Wyatt heard a stick crack off in the brush. He rose up onto his knees to see what it was. Instantly, the surrounding woods lit up with machine-gun fire. Tracer rounds buzzed overhead, flash-bang grenades exploded on each side of the path, and Wyatt's black helmet glowed Day-Glo orange and emitted an ear-splitting tone.

Hallsy ran over and screamed down at Wyatt. "I said stay down! Now your head is gone. Fifty push-ups."

Wyatt buried his nose into the muck and began pushing out push-ups.

"Out there," Hallsy motioned to the woods, "this entire week, ghosts are watching. Your every move. They will catch your every mistake. And Wyatt," Hallsy said as the tone cut off and the helmet turned back from orange to black, "I didn't expect you to be the first to screw up. Get it together. Or you will wash out. You hear me?"

"Yes, sir," Wyatt said, pushing out once more.

"All right, soon as Wyatt is finished, we begin again."

And so the slog continued.

Wyatt pulled himself up the flat rocky crest of the Caldera as the sun peaked over the horizon, yellow light spilling out over the surrounding islands and water.

"At ease," Hallsy said. "Take a fifteen-minute break for water and breakfast."

Hallsy looked off to the woods. As if materializing from a tall shrub, a staff member walked out of the forest carrying a large backpack and two gallons of water. This was the punk rocker Wyatt had seen on the first day at Valor, the kitchen helper, Fabian Grant, Mackenzie's brother. He topped off water bottles and replaced their MREs.

"Keep kicking ass," Fabian said. "Don't drop, don't stop."

Wyatt's spirits were buoyed.

Hallsy paced among them. "Make sure you eat and drink. You should not conserve your food. In the field, you'd be limited, but during Hell Week, we want you to keep your water and calorie intake high. You'll burn between seven and ten thousand calories a day, so be sure to drink and chow. Just don't gorge yourselves. We'll be moving again soon. Now eat."

The mud-splattered candidates shoveled and chugged.

When the campers finished eating, Fabian left the same way he came, disappearing into the woods.

Hallsy gave the next order. "We're going to be taking a swim soon, so we need to work up a sweat."

Of course they were already caked in mud, soaked in sweat, and practically swimming in the rain cascading down.

"Three 15-sets. Let's go!"

A 15-set was fifteen up-downs or "burpies," as they are known, 15 push-ups, 15 sit-ups, and 150 seconds of flutter kicks, followed by 14 up-downs, 14 push-ups, 14 sit-ups, and 140 seconds of flutter kicks, and on down to zero. The low number of initial reps was deceiving. 15 burpies? No problem. How about 120 burpies?

One 15-set included 375 exertions, all to be executed properly and not phoned in. To put it simply, three 15-sets was punishing.

Wyatt wasn't sure how far they were into the sets. He was trying not to count when Sanders, the tough-as-nails juvenile car thief from Kentucky, dropped his pack off his back and, gripping his stomach, staggered off into the woods. He'd gorged on MREs. Big mistake.

Sanders wasn't ten yards off the trail when his shoe snagged on a stealthily hidden length of fishing line. A booby trap. The ground directly next to Sanders erupted in a volcano of dirt, rock, and pine needles, knocking Sanders sideways. Like Wyatt's helmet had sounded off and flashed earlier, Sanders's helmet turned orange and shrieked like crazy.

"You are a sorry bunch," Hallsy said. "It isn't even 7 a.m. and we got two dead. Sanders, next time you need to take a crap, you best ask first."

"Ain't going to be a next time," Sanders said, clawing at the straps on the side of his helmet. "I want out. I am done!" He waddled toward Hallsy walking funny. Wyatt realized that when the explosion had gone off Sanders had crapped his pants.

"Give me the horn," Sanders said. Hand out.

Hallsy studied the boy, face red and getting redder. Shame building. "Tell you what," Hallsy said, his tone softening. "I'll let you change and wash up. Don't quit."

"Gimmie the goddamn horn!" Tears ran down Sanders's cheeks.

Hallsy nodded. The fog horn sounded and two more staff members materialized from the woods, put on cuffs, and led Sanders away.

Wyatt and the rest of the candidates watched Sanders leaving in shock. He was a hard-ass. And a good kid. He had quit and was gone without even time to say good-bye.

Wyatt adjusted his helmet and spat.

"Gone," Samy said. "Like that."

Hallsy shrugged. "No sympathy. If a little doo-doo in your shorts'll stop you, this ain't for you."

After the 15-sets, the remaining eleven candidates rappelled a cliff on the backside of the Caldera into frigid water. They were then told to swim, loaded with weapons and packs, to a nearby shore, where they found that three inflatable boats had been dragged up onto the beach and left at the base of a steep, narrow trailhead.

Another 15-set, and Hallsy gave instructions. They were to carry the boats to the end of the trail and await instructions. Each boat weighed three hundred pounds. They would need to split up into teams to do this.

Wyatt consulted his map, quickly estimating that the checkpoint was five miles inland through enemy territory. Meanwhile Annika, Wyatt's friend who looked and performed like an Amazonian huntress, hefted the side of one of the rafts, shook her head, and simply said, "Horn." It wasn't even noon yet.

CHAPTER 18

Winter 2015–2016
Monaco and Panama

Pablo's barstool in his casino sat empty for weeks, then months, then one day, some other fat butt smothered the sacred, shiny metal seat. Some other guy perched in Pablo's spot, like a toupee—a cheap, ill-fitting replica in place of the real article.

Pablo's vodka, ordered specially from Russia, piled up. The bartender dropped it from his order sheet. The casino's regular patrons, who originally came for the free drinks that Pablo dished out, initially inquired about his absence, but then quickly forgot about Pablo, preferring a peaceful environment without the domineering old blowhard jeering, "Prost! Prost!" So what if it meant paying for their drinks?

A few employees briefly considered calling the police to report his absence, but they had listened long enough to Pablo brag about his past with the Russian mafia. And their paychecks kept coming. Why mess with that? Even Pablo's best friends felt more at ease with him gone. It was easier to cheat the house without Pablo peering over their shoulders. All in all, Pablo's casino grew quaint and comfortable in its owner's absence.

Nobody really worried about Pablo. After all, he was last seen leaving the casino with a young pretty girl in a red dress. He was lucky. Most people assumed he was on an extended getaway or running elicit errands for an oligarch. Or on a drunken binge. A few people, of course, whispered that Pablo Gutierrez may have been decomposing somewhere musty. But this was not said openly.

Of all the possible speculation, no one who had ever known Pablo—friend, foe, or flunky—could have ever possibly guessed that the old paramilitary thug and strong-arm man had left Monaco for Panama to become a key player in one of the most disruptive start-ups of our time.

Yes, Pablo had traded in his ten-thousand-dollar suits for a hoodie, a ratty, pit-stained T-shirt, and a Bluetooth earpiece, attached to his sole remaining ear. Instead of slugging vodka all day, he now sipped Pu-er tea from an ancient rice bowl, hovering over a keyboard. Rather than spending days drunkenly sounding off to a bunch of washed-up lowlifes, Pablo now commanded the undivided attention of some of the greatest and most devious minds the tech industry had spawned.

Pablo didn't just work at Glowworm Gaming, he ran one of its most important and secretive divisions—a skunk-works affair code-named Project Prep School. Pablo Gutierrez led the team tasked with avenging the death of the Glowworm's father. Project Prep School had two clear targets: capture or kill Chris Gibbs and burn the program that trained him to the ground.

Of course, Pablo wasn't exactly getting paid for running Project Prep School. Not in dollars or euros or even Bitcoins. Pablo's remuneration came in a far more valuable currency— time tacked on to his lifespan.

Pablo had been both relieved and horrified when Raquel dispatched the hacker who had failed to discover the salt stain photos on Pablo's computer.

It sent a powerful message. Pablo knew that any failure to produce results would give the Glowworm and Raquel a welcome excuse to kill him horribly. And so it was by Pablo's progress and productivity, and by the Glowworm's grace, that Pablo continued to haunt the earth.

Pablo lived like a silicon slave. Long hours and pressure to perform. Slave that he was, Pablo surprisingly found his new job rewarding. And at times, he was even imbued with a sense of purpose, camaraderie, and learning. The health perks at Glowworm Gaming weren't bad either. In order to keep Pablo productive (and alive), the Glowworm had him on a medication regime similar to his own. This included human growth harmone, nootropics (smart drugs), 2000 mg of B-12 daily, and a hearty dose of good old-fashioned Adderall.

Pablo quickly shed his belly fat, often lifting up his shirt to show his cubical buddies his "sagging six-pack." He felt so great, in fact, he even signed up for the CrossFit classes held in the basement of the compound in Panama. Sometimes Raquel taught the class. Pablo savored those days at CrossFit, and soon was known as the King of the Kettlebells until he shattered his wrist in a one-on-one burpie competition with Raquel.

In many ways, Pablo was back in action, baby. He was ripped and geeked and, at eighty, looked like a grizzled, steroidal, geriatric hospital escapee. He felt younger and badder than ever, and he always kept the vision of Glowworm's Vitamix blender in the forefront of his mind. If Pablo was going to get out of there, his ticket to ride would be solving the riddle of Chris Gibbs and the American program that trained him.

Pablo knew the only way to do that was to match the past to

the present. The Chapan School for Boys, where Chris and Wilberforce met as boarding students, converted its paper files to digital
back in the early 2000s. This meant that Pablo's team could easily
hack the school's system and retrieve the files from the late '80s.
The problem was that nearly all records relating to Chris Gibbs had
mysteriously disappeared before the digital trail had been started.

What remained of Chris were a few photos and mentions
in the Chapan yearbook, *The Aegis*. There was Chris in a grainy
portrait, just another lanky freshman wearing a coat and tie,
smiling into the camera. His face dotted by a smattering of zits
and his mop of brown hair verging on a mullet. Chris could also
be found obscured by a teammate's afro in the JV football photo,
and skating down center ice, hockey hair out the back of his helmet. He was listed as a member of the debate team and the gaming club, and a contributor to the student newspaper.

Working with the *Aegis* photographs, Pablo's team created
a series of renderings of what Chris might look like today: a fairly
unremarkable man of fifty. Armed with the childhood photos
and the renderings and facial recognition software, the Glowworm's best hackers gained access to the U.S., Canadian, and
British passport offices and began searching for possible matches
to the renderings. They hacked into U.S. State Department databases for license, prison, and morgue photos and searched those
as well. Since the renderings depicted how Chris *might* look as an
adult, the results were mixed. A possible match would come in
and undergo a vetting process by Pablo's team. The closest con-
tending photographs would be taken to the Glowworm for his
inspection. No photo so far had passed the Glowworm test. If
this didn't change, Pablo was going to lose body parts.

CHAPTER 19

The raft bucked and plunged. Ebbie's body thrashed and jerked, eyes and tongue lolling, no clear signs of life, his blood streaming so heavily Wyatt could taste copper. Whitewater boiled up around their faces. They weren't submerged but they might as well have been. They raced down one final chute and shot out, listing into another calm stretch.

No one moved. They drifted in the foamy slipstream.

"Is he dead?" Hud asked.

Wyatt pulled himself up to Ebbie's face and listened. And heard breath. "Alive. Hurting, but alive."

They'd begun Hell Week as twelve, and they were now six zombies clinging to a half-sunken raft, heading down a frigid river. The end had to be near. Or they would die. Wyatt knew Ebbie needed medical assistance. He'd fallen from his raft and suffered a head injury.

The river flattened and deepened. And seemed to speed ahead. The fog lifted, but the day was cool and gray and a sleeting rain came down. A steep, tree-covered bank loomed up on the left. As they swept around it on a wide turn, Ebbie started coughing and his body began shaking. His eyes opened, eyeballs strained.

One word came out of his mouth. "Look."

It wasn't just the Old Man and Mum on the shore but the entire staff lined up. Torches burning. Soup boiling, blankets warming. Pizza boxes stacked. Group-C's souped-up inflatable at the ready. The *Sea Goat* anchored.

Cheers rang out from the shore. The Old Man yelled, "Congratulations, Group-C, you have completed Hell Week!"

Hallsy, Mackenzie, and Cass raced down the river on jet skis. Hallsy hooked the back of his jet ski to the raft. "Lift to shore?"

Wyatt spoke for everyone. "Is it over, is it really over?"

They trudged up the sand like the refugees they were. Their war had been Hell Week and they'd won. Bloody knees and elbows and hands rubbed raw. Borderline hypothermic. Bodies practically sucked dry by thousands of bug bites. No fat. All muscle and sinew, moving cautiously like wet, starved feral cats.

Stretchers were brought for Hud, who had smashed his ankle, and Ebbie. Samy fell on his knees and kissed the sand. Dolly's body shook, she sobbed with relief. Wyatt sat by the fire and silently and secretly prayed, thanking God for giving him the strength he did not have.

The Old Man walked over with a bowl of soup.

Wyatt moved to stand.

"Sit. Don't get up." The Old Man's knees creaked as he lowered himself to Wyatt's level and handed him the soup. "No one can take this away from you. Ever." He patted Wyatt's back firmly. "You can take this with you the rest of your life. I'm so proud. I know your father would be too if he were here."

What was that? Wyatt pulled back, scowling. "What does my dad have to do with this?"

"I'm sorry," the Old Man said, seeming genuinely apologetic. "I just meant any father would be proud. Any mother, too. Just look at Mum." Wyatt saw Mum headed his way, tears in her eyes, carrying a blanket.

Mum draped a blanket around Wyatt's shoulders and whispered into his ear, "I knew I made the right choice when I gave you that knife. Next step is to prove you are worthy of Top Camper." She winked.

Wyatt nodded, but in truth all he could think about was sleep. The Old Man read his mind. "Get rest, Wyatt," he said, "and don't get too cozy. You'll have a couple days to recover, then it's back on. A hundred percent, a hundred percent of the time."

For Wyatt, Hell Week began by staring at Dolly, and so it ended in the same way. Not long after staggering to shore, Wyatt lay in the stern of the *Sea Goat*, under a pile of warming blankets. Dolly lay beside him, their IVs pumping fluids, painkillers, sedatives, and antibiotics. Wyatt's eyes were heavy but he could not stop watching her, her hair blowing across green eyes, rimmed in red, staring at the water.

Under the warming blankets Wyatt felt a hand touch his. Her fingers were surprisingly calloused, like his, and still cold. She took his hand into hers and seemed to smile, before her eyes fluttered shut.

CHAPTER 20

Spring 2016
Panama and Places Unknown

The first credible photographic match Pablo's team found came from a newspaper article published by the *Bloomington Courier* on December 12, 1982.

"Have You Seen This Boy?" the headline read. "Friends and foster care officials have reported teen Eldon Waanders missing. The 14-year-old, who is 5'10" with sandy blond hair, was last seen leaving the Pound Ridge Sheriff's Office on Thanksgiving Day. Please call the sheriff's office with any information on his whereabouts."

The article had been converted from microfiche to digital and was especially grainy. The photo depicted a surly teenage boy taken from a school photo. It looked like Eldon Waanders could have been Chris Gibbs. Even the Glowworm thought it probable.

The problem with confirming the match was that a search

for Eldon Waanders produced a second article. This one from December 23, 1982. "Body of Missing Boy Found." The article went on to give details: "As we enter the holiday season, the town of Pound Ridge is struck by tragedy. On Wednesday morning, the body of Eldon Waanders was discovered in an abandoned vehicle off Hollings Road. The teen, a habitual runaway, had been missing since Thanksgiving Day. His body was identified by Sheriff Marion Bouchard, cause of death ruled as accidental carbon monoxide poisoning. Eldon had been taking shelter in an abandoned cargo van during the blizzard last week. He appears to have used a gas camping stove for heat as temperatures reached record lows. It is believed he sealed all doors and windows to conserve heat, unaware he was endangering himself."

The article contained memorial service and burial details. Pablo's team found copies of Eldon's birth and death certificates. Eldon Waanders had been fourteen when he died—a year and a half before Chris Gibbs attended boarding school. A frustratingly close match, the evidence seemed to point to a dead end, but it occurred to Pablo that Chris Gibbs had faked his death before. If he did it once, he could do it again. The new lead was not completely dead, but stalled until they could gather more information. Breaking this news to the Glowworm, however, was a different story.

Though the lead might still bear fruit, it was a failure, even if temporary. And as punishment for failure, the Glowworm, hacker that he was, let Raquel hack off Pablo's left leg below the knee. She used a tourniquet and her paring knife. Hurt like hell. Looked even worse.

And they ate his old hairy leg. Or rather, the girl ate some, and the Glowworm ingested it after it was blended into a slurry with farro and pumped into his stomach. In a show of self-serving magnanimity, the Glowworm had Pablo given antibiotics and outfitted with one of the world's most advanced prostheses, so Pablo could get around efficiently. The leg episode, however, had served its purpose. Pablo no longer had any fear of dying. He only feared underperforming.

While his team scoured the digital universe for any information about Chris Gibbs, Pablo set another, more traditional strategy in motion. He went old-school, convincing the Glowworm to put some money behind the problem. Pablo put out a bounty.

Working on the assumption that if the real Chris Gibbs might still be working for a U.S. spy agency, Pablo believed that someone out there in the criminal-spy underworld would know of him. And could be tempted into selling that information.

Through some of his oldest and sleaziest contacts at the Russian Federal Security Service and Foreign Intelligence Service, Pablo set out the bait. Fifteen million dollars to anyone who could deliver Chris Gibbs dead. Forty million, if they could bring him in alive. With the online and offline strategies in play, Pablo believed finding information leading to Chris Gibbs would be a matter of time.

Pursuing the program that trained Gibbs, on the other hand, was a trickier proposition. In the case of Gibbs, Pablo had evidence a person actually existed. He had attended a boarding school, had sucked up to the Glowworm and gotten invited to join the Degas family on Spring Break. Pablo had talked to him, watched him play video games, was asked to cook breakfast for him one morning. Point being, Gibbs was an entity Pablo had observed.

The training program, on the other hand, was a theory based on observing evidence of its existence. Logically, if a boy created a fake identity to get into boarding school, used a suction-cup climbing device to scale the hull of a boat, and assassinated a foreign leader who was a skilled assassin in his own right, the boy probably had some training. And if he'd received this type of training, there must have been a program that trained him. Logically, once again, that program must be highly clandestine, it must employ a support staff, it must be funded and shielded from public scrutiny by a government—all signs pointing to the U.S. in this case. And of course, there were the rumors Pablo had heard from his old FSB and KGB pals in Russia, rumors about a secret U.S. program to train young boys and girls to be spies and assassins.

That was the evidence he had—deduction and rumor. But had he observed the program in any shape or form? Pablo had never seen the program; everything he thought about it was speculation. He was like a hunter who had only discovered the carcass of a kill, but not the murderous animal. Pablo's hunter's instinct told him that it was an organization, or a pack of beasts, that had been able to take down the Colonel. Now Pablo needed to find that pack. The beasts were out in the game preserve sharpening their claws. Pablo figured he could do one of two things to find the pack: he could go poking around in the bushes, or he could do what poachers do—find the game warden and put a gun to his head.

The gun Pablo could use most easily was information. For years, the Glowworm had been worming his way into the homes and devices owned by hundreds of millions of people across the world. Some of those homes belonged to high-ranking officials in the U.S. government. Some, if not all, of those government officials would have something on their computers that they'd strongly like to keep private. And once the Glowworm got in, he was a master at finding those things.

So, Pablo thought. Let the blackmail begin!

PART FOUR

CHAPTER 21

Late Fall 2016
East Jerusalem, Places Unknown, and Panama

When most people think back on their lives, especially the formative years—the time spent in elementary school, middle school, high school, college, and first jobs—and they think about who mattered to them, the tendency is to recall friends or enemies, classmates, coworkers. If the memories are good, they're categorized by name, by face, a club, a sport, a haircut, sometimes even by smell—good or bad.

When the operator sitting in the hotel room in Jerusalem thought back on his life and tried to recall the lives who impacted him—the faces, the haircuts, the activities—they were all versions of his own.

Scott Watts, the high-school senior from Chicago who interned at the U.S. Embassy in South Korea and perfected his tennis and golf game with the daughter of the ambassador and the son of the president of South Korea. Tony Roy, the avid cyclist and student at the University of Tennessee, loved the sport of cycling so much that he spent a summer in Europe, participating in various races, all building up to observing the Tour de France, where he spent his time in the box next to a high-value target suspected of sharing U.S. secrets with the Belgians.

And right out of college, there was Travis Wilburn, the seed broker, who traveled extensively across the African continent, selling organic seed stock, meeting with rebel fighters, and, occasionally, permanently removing warlords from this earth.

The operator had, by his count, some seventy-three discrete identities in his thirty-odd years in the service of the American people. Some of those identities the operator would reuse, some had to be retired, but of all of them, the one he remembered most, the one that had the strongest impact on his life, was one of his first identities. Christopher Michael Gibbs, a boarding-school student at the Chapan School for Boys, where he was a member of the junior varsity football team, contributor to the high-school newspaper, member of the gaming club, a wrestler, and most critically, best friend to Wilberforce Degas, the son of Colonel Degas, who was, at the time, Central America's premiere butcher.

The reason the operator's assignment as Chris Gibbs was so impactful had to do with a number of factors. Of course, one's first kill is always memorable, especially when you're fifteen years old and you're unexpectedly forced to terminate a dictator. But killing Colonel Degas did not make his experience as Chris Gibbs as impactful as simply caring did. As Chris Gibbs, the operator actually cared about his rushing yards, touchdowns, and receptions on the school's rather mediocre JV football team. He cared about what he wrote in the student newspaper and about learning chess, and he cared about Wilberforce, or Wil, as he was known back then.

While the two made an odd pair, Chris Gibbs genuinely liked the pasty, nerdy, extremely bright Wilberforce, who was painfully eager for his attention. The friendship for the operator was genuine. The high-school experience was genuine. Everything leading up to the moment, and even, to a degree, the days following—the altercation with Colonel Degas—was genuine. Disentangling himself from that relationship was painful for the young operator (a lesson he learned and would not repeat). Far more painful, however, was the hurt that he must have caused Wil by taking his father—scumbag that he was—out of the kid's life.

This dichotomy of genuine emotion and caring juxtaposed with ruthless action was hard to reconcile, and so Chris Gibbs and his old friend, Wil Degas, were never far from the operator's thoughts. Whether it was conscious or not, he had always known that somehow those two boys from Chapan would re-enter his life.

That moment came earlier that day in East Jerusalem when the operator received a tip: a fifteen-million-dollar bounty had been placed on the head of an operator, known in his early years as Christopher Gibbs. Forty million to be brought back alive. Those kinds of numbers were enough to give even the most experienced of operators pause.

The operator had been in Jerusalem for the past month, on a relatively low-danger assignment. His cover was as a buyer of date palms for date paste, an industrial food ingredient used by cookie manufacturers in the United States. In reality, he'd been meeting with a Palestinian separatist group, trying to win their trust in order to gain information about certain high-value targets believed to be both financiers and directors of ISIS operations in Iraq and Syria. The Palestinian separatists were the kind of people whom the operator thought about as idealistic horse

traders. They were born negotiators, looking for a little deal here
and there. Give a little, get a little. The operator was very comfortable with them. Most of their business was conducted at
cafés and bars out in the public, trusted places. In a conflict zone,
sure, but nothing like a war zone. Hence, the operator had
come to the Middle East practically naked, as far as weaponry
went. He arrived armed with his clothes, a satellite phone, a SIG
Sauer, and three decades of experience.

The tip about the bounty came from the most trusted of
sources—a former colleague in his SEAL team, a former pro-
tégé, a lifetime friend and fellow operative, a member of the
Golden One Hundred. One of the few humans on this earth
who knew that the operator had been Chris Gibbs. His friend,
who had been operating in Syria on a DOD budget, offered to
come to Jerusalem and provide protection for the exfiltration.
And so the operator was not particularly worried about getting
out of the country and returning to the safety of the United
States.

After receiving the tip, as he had been trained, he calmly
returned to his hotel, quickly packed his personal items, light
weaponry, and articles related to his cover—sample fruit, bro-
chures, importation forms, and various business documents.
Transportation would be arriving outside the hotel lobby in a
matter of minutes. The operator moved into the hallway and
opted for the stairs instead of the creaky elevator. Though not
acutely concerned for his safety, if the rumors were true, forty
million dollars was a lot of money. The kind of dollar-value reserved for the likes of a Bin Laden or a Saddam Hussein, not an
operator who had lived a very careful and low-key life.

Still, as he descended the hotel's chipped marble staircase,
in the back of his mind were the Palestinian separatists he'd been
meeting with the past few weeks. The idealistic horse traders

who, undoubtedly, were tied into the same networks and chan-
nels that were whispering about the bounty and the operator
known as Chris Gibbs. He wondered if there was a photograph
of him out there somewhere, some digital footprint, something
that would make greedy minds go click.

Looking out from the smoky lobby at the street, the operator saw a black Land Rover parked outside the hotel, his friend
in the passenger seat, and he recognized a former Israeli Mossad
agent at the wheel. He didn't know the driver's real name, but
by reputation he knew him to be a skilled operator. And the
operator known as Chris Gibbs could not have chosen a better
driver. As an Israeli, he'd know the terrain and help get them
through checkpoints in the country.

Careful not to do anything that would draw suspicion, he
calmly walked over to reception, paid his bill, turned in his clunky
room key, a brass key tethered to a decorative tile that matched
the tile on the lobby floor. He received his passport and a receipt.
The operator slipped them into his pocket, thanked the recep-
tionist, walked out into the hot Jerusalem afternoon, and stepped
directly into the back seat of the Rover.

The driver had Metallica's "Unforgiven" playing on the radio, volume turned low. His friend, whose eyes never stopped
scanning the street, said, "Hey, buddy," as the operator got in
behind the passenger seat. The Israeli driver didn't wait for the
door to close, but pulled out, not speeding but not wasting any
time, either.

Jerusalem is both a modern and an ancient city, with a mix
of modern highways and narrow roads barely fitting a donkey
cart. The drivers tended to be reckless and eternally in a rush.
This included the many Orthodox Jews the operator had noticed,
driving minivans full of families with their large, circular velvet
hats on, at breakneck speeds through the ancient part of the

city. Navigating through the warren of streets, the two Americans and the Israeli driver discussed the exfiltration plan, the consensus being that driving south to the seaside town of Eilat would draw the least amount of attention. There, the Israeli would rent a boat and scuba equipment for himself. He would then take the Americans out into the Red Sea and make contact with an American naval vessel, drop off the Americans, and head back.

As soon as the details were decided, the operators settled in for a quiet ride, all hyper-alert as they made their way out of the city. The operator in the back seat was eager to speak to his friend in detail about what he knew about the bounty, the circumstances, the players involved, but he did not want to discuss this in front of the driver, who was not as well known to either man.

The farther they drove outside of Jerusalem, the more the tension eased. Not far from town was a famous Elvis-themed gas station with Elvis dressed as Jesus, Elvis dressed as a Hasidic Jew. Elvis printed on T-shirts, cups, every conceivable knickknack. It was, of course, a tourist destination. They stopped for gas and water, and the driver grabbed a falafel while the operator's friend picked up a tin of Skoal mint dip.

Departing the gas station, they opted for a circuitous route, not following the expressway that ran the length of Israel, but instead winding through a village to the northeast. The operator's friend joked about visiting a nearby restaurant famous for its hummus. They were in a dusty, hilly, nearly mountainous part of the country, driving down a narrow road. Ahead was an intersection where a villager pulled a reluctant donkey across the street. Attached to the donkey was a cart of what looked like farm equipment, very common in the area.

"Pull around them," the operator's friend said to the driver, who eased into the oncoming lane. The road ahead was clear to pass. Something pierced the windshield, and instantly, the Israeli's driver's head seemed to vaporize in red mist. The operator shielded his eyes, reached around his back for his gun, and groped for the door handle in the back seat, while the farmer let go of the now rearing donkey and emptied an Uzi into the Rover's engine block. The SUV careened off the side of the road and crashed into the rocky slope on the opposite side of the oncoming lane.

Upon impact, the driver's side of the vehicle exploded. The operator didn't know if it was due to the engine or some sort of ordnance inside the vehicle. He was thrust against the door, glass and fragments flying everywhere. Sharp bits of car swirled around him. The operator could feel the hair burn off the side of his head. He somehow managed to get the door open and stumble out into the street. His friend had already exited the vehicle and was crouched, firing up the side of the hill where gun barrels were aimed down at them. His friend was yelling something the operator couldn't hear because his eardrums had been blown out, but without pausing, he turned in the opposite direction and opened fire, killing the villager, whose Uzi sprayed in an erratic arc as he toppled backward onto the blacktop, firing into the donkey, which went berserk, stomping and kicking the car to pieces. The operator probably shouldn't have wasted the time or the ammunition, but out of mercy he shot the flailing donkey.

The operator thought he heard his friend yell, "This way!"

He glanced to his left and saw his friend sprint across the right side of the road and dive over a rickety guardrail in the direction of the steep slope down into the valley. The operator moved to follow, but something struck him from behind, something like an axe handle blow behind his ear. He fell onto the street, losing consciousness as his world turned bright white and then black.

.   .   .

Sometime later, the operator was vaguely aware he was bound, gagged, and in the back of a vehicle, speeding through what felt like winding roads. He knew since he was alive that whoever had captured him was likely beginning the process of collecting on the bounty, a process that would no doubt involve safe-houses, negotiations between untrustworthy parties, and innumerable opportunities for betrayals and human error. Chances of his survival were exceedingly low. His only hope, at this point, was that his friend had gotten out alive.

Halfway across the world, by way of the dark net, a laptop computer in a Panamanian gaming company chimed with a new email. There was a photo of a man in a trunk, a U.S. citizen who had been operating in the Middle East. Facial recognition to the high-school photo of Chris Gibbs was at eighty-three percent. The group that abducted the operator called itself the Brotherhood. They would be happy to sell the operator to Pablo, but there was one twist. The Brotherhood was holding an auction of sorts and Glowworm Gaming would be bidding against the U.S. government. The price for the operator believed to be Chris Gibbs had gone up to fifty million.

Pablo took this news to the Glowworm.

"I'll pay fifty million for him, I'll pay even sixty million. Whatever it takes, if it is the real Chris Gibbs," the Glowworm said. "But I want proof. Eighty-three percent is not good enough. I need DNA or a fingerprint to match Gibbs. Or I don't pay. It's that simple."

And so Pablo had his new directive. Find a print, blood, hair, or tissue sample from a high-school student who had disappeared thirty years ago.

Yeah, real simple.

CHAPTER 22

August 2017
Camp Valor

The Cave Complex had a locker room and showers. Hot showers. Wyatt took his time. After twelve straight hours of close-quarters pistol training in three different environments and simulated situations—hostage, terrorists on plane, school shooter—Wyatt leaned against the tile wall and let the piping-hot water course down his shoulders, neck, and back. When his muscles loosened and his back was bright red, he shut off the spigot, grabbed a towel, and went back to his locker, where he cleaned, oiled, and stowed his gear. He changed into his now extremely thin Tony Hawk T-shirt, shorts, belt, and sheath with the knife, which he'd officially been allowed to keep since completing Hell Week. He then returned his H&K MP7A1 and Glock to the gun locker and secured the weapons.

The rest of the Group-Cs had long ago headed back to base camp and to the Mess Hall. They'd learned that to wait for

Wyatt meant they'd starve or eat cold food. Wyatt was happy to eat icicles if it meant a little alone time.

He stepped from the Cave Complex into golden late-afternoon sunlight. He was tired. To his core. But he felt good and clean, like a wet sponge wrung dry. A drone buzzed toward him and dipped its wing. Rory must be at the controls, he thought. Even though she had originally been slated for explosives, Rory had shown a proclivity toward aviation and drones, so the staff transitioned her to that program.

Wyatt gave a wave. The drone banked hard and disappeared into the mouth of the cave, the image reminding Wyatt of a children's book he'd read about an old lady inhaling a fly.

He smiled and started up the interior slope of the Caldera at a crisp pace. He remembered the first day he'd walked up the opposite side of the Caldera and how winded he'd become. The day was hotter than his first day and the interior slope was steeper and he was far more tired, yet he felt like he could start running and not even break a sweat.

As Wyatt summited the high ridge that ringed the Caldera, he noticed that a second, smaller drone had been following him, but fell off as he crossed out of the Caldera. Wyatt suspected this second drone, the stalking drone, must be manned by Avi. Avi had never warmed up to Wyatt. The security guru was prickly with everyone, but especially with Wyatt, and Wyatt couldn't understand why. The only thing Wyatt could chalk it up to was that Hallsy clearly liked Wyatt and if there was any-one Avi liked less than Wyatt it was Hallsy.

The heavily wooded path down to base camp was now in the shadow of the Caldera and was particularly dark. Not quite cool, but cooler than the Sugar Bowl. And it felt good.

A pebble landed at Wyatt's feet. He froze and scanned the hillside, searching for movement in the dusky light slanting through the trees. He smelled dinner wafting up from base camp. Who would be out in the woods besides him? He glimpsed movement to his three o'clock and decided to investigate. But instead of taking a direct line to the source of the movement, he ambled down the path and then looped back uphill, around a large rock outcropping. He unclipped his knife and gripped the bone handle.

He slowly and silently crept up a narrow ravine into a dense thicket of trees and discovered a figure with its back to him, looking down at the path.

"Dolly?"

She jumped and put a finger to her lips. "Shhh." She pointed, indicating they should walk deeper into the forest.

He followed. They came to a cavelike cutout that was shielded by the thick pine boughs. Dolly entered, her eyes and posture hyper-alert. She vibed nervous. Borderline scared. Wyatt had never seen her like this. He kinda liked it. Wyatt followed, his breathing quickened too. They had not been alone since the night before Hell Week, when their bodies touched in the water.

"Yeah, I know this is weird, but I wanted to talk to you, alone," Dolly said, a little raspy, throat dry. "Avi is all crazy with his drones. And Hud . . ." She hesitated. "I didn't want anyone else to see me."

They were very close in the enclosure, less than a foot apart. He could smell the soap on her skin. He could even smell her lip balm. Roses. He could feel her breath. Wyatt's mouth was so dry, he felt like he had a tablespoon of cinnamon in his mouth. He had to say something. "So what did you want to talk about?"

Her eyebrows scrunched a little. Dammit. He should have just shut up. He felt all the warmth leave her.

"The Old Man," she said. "Have you noticed? He's acting

strange. I think something happened. I don't know. Like in the world."

Wyatt thought for a moment. The Old Man and Hallsy had been meeting privately lately, taking long conference calls in the Cave Complex. Everything hush-hush.

"Yeah, I've noticed," Wyatt said, "but what have you seen?"

"I've heard rumors . . . of a capture."

"From who?" Wyatt asked.

"Fabian Grant."

"Mackenzie's brother?"

"Yes, he works closely with Mum so he hears everything. I'm inclined to believe him," Dolly said.

"I get it," Wyatt said. "What did Fabian say?"

"Supposedly, an operator, a former member of Valor, has been captured by an Islamist terrorist group. They wanted a big price tag, and the Old Man and Hallsy are pressuring the Department of Defense to get the operator back. But the negotiations are complicated. And they don't know which way it'll go."

Wyatt nodded, leaving out his own experience eavesdropping on the Old Man and Hallsy as well as his sense that somehow he factored into those discussions. Right now, he did not care about anything other than being close to Dolly. Staying close. He just wanted to be a boy with a girl. Not a Valorian. Just a kid again. He told himself to shut up. Don't move. Say as little as possible.

"Can we do anything about it?" Wyatt finally asked. "Or can we forget about the outside world . . . and Valor . . . for just a little bit?"

"That's why I wanted to talk to you," Dolly said. "You're the special one."

Wyatt made a face. "Special? They pulled me out of a jail. Like everyone else."

"No." She scowled and shook her head. Wyatt had a hard time not staring at her lips. "They don't let anyone skip indoc. You did. Hallsy and the Old Man are tracking you. You're their top recruit. That's why Hud is competitive with you. He used to be their golden boy, now you are."

"That's not why Hud doesn't like me," Wyatt said, holding her with his eyes.

"What? Because of me?" she said.

Wyatt nodded slowly.

"Maybe. But whatever was between Hud and me, whatever happened in past summers, it's over. Completely over."

"I'm not sure Hud thinks that," Wyatt said softly.

She grew colder, eyes downcast. "This is why we don't . . . get emotional in the program. This is why"—she looked around at the trees and their confined space—"I shouldn't be out here with you." She took a step back. "There's no place for any . . ."

"Any what?" Wyatt stepped closer to her.

"Feelings. At Valor. Too dangerous. Getting emotional, thinking with anything but a clear head, can get you killed. We need to clear our heads. For you, for Hud, for me . . ." She looked up at Wyatt, her breath now heavy.

"My head is very clear," Wyatt said. "I only have one thought." He reached out and took Dolly's hand.

She didn't pull back, sliding her hands up to his face and neck. She raised her lips and pulled him to her. And they kissed. Crushing into each other. Tightening. Having waited so long.

Time tumbled forward, both lost in the moment until they heard the siren wailing from the base of the Caldera.

"Thank you for joining us, Wyatt," Hallsy said sarcastically as Wyatt entered the Ready Room. The rest of Group-C sat in folding chairs with their notepads out. Wyatt had given Dolly a head

start, so she had taken the seat in front of him. He lowered himself into a chair next to Samy. "Sorry I'm late."

Hud glared, jaws clenched, eyes burning. Did he suspect
something?

"The alarm you heard is not a drill," the Old Man said from
the back of the room, a cup of coffee steaming in his hand. "Our
intelligence network has been tipped off to a credible threat. Sergeant Hallsy will tell you the rest."

The screens behind Hallsy glowed to life. Photos of two
teenage boys: one seventeen years old, dark-complected; the
other fifteen or sixteen and fair with large, puppy-dog brown
eyes. They looked eastern European, maybe Russian. "Meet
Chokar and Jawad Alamariah. Brothers. Both naturalized
Canadian citizens and phenomenal athletes. Chokar, the older
brother, recently qualified for the Canadian Junior Olympic
boxing team."

Wyatt stared at Jawad's face, trying to place where he had
seen it before. Something about the boy was unnervingly familiar. Where had he seen him? The screen clicked through images
of Chokar brandishing boxing trophies, big thick belts. Smiling broadly.

Hallsy continued, "The brothers emigrated to Canada from
Chechnya in '02, seeking political asylum. Canadian authorities
had been told that their father died of cancer. The Canadians
were not told the truth."

An image projected on the screen of a radical Islamist fighter
holding up a human head, big grin on the fighter's face. Pure evil.

Hallsy let the image stay up on the screen. "This was Chokar's daddy shortly before a U.S. SEAL team eliminated him.
Back then, Chokar was three, Jawad just an infant. So you
wonder, could the family start a new life in the West? The answer, of course, is yes. They could have and—"

Hallsy changed the image on the screen to show Chokar and Jawad smiling, arm in arm with their mother. "By all accounts, they had started over. Until last summer."

The screen showed Chokar in a foreign land, surrounded by older bearded men. "Chokar returned to Chechnya for a visit. We believe an uncle radicalized him and when Chokar returned to the U.S., Chokar in turn radicalized his younger brother, Jawad, who, it turns out, is not a meathead like his older brother. Jawad is pretty damn smart."

Hallsy zoomed in on Jawad, into his big brown eyes. "So smart, in fact, he's become a master bomb maker." Hallsy brought up images of a remote athletic facility. "This is a U.S. Olympic training facility for boxers. The Canadian team has been invited to participate in a competition. Chokar has been there for a month. Last week, it was announced that the president of the United States and the Canadian prime minister will tour the boxing facility."

Hallsy paused for effect. "Two days ago, guess who decided to pack up his bags and visit his older brother?" Hallsy nodded, "You guessed it. Baby Bamm-Bamm."

The image switched back to Jawad's innocent puppy-dog eyes.

"What about the Secret Service?" Dolly said. "Haven't they cleared the area already?"

"Of course. They found no evidence of a threat. And there may be no threat. We *hope* there is no threat." Hallsy paused for emphasis. "So what do we do?"

"Can't rely on hope," Ebbie said, echoing lessons he'd learned since arriving at Valor. "Hope is not a strategy. And the Secret Service is far from perfect. This is one of these tricky situations where a sovereign nation and ally, Canada, is a guest in our country and we suspect a member of their Junior Olympian team may be a terrorist. We can't send in the cavalry or even the diplomats. We need to come in under the radar and just make sure everything is okay."

"That's exactly right, Ebbie," Hallsy said. "This scenario is tailor-made for Valor. We can get in and determine if there is a threat. If all goes well, we get out and no one ever knows."

Avi entered the Ready Room with a scale model of the training facility and placed it on the center of the conference table.

"Thanks, Avi." Hallsy picked up a pointer with a toy helicopter glued to the end. "Our insertion point will be three miles offshore. We'll make aquatic entry, and utilize diver propulsion vehicles to reach shore. Rory will operate an infrared drone from a remote site. The insertion team will be disguised as attendees at the training facility; however, I warn you—this will not pass much scrutiny. The facility is small and tight-knit. Avoid detection at all costs. From the beach, we'll split into two teams. Ebbie, Dolly, Samy will be Team One. Team Two is Wyatt and Hud."

Wyatt held out his fist for Hud to bump, but it hung in the air.

"You all right?" Wyatt whispered.

Hud gazed back, eyes unnervingly empty. "All good." He smiled. And pounded Wyatt's fist.

"The last thing I want to tell you," the Old Man said, "you have all performed superbly. We are now in the last weeks of summer and you have the opportunity to distinguish yourselves. It is on missions like these where we decide who receives Top Camper and, more than that, who will be with this program for the long haul."

CHAPTER 23

August 15, 2017
Near Olympic Training Facility, Pacific Northwest

"You're up." Hallsy nudged Wyatt toward the open helicopter door. Some thirty feet below was a frothing sea, only dimly visible in moonlight. Wyatt knew the water was cold and unrelenting. But unlike during Hell Week, Wyatt now wore protection: a 5mm neoprene scuba suit, a pair of flippers, and a closed-circuit MK 25 rebreather, which would allow Wyatt to breathe underwater without discharging oxygen into the environment. That meant no bubbles. He also carried a SubGravity RS scooter, a diver propulsion device (DPD), which would help Wyatt swim up to 280 feet per minute. His kit was strapped to his chest. In it, he carried various mission-critical odds and ends, including a lock pick, night vision goggles, a 9mm Glock, and compact Heckler & Koch MP7A1 submachine gun he'd trained with for close-quarters combat. He'd packed four extra clips of 4.6mm rounds for the H&K, in case things got hairy.

Thanks to the rapid neural growth of teenage minds and the teaching techniques at Valor, Wyatt had become an expert diver, parachutist, and marksman. He was trained to use a vast array of weapons and could operate, among other things, a tank and a Mark V SOC, the souped-up inflatable SEALs use. Wyatt could guide a missile strike from an F-18 with the use of a SOFLAM laser target designator. He could craft lethal weapons out of most household goods. Thanks to Cass's ordnance classes, if he had five minutes alone in a hardware store, he could make an IED that could take down a tank. He was trained in several forms of martial arts, and if a vehicle had either two or four wheels and an engine, he could probably figure out how to take it on a joy ride.

Even with all the training that had been packed into his brain and body in the past six weeks, as he prepared for his first mission in the field, he felt like he knew nothing. More importantly, he wondered if he was ready to engage a target. Wyatt was armed to the teeth, and if engaged, might be called upon to use lethal force. Was that something he could do? Would do? Sliding into position, doubt crept into his brain and body, and his legs turned rubbery.

Hud did not seem to experience this kind of anxiety. Nor did Samy. Or even Dolly. To those three, the barrel of a gun looked the same as a garden hose. When you turned it on, something came out the end. If you didn't want to get hit, get out of the way.

On the other hand, Ebbie, who had rejoined Group-C after a week recovering from his concussion, had a healthy respect for fear and was transparent about when he felt it. He'd say things like, "Right now, I'm scared as a damn boy can be." Then he'd laugh and do something insane.

Because Rory had transitioned to flying drones and did so

with surgical precision, she was denied the joys of jumping out of helicopters and staring down the business end of gun barrels.

For Wyatt, the only thing that made the uncertain feeling and self-doubt go away was action. Action, discipline, and repetition. Stop thinking. Get out of your head. Act. Heart hammering, feeling like a giant cold hand was gripping his chest, Wyatt did what he knew would make him get on point—he leapt into the void.

The fall was brief. Wyatt broke the surface of the water, heels down. The diver propulsion vehicle jerked in his hand at the surface, but then sank with Wyatt as he plunged several feet and everything grew calm. It was dark, but he could see the rest of the team waiting for him ahead, their lights glowing, lights that would be turned off as they got closer to shore, about three miles directly to the east.

Wyatt used the DPV to pull himself over to Hud. The final member of Group-C to enter the water was Ebbie. There would be no staff supervision in the water or on the land on this mission, as their presence in a youth environment would immediately draw suspicion. Group-C was truly on its own for the first time. No ghosting. It was all them.

Using hand signals, Samy instructed the five members of the mission to proceed. Wyatt noted with pride that Samy, who had been the poorest swimmer in the group, led the water portion of the expedition.

Guided by compass, GPS, and Samy, they arrived at the beachhead with pinpoint accuracy. Traveling with the currents at around 280 feet per minute, it took them a little over an hour and a half to reach land. As the teams had rehearsed, they made sure the beach was empty before proceeding onto the shore, which was very un-beachy, in fact. It was extremely rocky with a light wind on an otherwise placid summer night. In the distance over the cliffs that lined the rocky shore, Wyatt saw lights from the boxing training facility and the dorms.

The insertion teams stashed the SubGravity RS scooters along the edge of the cliff with the rebreathers and their neoprene wetsuits and flippers for collection after the mission. They would exfiltrate the area the same way they had come. From their kits, each team member drew out the hoodie and sweatpants worn by the visiting Canadian Junior Olympic team and put those on. They also donned night vision goggles, and each slung an athletic bag over their shoulder. In his bag, Wyatt had the Heckler & Koch submachine gun, ammunition, glass cutter, and lock picks. He tucked the 9mm into the waistband of his sweatpants.

It had been decided that Wyatt would run point on the ground, so at the appropriate time, when the group was ready, he moved ahead and crept up over the cliffs to sweep the surrounding area with his night vision goggles. All was clear. He signaled and proceeded carefully, making his way toward the dorm and training facility with the rest of Group-C following close behind.

As he neared the buildings, Wyatt signaled the rest of the team to stop and kneel. Over to his right, he identified the outline of two bodies. Security, he thought. He edged closer and saw it was teenagers necking behind shrubs. Recognizing that this was not a threat and that they were at no risk of detection—after all, the two were fairly lip-locked—Wyatt simply guided the team in a wider arc around the couple and crept up close to the buildings.

When they were close enough to be seen from inside the building, they removed their night vision goggles and put them in their bags, proceeding toward the buildings along a path as if they were any other Junior Olympians visiting the facility. Since they were approaching the building from the rear, they did not encounter any of the actual athletes. As rehearsed, they eventually came to a fork in the path, and at Wyatt's signal, Insertion Team One moved quickly toward the dorms, while Wyatt and Hud approached the training building from the rear.

Through an earbud, Wyatt communicated with Rory, Hallsy, and the Old Man.

"Insertion Team One is en route to the dorms. Team Two, head to the boxing gym."

"Roger," Rory said. "I have you on infrared. I can see your movements. Nothing ahead of you."

As they made their way toward the basement windows— the designated entry point to the building—Hud clicked off his radio, indicating he wanted to talk without others listening. He motioned for Wyatt to do the same.

"What's up?" Wyatt said.

"You tell me what's up. What's up with you and Dolly?" Hud had an edge to his voice. "You got to cut that out. That type of stuff has no business in Valor, or on these missions, or at the level at which we are operating. That's why Dolly and I cut it off. You gotta get wise."

Wyatt's temper flared, and he wanted to tell Hud that was none of his business, tell him to butt out. If they'd been back in Millersville, Wyatt might have even taken a swing. But he suppressed his anger. "Hud," he said calmly. "We can't discuss this now. Leave it for later. Stay on mission."

Instead of calming Hud, this seemed to make him even angrier. "That's exactly why what you're doing has no place. It's already affected the mis—"

Wyatt stopped Hud, "—It hasn't affected the mission. It's affected *you*. You need to get your head straight. You read me,

Hud?" Wyatt looked deep into his eyes, seeing the same hollowness from the Ready Room. Something wasn't right. He wasn't there. "If you can't get your head straight right now, I'm aborting this." Wyatt reached for his radio.

"Wait." Hud shook his head, the old Hud now coming back, smirking again. The arrogant Hud returned. The guy you didn't love but wanted on your side. "You're right. Forget Dolly. Who cares? It's game on."

Wyatt didn't take his eyes off Hud's. "Are you sure? Are you good?"

"I am gold. Let's cut this powwow short and go take the Bamm-Bamm brothers down."

"All right. Let's move."

Back on mission, Wyatt and Hud approached the building, the classic sounds of a boxing gym wafting down from the open windows on the third floor, fists thudding against bags, feet shuffling, a crowd quietly chatting, whistles, instructions, and the rhythmic ringing of the bell.

Wyatt had planned to use his glass cutter to cut a section of a ground-floor window, but one of the basement windows had been cracked for ventilation, so they simply had to open it more and slide in.

The basement was, in fact, a crawl space with a sump pump and a humidifier, little more than five feet deep of head space and smelled of mud, earth, and wet concrete. Grit and rodent scat on the ground under their feet. Working from a blueprint, Hud quickly found the trapdoor to the first-floor storage room. Wyatt leveled his 9mm as Hud pushed up the floorboard. The moment of truth. Thankfully, the room was empty, filled with boxing equipment and cans of powdered sports drinks.

They climbed into the building, replaced the floorboard, and moved to the door of the first-floor hallway. There was no one in the storage area, though through windows to the west, they could see several security personnel prowling outside, roaming the grounds.

Wyatt and Hud moved quickly to a staircase in the rear of the building and followed it up to the third floor. There they paused outside the door. Now, the sounds of training were loud and close, and the familiar smell of a gym—sweat and must and the faint odor of cleaning products—seeped into the stairwell. Hud nodded, they tucked their weapons into their clothing, and pushed open the doorway.

They stepped out into a hallway casually, as if they were simply arriving late to the gym for a workout. Down the hall, two double doors opened to the training floor, where the young Junior Olympians worked out, the training staff coached, and observers milled around watching. People were scattered around the large, open floor of the gym, shadow boxing, jumping rope, shooting the breeze.

A small crowd had gathered around one of the boxing rings, watching a boy Wyatt recognized as Chokar sparring with an American, the two fighters completely focused on one another, moving like cats, jabbing, ducking, stalking each other. Chokar's younger brother, Jawad, watched ringside, consumed by the spectacle. A couple members of the press snapped photos. As Wyatt and Hud made their way to the locker room, Wyatt noticed one of the coaches from the American team staring at him.

Wyatt smiled and nodded. The coach waited a beat, then nodded back and returned to watching the match. Wyatt and Hud pushed open the door to the locker room.

"We're in the locker room," Wyatt whispered into his comms

system. The room stunk of sweat, moldering clothes, and uric acid. They quickly checked to see if the locker room was empty. They rounded the corner to the shower area near the entrance, and Hud saw a pair of feet with pants at the ankles in one of the stalls. Someone was taking a dump. Then, the familiar sound of a page turning. This guy was going to be there a while.

Wyatt signaled Hud to stay in a lookout position, keeping eyes on the bathroom and the entrance to the training facility.

Hud held up his hand, signaling "OK" with his pointer and his thumb.

Wyatt entered the locker area, swiftly locating Chokar's locker, his name written in tape along the top. The lockers in this facility were not the typical kind of narrow lockers found in a high school or men's room. It was an Olympic facility, and the equipment was similar to what you might find in a Major League Baseball locker room, with grates for ventilation. Almost all of the lockers were unlocked, except for Chokar's, which was secured with a big brass Master padlock.

Wyatt set his bag down, removed his pick, and went to work. He had the lock open in about thirty seconds, and whispered into the comms, "Have access to locker, now performing search." Wyatt wore a body camera, so not only was his point of view recorded, it was also broadcast to the Old Man and Hallsy back at Valor.

Wyatt dimly heard a toilet flush. "Hud," Wyatt asked. "How are we doing?"

A second or two passed as Wyatt rifled through several pairs of shoes and gloves.

"All clear, Wyatt. He's still on the can. Looks like it was a courtesy flush," Hud said, his voice a quiet whisper. "Take your time."

Wyatt found rolls of tape and wrist wraps, along with the

Koran, bandages, aspirin, tins of creams and ointments, a pile of dirty jock straps in the corner, wet boxing shorts, and several pairs of nylon workout suits on hangers. The locker smelled like a wheel of old pungent cheese. Wyatt quickly searched the loose items, but found nothing. He turned his attention to the two gym bags that had been placed at the center of the locker.

The first gym bag Wyatt opened belonged to Chokar, the standard bag used by the Canadian Junior Olympian boxing team. A quick peek inside and Wyatt saw nothing suspicious. Wyatt zipped up the bag and unzipped the dingy backpack, which he recognized from an earlier photograph as belonging to Jawad. It was the kind worn by millions of students across the world—smallish, slightly frayed, unassuming.

Wyatt unzipped the bag and looked inside. He immediately felt the hairs on the back of his neck stand up. "I think we have something," he said. "I'm seeing electronic equipment, an iPad, loose wires, and a heavy, cylindrical object. Taped to the top of the cylinder is what looks like a blasting cap connected to a . . . phone detonator."

"Is the device armed?" the Old Man's voice broke in over the radio.

"I can't tell. I don't think so. And I see a box of ammunition in the bottom of the bag. But no gun," Wyatt said, reflecting on what this meant. Jawad was likely armed.

"Secure the device," the Old Man said but Wyatt zoned out, hearing footsteps approaching down the row of lockers.

Wasn't Hud guarding the entrance? He hadn't signaled.

"Hud?" Wyatt whispered.

But the feet took big steps, running now. Wyatt had no time to think. Wyatt drew the 9mm just as Jawad rounded the corner, his own gun drawn. Zero hesitation on Wyatt's part. He aimed and pulled the trigger twice. Jawad fired back at the exact same time.

Neither Wyatt nor Jawad stopped pulling his trigger. Each unloaded his weapon into the other, and the room filled with the sound of gunfire and the smell of smoke as shells were ejected from the weapons. Still, neither boy fell. They just kept firing, point-blank into one other. Wyatt imagined the wall behind him was riddled with bullets and blood splatter and that any second he would topple over and die. A question pinged in his mind. Where was Hud?

Had Wyatt's mind and body not been flooded with adrenaline and sensory overload, he might have noticed that his 9mm did not recoil. And while there was plenty of smoke and sparks, there was no blood.

Wyatt and Jawad stared at each other, puzzled. Then Hud came running up, screaming, "Wyatt, get down!"

Hud fired at Jawad's back in rapid succession, emptying his clip, screaming "Ahhhhhhh!"

Again, Jawad did not fall. Now Wyatt knew something was off, like the way someone recognizes that they are dreaming.

"A little late, aren't you, Hud?" Hallsy's voice broke through the silent locker room as he entered with the Old Man.

Wyatt's mind raced, his heart jack-hammered, and his ears rang. Then the realization hit him. "This was a training exercise?" he said, his voice tight and dry, conflicting feelings flowing through him.

The kid, Jawad, was snickering now, tucking his gun in his pants. "Yeah. Blanks. Feel like you got punked, huh? That was how I felt my year as a Group-C."

"Who . . . are you?" Wyatt asked.

"Wyatt, meet Jawad Mossa, or Jo, as we call him," Hallsy

said, and instantly Wyatt knew where he had seen the boy before. "Jo was a member of last year's Group-A."

"Yeah. And he was Top Camper. I knew I had seen him. I just couldn't place it," Wyatt said, recalling the photograph of last year's Top Camper. In the photo, Jo had a scraggly beard and wore sunglasses, but now was clean shaven. Still, Wyatt kicked himself. He should have figured it out. "Can't believe his photo was right there on the wall and I didn't put it together." He shook his head.

"Neither did I when I was in your shoes." Jo patted Wyatt on the shoulder. "Don't take it too hard."

"None of you made the connection and saw the obvious," Hallsy said. "Shows me just how much we all have to learn about being observant. As well as the power of suggestion. Jo came back for the end of the summer to help with training. Same goes for all the boxers you saw out on the training-room floor, in the boxing gym. Even the kids you saw making out outside."

Wyatt steadied himself against a locker, still floored, still processing. "It was all fake. A total setup."

Hallsy nodded again. "Yes. A test. Elaborate, but completely necessary." Hallsy turned and glared at Hud. "Especially after what we saw you do today."

Hud took a step back, looking cowed and pale.

"Yes, Hud," Hallsy said. "We were watching."

Hud swallowed a few times, put his head in his hands, and sat down.

"Saw what?" Wyatt asked. "What happened? Hud was exactly where we rehearsed."

"Wyatt," the Old Man said. "I want you to leave with Hallsy. He'll take you to your debrief. Hud, you're going to leave with me." The Old Man's voice was firm but heavy with sadness.

Hallsy stepped to Hud and placed handcuffs on his wrists.

"What do you mean?" Hud stammered. "Like Wyatt said, I . . . I . . . was covering him. I was distracted by the person in the bathroom. They were getting ready to leave when Jawad entered. It was a mistake. I missed him. He got past me." Hud seemed to collapse in on himself, shrinking as a human. His chest heaved as he cried, and he looked at Wyatt. "I'm so, so sorry, Wyatt. Please. Please forgive me." And then he looked at the Old Man, "Let me stay at Valor. It was a mistake. I don't know why it happened."

The Old Man's voice took on an edge. "Wyatt, you are dismissed."

CHAPTER 24

August 2017, Predawn
Camp Valor

They did not know where Hud had been taken. Group-C returned to base camp and was debriefed on the mission back in the main lodge over a breakfast made by Mum. Wyatt's body was starved. Pre-mission jitters had killed his hunger leading up to the insertion. The swim alone was ninety minutes. They had been tested emotionally and physically. Every cell in Wyatt's body screamed for calories.

And yet, Wyatt couldn't eat. Nor could anyone else in the group. They'd lost a man. The rumor circulating through Valor was that Hudson Decker was being washed out.

Heads hung low and piles of biscuits, eggs, sausage, and bacon were picked over. Mostly coffee and water were consumed. Hallsy lowered a screen, a video projector was brought in, and he played footage from the training exercise. The debrief covered and critiqued all aspects of the training exercise—the insertion, the beach landing, crossing to the dorms and boxing facility—all but what everyone was thinking about—what happened in the locker room.

On Screen: As Jawad continues his approach toward the locker room, Hud retreats into the bathroom area and appears to hide behind a corner as Jawad enters.

Wyatt says, "Hud."

Jawad breaks into a run. Wyatt draws his weapon and the two fire upon each other as Jawad rounds the corner. Hud emerges after shooting has begun, comes up behind Jawad, and fires.

The video goes to black.

Finally, Hallsy spoke: "The Old Man and I have determined that Hud intended to put Wyatt in danger. This intent—not mistake—is cause for removal from Valor. The only way Hud stays is if you, his fellow Group-C members, unanimously choose to have him return." Hallsy added flatly, "So what do you want to do?"

The question dangled in the tense air in the room. No one dared touch it for a long time.

"I know Hud rubbed a lot of people the wrong way here, but Hud is one of my dogs," Ebbie broke the silence. "So I hate to be the one to admit it, but this looks bad. Looks like Hud hung Wyatt out to dry."

"Hallsy asked about intent," Wyatt jumped in. "Clearly Hud made a mistake. But the video can't show you what's in Hud's mind. We have no way of knowing what he was thinking. I don't think it's fair to speculate."

"Whatever was going through his head," Samy said, "had that exercise been in the field, Wyatt's brains would have been sprayed all over that locker. That kid Jawad would be dead. And we'd have to take Hud's word for it 'cause we wouldn't have had anything else."

"But we weren't in the field," Wyatt said.

"He didn't know that," Rory said. "None of us did."

"That doesn't matter," Wyatt said. "Our instructors didn't put us out in the field because we still needed training. This was training. We needed to learn the lesson. We have all made mistakes that might have cost lives in the field. Now Hud has learned."

"But what does it say about character?" Rory asked.

"Character?" Wyatt laughed. "We're all criminals. Every one of us has lied or cheated or stolen. Betrayed ourselves and others. That's how we got here. If character isn't something that can change, then we all should leave."

"Ok"—Ebbie looked at his comrades—"Hud stays, right?" Wyatt nodded and everyone followed suit. Everyone except Dolly.

"I think I know him better than anyone else in this room," Dolly finally piped up. Her eyes moved from face to face. "I don't know if he wanted Wyatt dead, I don't think so. Hud is not that type of a person. He's not an evil person. But I do think he wanted to see what would happen if Wyatt were alone with danger. He wanted to test Wyatt. That's what I think. Wyatt drew first. Wyatt would have survived, in my mind. But Hud failed. As much as it hurts for me to say this." Tears welled in Dolly's eyes. "Hud is strong, maybe the strongest of us all here. But he needs to go. Let's never lay eyes on him again."

With that, Dolly stood and left the lodge. It had been decided. Hud had to go.

CHAPTER 25

August 2017
Camp Valor Cave Complex

Hud lay on a hospital bed in the Cave Complex, hands cuffed together, his blue and green eyes watching the resident physician, Dr. Elaine Choy, ready a course of pills, injections, and the ECT machine beside his bed. The ECT machine, used for electroshock therapy, looked like it came right out of the 1970s, a clunky stereo tuner. Tune in, tweak your brain out.

Choy was waiting on the final word to see if Hud would be expelled or not before she commenced with sedation, the first phase of the brain-wiping process. Hud couldn't stand the suspense or the sight of the doctor sharpening her axes, so to speak.

Something rang close to Hud's head, and he jerked up in bed—a wall-mounted phone. The antiquated device matched the ECT.

Dr. Choy answered. A string of mumbles and "okay"s followed. She hung up and eyed Hud, who was trying to play it cool.

"So what's it gonna be? What did they decide?" he asked.

Dr. Choy approached Hud's bunk and held out two blue pills. "I'm sorry, Hud. You're going home."

He forced a laugh. "Figured." The tears brimmed in Hud's eyes. Anger, too, if you looked deep into them. "Fair enough." He took the pills in his fingertips, tossed them in his mouth like M&Ms, and swallowed. "Okay, Doc, just do me one favor when I knock out and you get your machine all fired up. Get all the memories out. I don't want nothing. Not the Old Man. Not Hallsy. Not Mum. Not any of Group-C."

"Once you fall asleep, any memories of Valor will seem like only a dream," the doctor said and flipped on the ECT machine. It thrummed like an electric guitar being plugged into an amp.

Hud's heart rate jacked.

Choy was used to this. "Don't worry, Hud. This will be painless."

"Sure. Sure. Hey, Doc. Will you sit here with me?" Hud shifted in his bed to give her space. "Just for a little while?" Tears, which had pooled in his eye sockets, now rolled down his cheeks. "Just wait, until I'm asleep."

"If it helps you calm down," Dr. Choy said and sat gingerly on the edge of the bed.

"Hold my hand." Hud's breathing was deepening and slowing. "Please."

The doctor took his hand. More tears squeezed out. She watched as Hud's eyelids grew heavy, fluttering as the sedative took hold, pulling Hud under. All tension in Hud's grip slackened.

"There," she said. "That wasn't too bad." Dr. Choy moved to let go of Hud's hand and Hud pounced, seizing her by the wrist and pulling her onto the bed with him. As the doctor screamed, Hud spat the two blue pills into her mouth and then clamped his hand over. He pinned her down and waited until the little blue pills worked on the doc.

Ninety seconds later, Dr. Choy was out cold. Hud removed the keys from her belt and uncuffed himself. Rubbing his wrists, he took a moment to plan his next move. Hud was leaving Camp Valor, that was for certain. And he'd be taking his memories with him.

Wyatt had not been asleep an hour when the alarm sounded. Again.

"All hands on deck," Hallsy yelled over a megaphone. "Man-hunt under way. We need all campers who can walk or crawl. You have five minutes."

"Gotta be kidding me," Samy grumbled. "If this is another drill, I'm gonna lose it on someone. Don't care if they're staff or not, this camel needs some sleep."

Bright light shone into the cabin. All the boys inside groaned at the light, squinting. Dolly stood in the doorway.

"Wyatt," she said. "It's Hud. He's escaped from the Caldera."

PART FIVE

CHAPTER 26

August 2017
Williamsburg, Pennsylvania

Driving was treacherous. It was near midnight and fog banks rolled over I-80. Visibility varied between two car lengths and a hundred yards, depending on elevation. State trooper Bill Jefferies trailed a safe distance behind a late-model Chrysler Town & Country minivan struggling in the soupy conditions. Or was it something else?

The trooper recorded the taillights veering off to the shoulder and jerking back, twice. The Seattle plates on the car told Jefferies the driver was passing through, and not in familiar territory. The swerving told Jefferies the driver might be tired, drunk, or unable to see. Possibly all three. Time to find out.

Lieutenant Jefferies accelerated, pulling up directly behind the T&C. He flipped on his lights and chirped his siren. The van abruptly swerved, the driver perking at the wheel. Not an uncommon reaction. Jefferies engaged the cruiser's speakers—he loved the speakers. "Pull over," he said, a lilt of pleasure in his tone.

But instead of complying, the minivan sped up, edging into the middle of the two lanes. Jefferies thumbed his radio, "502 headed eastbound on I-80, vehicle not responding to commands to pull over. Can you run the plates for me? Wait—" Jefferies watched as the minivan drifted wide on a turn, driving nearly off the shoulder. Then in a wildly dangerous move, the driver slammed on the brakes and cut the wheel to the left, crossing back in front of the cruiser at a hard angle and skidding toward a turn-around in the median of the highway.

Jefferies nearly clipped the minivan's rear bumper and shot past. The T&C turned a full 180 degrees as it slid off the express-way into the median, now headed in the opposite direction.

"Holy mackerel, vehicle is now heading westbound on 80." Jefferies punched his brakes, attempting his own three-point turn, but overshot the median. The next turn-around was two miles ahead. The minivan would be long gone. Screw it, he thought. And banged a U-turn and drove east on the westbound left-hand shoulder back toward the median, praying no cars would be headed in his direction.

He had lost sight of the minivan until he came up to the median and saw the two red taillights stacked vertically in the grass, a swath of mud cutting across the median. The van had flipped and was on its side, engine smoking. The driver's head poked out of the passenger-side window, blood streaming down his face. He hoisted himself up onto the doorframe, perched like a cat ready to spring off.

Jefferies lit him up with his spotlights and opened his own door. He stepped from his cruiser, gun drawn, hunkering down in shooting stance behind the door.

"Hands up and face his way."

The driver seemed to contemplate a run. Jefferies was prepared to fire when he saw hands slowly interlace behind a close-cropped head.

"Turn around!"

The body twisted on the doorframe. The driver was just a boy, maybe not even sixteen. Black hair, one eye blue, one eye green. And he looked feral.

CHAPTER 27

Summer 2017
Glowworm Gaming Headquarters

After nearly nine months, negotiations with the ISIS affiliate for the captured operator had nearly ground to a halt. The Glowworm wanted Pablo to negotiate that, too. Which he would. But the price was going up because someone else was bidding high. Maybe the U.S. And maybe the Glowworm would pay fifty million dollars if they could prove the captive was Chris Gibbs . . . but that was still uncertain. They needed proof that the HVT was the real article. Pablo's biggest fear was that they'd shell out fifty million dollars for the wrong guy, for some poor schlub yanked off the streets of Jerusalem. When did human trafficking and bounty hunting get so complicated? And expensive? Pablo shivered to think what Raquel would cut off and eat if he messed up.

But good news came one morning when Pablo saw Fouad running down the rows of cubicles, waving a printout. "Hola,

hola, Pablo. Think we got something." Fouad slapped the papers down on Pablo's desk and slid into the chair next to him.

Pablo studied what looked like a copy of a police report. "Arrest report? What is this?"

Fouad spoke quickly, "Early Tuesday morning a Pennsylvania state trooper attempted to pull over what he thought was a drunk driver. The car gave chase, the trooper radioed in the number of the Seattle plates, and they came back as belonging to a different vehicle. Mid-chase, the car crashed. The driver was injured but still tried to flee the scene of the accident."

Pablo shrugged, "Maybe he'd stolen the car and was trying to make a run for it."

"Sure, yeah," said Fouad. "But when the trooper finally made the arrest, he discovered the driver was a boy, teenage, and had no ID. Cop guessed between fifteen and seventeen years old. And the car was a mess. It looked like the boy had been on a road trip, living off of what he could hunt, fish, or steal. The car was filled with camping gear and a variety of license plates, which he was apparently swapping out. Tracing the VIN, they learned it had been stolen from a SEA-TAC long-term parking lot a week before the accident."

"SEA-TAC?" Pablo asked.

"Seattle–Tacoma airport."

Pablo was squinting, confused.

Fouad held up a finger. "Hang on to that detail. Just wait. In the car, they also found a military issue M4 assault rifle, which the police traced to a munitions depot in Florida."

"Wait," Pablo said, still squinting, "he was in the military?"

"Hold on to that detail as well. Here is how it works. The military buys weapons, they trace and track each weapon with a serial number. The gun the boy had in his possession had last been in Florida. Now this kid, this car-stealing survivalist, would not speak, would not even give his name. So we don't know how he got the gun. But when he was printed, a juvenile record came up. Several priors, all pretty minor stuff: shoplifting, joyriding, truancy, and an assault charge for a fight with a teacher. All when he was younger. There's nothing on the kid for the past three years . . . which is where it gets really interesting." Fouad grinned, yellow teeth forming a crescent in a scraggly beard. "He had been remanded to spend his summers at a juvenile detention facility where he's supposed to work cleaning up trash, paying off his debt to society."

"Okay," Pablo said, "I see a lot of interesting pieces, but how do they fit together?"

"They don't. That's the point. The juvenile detention facility where the kid was supposed to be this summer was in upstate New York, a place called Fishkill. He was picked up in Pennsylvania. He'd stolen a car in Seattle. He had a military-issue rifle from Florida. The kid couldn't have possibly escaped from New York the same day he stole a car in Seattle and picked up a gun from a munitions depot in Florida. Plus, he not only knew how to live off the land but apparently could steal cars, too, live off the grid."

"Pablo," Fouad said. "What's missing, the thing that puts the puzzle together, *is the program*."

Pablo considered this for a long moment. "Yes. I see what you are saying." Pablo shrugged. "Or, he's just another juvenile delinquent runaway. . . ."

As soon as Pablo said the words, the hairs on his arms and neck rose. Puzzle pieces weren't just coming together now, they were crashing together. On all fronts. Pablo stood up, wobbling a little on the prosthesis, and steadied himself with a cane.

"Follow me to the Glowworm's office. He needs to hear this."

Pablo limped out into the endless rows of dark cubicles, Fouad trailing behind him.

"The police," Pablo said to Fouad. "They found his record. Who is he? And where is he?"

"He's being transferred from Pennsylvania to New York City." Fouad hurried to catch up with Pablo, an eager puppy. "In terms of who he is, I saved that little nugget for you too. Hudson Decker is his name."

"Why does that name sound familiar?" Pablo asked.

"The Decker Library, the Decker Museum, the Decker Institute of Arts. Those New York cultural and historical institutions ring a bell?"

Pablo nodded as if he knew, but the truth was, if there wasn't a Decker casino, he probably wasn't aware of the family. "Pablo, Armand Decker is the kid's great-great-grandfather. He basically built what we know as modern New York. Just think about the kind of connections that kid must have to the military, to the judicial system. . . ."

Pablo was thinking all right as he came to a stop outside of the Glowworm's office, two heavily armed guards clad in black on either side of the thick black doors, the smell of meat wafting out. "Go see about the plane."

Travel for the Glowworm was never easy. Given his abhorrence of sunlight, and security requirements, getting the Glowworm to move around the world required the support of a small army of logistics experts, support personnel, specialized vehicles, and safe houses. It also required a specialized plane for the Glowworm himself.

The first thing the Glowworm did after buying his personal 747 was to completely black out all windows. He gutted the interior and divided it into two sections. The first was his personal space, which was in the darkest part of the plane—the rear. This was outfitted with high-speed Internet, cloud service, a Vitamix blender, his pump system so he could eat, and all of the spy equipment you'd find on a P-3 spy plane.

The front section of the plane was where the Glowworm's goons, hackers, and captive workers—like Pablo and Fouad— would travel. It was actually pretty luxurious. There was a gaming room, a workout room, a shower, tea and coffee bar, and lay-down beds, like the kind you'd find on a first-class Asian airline.

En route from Panama to New York City, Pablo watched the classic film *Gone with the Wind* after a snack of PowerBars and injections of steroids. A song lyric from the 1960s came to his mind from the hippie band the Grateful Dead. "What a long, strange trip it's been."

Certainly, it had been strange, but long . . . long was relative, and Pablo hoped—prayed—that in Hudson Decker he would find the answers he needed to keep lengthening his own trip. The truth shall set you free, as they say. Can the truth return you to limitless vodka and long days berating the patrons from the seat of your casino bar? Can it save you fifty million dollars? Or at least save your critical appendages?

Pablo gazed over at the beautiful Lebanese blond killer-child sitting across the aisle. Raquel in repose. A demon reclining in a Sharper Image massage chair on a 747, reading the latest issue of *Teen Vogue*.

Pablo wondered what was going through her mind as she wetted her fingertips and flipped through pages of pumps, gossip, and cashmere sweater ideas. Did she think about killing the people in the photos? Or, like most people, did she think about wearing their clothes? Or wearing human skins as clothes? More likely the latter.

Pablo was a killer. His whole life, he had dealt with, be-friended, worshipped, and hunted killers. But creatures like Raquel and the Glowworm, he just couldn't understand. God save us, he thought, crossing himself.

He heard the Vitamix blender buzzing in the rear of the plane. God save us.

CHAPTER 28

August 2017
Decker Apartment, Manhattan

Hudson Decker lay on the enormous couch playing *Grand Theft Auto V*, his cell phone repeatedly buzzing against leather. News, social media, texts, pokes from old friends who'd heard he was back, back in action. Word had traveled fast.

"Dude, weren't you like already in juvie this summer?"

"What happened?"

"Your parents get you out?"

And of course: "Want to come over?" Hud didn't want to see anyone. Not yet. And not immediately with his New York friends. They were good enough people. But they were talkers, the kinds of kids who liked to hang out, to keep things on the surface. Hud liked deep connections built on experience. He liked friendships that didn't need words, or time spent "chillin'." Maybe this was why Hud had so few real friends and preferred those at Valor.

The ankle bracelet on his leg meant he couldn't leave his family's apartment in the city, which occupied two floors of a prewar building overlooking Central Park. The Decker family lawyers had swarmed the Pennsylvania courts to get Hud released and placed under house arrest. But where were his parents now? Mom shopping, Dad in his wheelchair rolled up to a giant credenza in a skyscraper somewhere, probably drooling. Doing anything not to be with Hud.

The place wasn't bad. Better than most ultra-luxurious apartments in the city. Hud had some friends with swankier digs, but not many. Certainly the double penthouse beat the hell out of jail. But did it beat the hell out of a dirty, dusty tent? Or a shady spot near the water on the far side of the Caldera?

The apartment, the city, Hud's life, couldn't hold a candle to the crappiest bunk at Valor. He wanted it back. He wanted to be back more than he could take. He'd screwed up big-time—with Wyatt, with Valor, with Dolly. With his own life. What's worse, Hud knew he was putting the camp and his friends at risk by remembering. By taking the memories with him. And because of this, Hud knew that above all else it was just a matter of time before Valor came for him, for their memories. But when would they come? And how would he know they were coming?

Hud had been playing Grand Theft Auto in multiplayer mode, going head to head with someone in Ireland. Then around 2 p.m., the game lost connection. Internet was out, cable was out as well. Hud rebooted the modem and tried the game again. No dice. Hud knew one of his neighbor's Wi-Fi passwords and tried that. His neighbor wasn't getting a connection either.

Moderately annoyed, Hud grabbed his cell phone and thought about who to call—Mom, Dad. Or Carlos, the building manager. Bingo.

Hud queued up Carlos's number and called, but he couldn't

dial out. There was no signal. Maybe Carlos was down in the lobby or in the basement.

Hud tried the in-apartment elevator. Called it several times. Didn't come. It was possible that because he was on house arrest, the building managers had programmed it that way, but Hud's instincts told him he needed to move. To walk. To change locations. Ankle bracelet be damned. They could throw him back in jail if they wanted. He hoped they did. Or tried. He'd be safer in jail or on the run than he would be with Valor after him.

Hud started out into the cold stone stairway and started down. He had eighteen floors to go and stopped halfway down the first flight of stairs. He listened.

Footsteps. Four people, maybe five in total. A small party coming up. Hud peered down the stairwell and saw a hand sliding up the wood balustrade. Hud's first thought was the Old Man.

He backtracked, using the quiet heel-toe movement he'd been taught at Valor. He tucked his body into the cutout that gave tenants on lower floors roof access in the case of a fire.

The footfalls stopped at the door to his apartment. Someone whispered—a girl—possibly Middle Eastern, lightly accented.

"Open it," she said. Who at Valor had that voice? Hud couldn't place it.

A man whispered back, Latin-sounding but unintelligible.

The girl said louder, "Do not kick it in. Use the pick."

The hairs on Hud's arms and on the back of his neck stood at attention. These were not people from Valor. Hud listened to the efficient metallic sounds of tools expertly handled.

The Latin man whispering, again, deep and low. "Remember, do not kill him until we can interrogate. No prints. Gloves on."

Hud heard the door creak open. Footsteps shuffled. The door closed. The people, whoever they were, had entered the apartment. Now was the time to move, to sneak past the apartment, and run. To run like hell.

Hud stepped from the alcove and saw a startlingly beautiful girl, with blond hair and olive skin, so pretty that had he seen her on the street he would have stopped to pick his jaw up off the ground. And he wanted to keep staring . . . except for the syringe he noticed in her hand.

"Here!" She ran at him, yelling. Cable ties clutched in her other hand.

Hud pivoted and ran back toward the roof. He took the stairs three at a time and slammed his shoulder into the door, blasting it open, feeling something sharp jab into the back of his calf. Hud kicked as hard as he could, foot to face, catching her right in the pretty little mouth.

The blonde tumbled back down the stairs, crashing into the men now scrambling after Hud. Hud swept his hand down to pull the syringe out of his leg, and ran out onto the roof, glancing down at the syringe in his hand, seeing the plunger depressed and the tube empty. Whatever had been in the syringe was in his blood now. And he could feel it. A sedative. Strong. Damn strong.

He felt like he was running through concrete, his mind dimming, his vision fading. He had a single thought—Valor. Protect Valor. With the last light remaining in his eyes and in his mind, Hud sprinted toward the street side of the rooftop, toward Central Park, lush and green and glorious in the late summer.

Unlike the young bucks, Pablo had not scrambled for the roof after the boy Hudson Decker. At eighty-two, he was never much of a sprinter. Not to mention his prosthesis. He stayed in the apartment, listening to the scuffle in the stairwell, footfalls on the roof. Pablo kept his eyes on the giant floor-to-ceiling windows facing the park, where he saw a teenage boy sail past view, in a free-fall dive, head down, arms to his sides, hooded sweatshirt flapping. Pablo could have sworn he was smiling.

Damn him, Pablo thought, and damn Raquel. He heard a thud, followed by screams coming up from the street, and decided it was time to get out of the building. Pablo turned back toward the staircase and saw a young woman step inside the door to the apartment. She was probably early twenties, breathing heavy. She'd clearly just run up the stairs. And she held out a gun, a pistol, aimed at Pablo.

"Put your hands up and get on the ground," she commanded, and by her stance, he assumed she must be law enforcement, but she did not carry a badge. Strangely, Pablo noticed half her face was webbed in scars. Burn scars, he thought.

"Where is he? Where is Hud?"

Pablo said nothing but raised his hands slowly and signaled toward the window. The girl's eyes shifted that way, registering the screams rising up from the street.

Watching her reaction to the screams, something clicked for Pablo. She knew him. It was personal to her. "You are one of them, aren't you?" he said.

Her hesitation was only a millisecond, but he watched her process his words. And he knew. Pablo knew. He was right.

"On the ground," the woman repeated, eyes moving back as she readjusted her aim.

A flash of movement, like a club swinging, behind the woman. Silver and hands and a flash but no sound. The woman's head spun to the side and her body crumpled to the floor of the apartment.

Raquel stood where the woman had been, a 9mm with a long

silencer in her hands. "Are you trying to get caught?" She glared at Pablo. "You need to move, now."

"That was one of them," Pablo said. "You just killed two people who could have taken us to them."

"I can make it three if you push me." She aimed at his head. "Move. Now."

CHAPTER 29

August 2017
Camp Valor

They sat around the fire grieving. Dolly, Ebbie, Samy, Rory, Hallsy, Avi,
Mum, and the Old Man. Tears in eyes, hearts broken. Dolly by
far the worst.

Dolly would not make eye contact with Wyatt. Hud had
died. Cass was only slightly luckier, but not by much. She
lay in a medically induced coma as surgeons at NewYork–
Presbyterian Hospital debated how to remove the 9mm shell
from her brain without killing her.

The Old Man rose slowly, bone-tired and gaunt. "Normally, the final days of the summer are a time for celebration.
As all of you have heard by now, your former Valor candidate,
Hudson Decker, has died, and Cassidy Allen is in critical condition."

Dolly put her head in her hands, sobbing silently. Hallsy
kneeled next to her. Wyatt had heard the rumor Cass and

Hallsy had once been together. Whether it was true or not, Hallsy too was struggling with the news. He patted Dolly's back. "Your sister will be okay," he said. "She's tough as hell. She won't give up."

Dolly nodded, wiped her eyes, and looked back at the Old Man.

The Old Man continued, "The official cause of Hud's death, and what will be reported in the news, is suicide. However, we know that is not what happened. We lost track of Hud briefly after his escape. But from the moment of Hud's arrest in Pennsylvania, Cass had him under surveillance. She was awaiting word from me for the proper time to reengage him."

"You mean to wipe his brain?" Dolly said.

"Yes." The Old Man did not flinch. "The plan was to complete the memory removal process. But around 2 p.m. yesterday, Cass discovered that all communication in a several-block radius had been compromised. Internet service ceased, security cameras were shut down, and all cellular phones, cable, and radio were scrambled. When Cass went to investigate, she was ambushed by whoever had come for Hud. Thanks to our partner agencies, her involvement has been made completely confidential. And I am sure we will learn more when she recuperates. For now, the only clue to go on is that there were reports—a visual sighting—of a blond girl on the roof. Other than that, we have not a single lead."

"Sir," Ebbie said. "I don't mean to be thick here. But are you trying to say that Hud jumped to his death from a rooftop in New York and there isn't footage of it anywhere?"

"As of right now, that's what we are saying."

Wyatt said, "How could that happen? Who could do that?"

"I'll let Avi answer that in more detail." The Old Man nodded to his security man.

"Thank you," Avi said and cleared his throat. "We think an agent—a sophisticated state player or organization or country—has been trolling for Valor. We do not yet know who they are, and I believe . . . at least, I don't see any evidence that suggests that any of our systems here at Valor have been compromised. But in the hours after Hud's arrest, the Williamsburg, Pennsylvania Police Department was hacked. And other databases a hacker might use to find us have also been compromised."

"Such as?" Ebbie asked.

"Every juvenile detention center in the United States, the Department of Defense . . ."

"Those systems can be hacked?" Dolly said.

"Of course." Avi nodded. "I could teach some of you to do it in a couple hours. Any other questions?"

"Yes." Wyatt kicked a log into the fire, sending a cloud of sparks roiling toward the sky. "So what now? What do we do about it?"

"It's not *what do we do*," Dolly said, "but *when* and *where*."

"I can understand how you feel," Avi said. "But that is not my question to answer."

Avi turned to the Old Man, who stepped back into the light of the fire. He stared into the flames. "I have been wrestling with that question all day," the Old Man said. "On one hand, we have an agent clearly trying to do us harm. On the other hand, we have a young and inexperienced group of operators. In most years, I would not take a Group-C into the field where we might encounter an enemy, let alone one we do not know. But as I mentioned earlier, this summer is not typical. And Valor's security is at risk. I can pull in some members from Group-A and Group-B from their deployments, but we need them sooner than they can get here. Furthermore, you are not a normal Group-C. You are five of the most promising Valor candidates I have seen in my lifetime. And we have no other options. We must act quickly and decisively.

"So, tomorrow morning, all remaining members of Group-C and staff will be flying to New York to attend Hud's funeral. We'll mourn him and we'll pray for Cass, and then we'll find those who are responsible. I have little doubt those very same people will be at the funeral, looking for us. It will be our mission to identify these players without revealing ourselves. We will not make contact, only observe."

The Old Man paused to make sure his words were heard clearly. "If this group is as dangerous as I believe it is, this mission could absolutely see an engagement. We will do everything we can to avoid that. But it is a possibility. You must go into this with eyes open. This is live. This is not a test . . . not one I have devised, anyway."

CHAPTER 30

Like his plane, the Glowworm's limousine had been modified to suit its star occupant. The windows blacked out, stocked with computer gadgetry and his blender, which currently contained a hunk of flesh from Pablo's rump and the tip of his nose—both removed mid-flight as punishment for Hudson Decker's dive off the roof of his Fifth Avenue apartment. It had actually been Raquel's failure. She was the one who terrified Hud into jumping. But the Glowworm would not see fault in the little demon he used to lure people to their deaths.

Whatever the case, there was nothing he could do about it. Pablo took the hit for the mistakes and now sat precariously trying to balance his weight on his left butt cheek, his nose bandaged.

The Glowworm grinned in the back, a slimy legume from

hell, chuckling. "Enjoy your flight?" he asked. Raquel sat beside him, perched like a cat, drinking milk.

Pablo ignored the question, enduring crippling pain and silence as they drove to Pound Ridge, Indiana, to the home of the widow of the late Sheriff Bouchard. They were following up on a hunch Pablo had about a long-dead teenage runaway, Eldon Waanders.

Pablo and Raquel stepped from the modified party bus and leaned into the wind and drizzling rain as they made their way up the cracked drive. Off to their right, in the foggy darkness, they could make out two buildings—a dilapidated barn and shed, the roofs thick with moss and collapsing.

Evidently, at some point, there had been livestock on the property. Those days, however, were long gone, and the only animals in the yard were wild. The main house, the farmhouse, looked like it had once been maintained and well appointed. But now, like the barns, the main house had fallen into disrepair.

The rain poured over the dented gutters, choked by many autumns of leaves. A chunk of stone was missing under the steps to the front door. A light glowed somewhere deep within the house, and even with his disfigured nose Pablo could smell the tang of a microwave dinner wafting from a distant open window. He looked at Raquel. "Let me talk." He pressed the doorbell.

It took a good three and a half minutes for someone to come to the door. It opened without creaking, revealing a walker, a tripod of three chewed-up tennis balls, a pinkish robe that was either silk or the oldest polyester known to man, dingy pajamas, and the face of an old lady whose halo of hair was so white and perfectly round that it looked like her wrinkly face grew out of the center of a ping-pong ball.

"Madame, we spoke earlier," Pablo said, putting on his most exotic, most tropical voice. He removed his hat, bowed, mindful of the bandages covering his missing ear and nose. "I am Pablo Gutierrez and this"—he turned to Raquel—"is my granddaughter. I do apologize for the late hour."

Nancy Bouchard looked out into the rain. "You made good time, despite the weather. I didn't expect you to make it until tomorrow, otherwise I would have put on something a little nicer."

"You look like a woman enjoying a summer night," Pablo said as warmly as he could. "Do you think it's too late for us to come in? If it is, we can come back in the morning."

"Oh no," Mrs. Bouchard said. "I was just about to start watching *Dr. Phil*. I tape it so I can watch it twice," she said with a sly grin. "Follow me."

Pablo and Raquel trailed the elderly woman into the dark house, the old lady navigating around clutter like a bat. Her destination, of course, was the kitchen, brightly decorated in two-tone pink and lime-green styling and dotted with many photographs.

"Is this your husband?" Pablo asked, motioning to a small silver frame that needed polishing.

"Sure," she said. "That was in Laos." In the photo, a young Sheriff Bouchard sat in the jungle, a Russian-made AK-47 slung over his shoulder, wearing a green beret and a mischievous smirk.

"So your husband was special forces during the war?"

"Oh yeah," she said, "he was in the early days of all that SEAL and CIA business. Was surprised he wanted to move back to Pound Ridge after the war. But guess he'd had enough." She smiled.

So had Pablo. More elements fitting together.

"Sit, please," she said.

Pablo and Raquel slid into a breakfast nook overlooking the backyard shrouded in fog. The old lady groaned as she lowered herself into the seat across from them. "I'm sorry I don't have any coffee made, but I can offer you a Sanka. Or an aspirin for your nose." The old lady squinted at Pablo. "That a sunspot you had removed? Looks like it stings."

"Yes," said Pablo, awkwardly touching the bandage on his nose. "Early cancer spot. But it's okay," Pablo said. "Thank you. It's kind enough that you would talk to us."

"Don't have anything better to do. Now, let me get this straight," the old widow said. "You two think you're somehow related to Eldon Waanders?"

"Yes, that's right," said Pablo. "As I told you earlier, my granddaughter and I are from España. Some time ago, we learned that I was actually a twin, separated at birth. We believe that my missing twin brother is the father of the boy, Eldon Waanders, and we are simply trying to confirm it. With DNA, or perhaps police records, or even a fingerprint."

The woman nodded, a little confused but rolling with it. "And how did you come to find me?"

From his pocket, Pablo removed a printout of the article, reporting that Eldon Waanders, who had been missing since Thanksgiving, had been found dead before Christmas. "I found you through this article, which mentions your husband. He found the boy . . . after the boy had died. But did he know Eldon in life?"

"Yes, he did," she said. "We didn't have any children of our own. My husband, Marion, was very involved in youth sports, the Boy Scouts—things of that sort. He took a particular interest in some juvenile delinquents we had in the area. Particularly, the ones he thought showed promise. And Eldon was one of the hardest cases he'd ever dealt with. The boy was in and out of trouble, very tough. Very mean. As you know, his parents—your brother, I guess—died when he was young, so he was a foster child. Bounced around the area. He seemed to live either in the jail, in the lockup, or with a rotating list of families.

"For some reason, my husband just took a liking to the boy. He was very smart, and just . . . I don't know. Restless. I think Marion believed that if he put the boy to work and set his hands in motion, they wouldn't do bad things." She motioned out into the backyard and the fog swirling around the crumbling barn and shed. "Marion and Eldon got the barn and chicken coop in tip-top shape. Fixed them up. Painted them. We had two dozen birds, a horse, a couple goats at one time."

"They worked together fixing things up? Your husband . . . and Eldon?" Pablo asked.

"Yes. He really responded to the work. Came out of his shell." The old lady rubbed her swollen, rheumatoid knuckles. "And so did Marion. Marion just loved the kid. And Eldon started spending a lot of time over here. Always doing something, whether it was taking care of the animals or painting. In fact, we got so close to the boy, and he had been staying out of trouble so long, that my husband thought we might make a room for him here, which we did. The boy painted it himself. Fixed all the tongue and groove. Sanded the floor, waxed it. Did it all by himself."

"Did he move in?" Raquel asked. "With you and your husband here?"

The woman startled, hearing Raquel speak for the first time. "I just got to tell you, darlin', you are gorgeous." The widow smiled.

Raquel sighed in annoyance.

"No, is the answer," the old widow continued. "Unfortunately, he did not move in. Couple weeks before we were going to take custody of the boy, Eldon up and disappeared. I was the one who reported him missing. Marion found him in the van on the outside of town after the blizzard."

Pablo nodded. "Terribly tragic."

"Marion was devastated. Crushed. We all were. In fact, I never did anything with the room that the boy had made for himself here."

"You mentioned that he had painted the room himself?" Pablo asked.

"I did," she said.

"He did *all* the work himself?" Pablo repeated.

"Oh yeah. Every last brushstroke."

"And the room has not been touched in the intervening years?" Pablo asked, voice all sunshine.

"Well," she said. "That's not entirely true. I've put a few things in there, but nobody's slept in it. You're welcome to take a look, long as you don't mind showing yourself up there and leaving me with the good doctor." She swiveled toward her old TV, *Dr. Phil* reruns on mute. She plucked up the remote like she was a six-shooting sheriff herself, snapped a button, and the volume came roaring back.

Across the landing from a steep, narrow staircase Pablo and Raquel found the room intended for Eldon Waanders. It was indeed filled with a few things, something like a ton and a half of hoarded boxes packed with magazines, candy bar wrappers, and freaky collections of dolls and doll body parts, all stacked to the ceiling and spilling out like a volcano spewing all things weird and junky.

"Do you have a flashlight?" Pablo asked Raquel.

"I have this." She drew out her iPhone and snapped on the flashlight.

"Thank you," he said, taking it from her pretty hand and holding the light up close to the surface of the white paint.

It took him a while, but eventually he found what he was looking for. On the inside door of the laundry chute, Pablo discovered four fingerprints. Pablo photographed the prints as a cluster and then again individually. He then used the tip of his penknife to unscrew the bolts from the latch and remove the small laundry chute door from the wall. He tucked it under his arm. "I'm sure the old lady would not mind if we take this," Pablo said.

"I'm sure too," Raquel said and Pablo noticed a glimmer of ash swirl in Raquel's black eyes. "But let me go ask." Raquel turned and descended to the lower level.

Pablo moved slowly down the steep steps, one arm tightly clutching the laundry chute door and the other holding the wobbly railing, stairs still tricky on his fake leg.

Minutes later, he found Raquel in the kitchen, her back to him, sorting through the cupboard, where she remqved a 1960s-era Oster blender. A wad of red and white gristle sat on the cutting board. The old lady was on the floor, shoved under the breakfast table, her ping-pong ball hairdo sopping up a puddle of blood.

"Buenísimo. Very good," the Glowworm said warmly, clapping his long, moon-colored hands. "You, my friend, have redeemed yourself. You are back in the inside circle. On the Dream Team again. Come give Daddy a hug."

Pablo inched forward on the bench and leaned into the Glowworm's bare chest, feeling the slime that covered his skin and smelling his weird and pungent B.O.—a chemical scent like a urinal deodorizer smothered in CK1. Awkward as the hug was, Pablo felt a surge of pride as his captor patted his back.

"What's next?" the Glowworm hissed into Pablo's ear.

"We have almost everything to determine if Eldon Waanders is in fact the prisoner held by the Brotherhood," Pablo said as the party limo snaked its way back down toward the interstate. "One last stop to be sure. Perhaps on the way, we can buy a shovel."

CHAPTER 31

With its short runway and sheer cliff walls, the Caldera was always terrifying at takeoff, especially in a jet. The crew, staff, and members of Group-C braced themselves as the Embraer Phenom 300 raced down the runway, went nose up, and climbed, screaming toward blue sky just over the lip of the Caldera.

They leveled off and the captain announced their flight plan, followed by the final in-flight briefing, which was short and businesslike.

Wyatt tried to check in with Dolly. Wyatt of course knew she was the most distraught of the lot, though she tried not to show it. Since the bonfire she had remained stoic and distant. All business.

"Far as I am concerned, you and I helped push Hud out. And as for my sister—" Dolly paused, keeping her emotions in check.

"If we get a chance for revenge, I'm taking it. We owe it to Hud and Cass. We owe it to ourselves. Are you with me?"

Wyatt looked her in the eyes. "Yes."

Group-C was issued detailed plans of the cathedral and drilled on where and when each team member would sit, stand, or kneel. They were issued appropriate clothes for the funeral, fake IDs, cover stories, and, given the data breaches, heavily encrypted smartphones.

As the small jet descended toward Teterboro, Wyatt conducted a final weapons check. He carried a Glock 26 and a Colt Mustang XSP, a knife, a silencer, and four extra clips, and the back of his belt was ringed with two flash-bang grenades, two M67 fragmentation grenades, and mace. It was a lot of ordnance for a funeral, Wyatt thought, but he had a feeling he might need it.

CHAPTER 32

August 2017
Pound Ridge, Indiana

Pablo found the groundskeeper and night security guard at St. Jude's Cemetery asleep at his desk, a copy of *Maxim* in his lap and a jar of peanut butter with a spoon sticking out of it on his credenza. Pablo roused him with ten thousand dollars, fanned under his nose. They wanted access to the graves? No problem.

With all the rain, the ground was soft and muddy. Pablo, Raquel, and Fouad did the digging and slinging while the Glowworm stayed in the modified limousine, dialed into the dark net, requesting that the Brotherhood send a copy of the HVT's fingerprints.

Unearthing the coffin took several hours, and even with the steroids, stimulants, and other drugs coursing through his system, Pablo struggled with the shovel. After all, he was old. He tottered, chest heaving, slick with sweat and rain, peering down into the deep wet hole in the ground, the coffin's lid visible under a slick of muck.

"Moment of truth," Fouad said, lowering to his knees. He leaned into the hole, hooked the lid with the edge of the shovel, and pried it open. A fine, dry dust swirled up, into the rain, still slanting down. Fouad swung an LED lamp into the hole, illuminating the soft interior of a mid-grade coffin. Pablo peered over the edge. They had found just what they were looking for— nothing.

Where the body was supposed to have been, there were only three large sacks of gravel, the pebbles spilling out of the old canvas.

Raquel purred. "You were right again. The Glowworm will be pleased."

Pablo nodded, took off his hat, and rubbed the dirt from his forehead. The bandage on his nose had come off long ago and a trickle of blood ran down the center of his cratered face. "And I hope after this I will have proven myself. I will get to go home." He looked off in the direction of the groundskeeper's office, getting an idea. "If you're going to kill the groundskeeper, we might as well stick him in a coffin before we rebury it."

"I have a better idea." A voice came from the darkness behind him. Pablo turned as the Glowworm, naked save for his diaper-like shorts, stalked toward him, his muscles bristling and feeding tube capped.

Pablo had been in the hitman game long enough to know what the Glowworm had in mind—"a two-fer," as the Americans say. Two bodies, one coffin. And Pablo would be part of the deal.

"But why now?" Pablo asked, backing up to the edge of the grave. "After I have helped you? Why would you do it? You now know beyond any question that I did not kill your father."

"Yes, you have showed this to me," the Glowworm said, squaring off across from him.

"Haven't I repaid the debt to you? Haven't I been a good servant? Proven my loyalty? Surely my work for you has made up for raising my hand against your mother."

"Yes. Right again," the Glowworm said, smiling a weird, toothless grin. "Your debt to me for what you did to my mother has been more than repaid. You are off the hook completely."

"So then why hurt an old man?" Pablo forced a chuckle, trying to make light of the situation.

The Glowworm wiped rain from his shoulders and looked at his hands before looking back up. "Because I am a killer," the Glowworm said matter-of-factly, "and both you and my father helped to create me."

He charged Pablo, and the old man could only put up his hands in feeble defense as the thing that used to be Wilberforce Degas flew through the air like a human missile, an all-pro linebacker, slamming into Pablo. The Glowworm's fingers were already wrapping around Pablo's throat as the two bodies fell straight back into the grave, smashing into the muddy side of the pit, falling into the open casket.

Raquel could see the Glowworm needed a little alone time. After severing the last tie to his old life, the Glowworm sat under a tree in a fetal position, pelted by rain, shivering as he unloosed tears and emotion, baggage from youth. Raquel came and sat next to him. An odd pair. A humanoid hacker and his beautiful demon-child.

"I need to ask you a question," she finally said.

The Glowworm sniffled, and with his unsettlingly large hands, wiped away tears.

"Anything, my dear."

"Why did you kill him?"

The Glowworm looked up, a little surprised. "What do you mean, why did I kill Pablo? I was always going to kill him."

"No, I don't mean why. I mean why now?" she asked. "We have yet to find Chris Gibbs and we have yet to find the camp. I thought that's why we were keeping him alive?"

"Ah, you are right, of course, in thinking this," the Glowworm said. "But while I was in the car, I determined the fingerprints are a match. Eldon Waanders is the same man as Chris Gibbs. And Gibbs is the operator captured by the Brotherhood. He will be in our company as soon as a wire transfer goes through. The Brotherhood is bringing him to New York for collection."

"Ahhhh . . . that is good," she said. "But what about the camp itself? How do we find that?"

The Glowworm grinned. "My dear, that is easy," he said. "You. You're going to be the light that lures them in."

CHAPTER 33

The operator known as Chris Gibbs was pretty sure he'd been smuggled out of Israel by way of Egypt, but in the ten months he'd been in captivity he'd been given very few clues as to his whereabouts. He was moved often, first hidden in basements and bomb shelters, and later a shipping container. He could tell from the movement he was driven in a truck and then loaded onto a boat and then the boat went to sea. He assumed he was kept in a ship traveling up and down the coast of Africa.

He was manacled at all times and guarded by at least two men, who wisely kept their distance and their weapons trained on him. Given the chance, he would have disarmed the men or at least tried. He was beaten for the slightest infraction or for no infraction at all. And he was allowed to take off his hood only to eat. The toilet he used was a bucket that would be emptied every few days. Whenever he took his hood off, his captors would be wearing theirs. Aside from during the gun battle in which he was captured, he never saw their faces.

Still, as a trained operator, he was able to figure a few things out. For one, he'd counted at least six different guards and could identify them by voice and the look of their sandaled feet and hands. Should he live to be a hundred, he would never forget those hands and feet. He would recognize them anywhere. Drawing on the little Arabic he spoke, he quickly gleaned that his captors were part of an ISIS faction that called itself the Brotherhood.

The operator also knew if there was any chance for his survival, it would have to do with greed. The Brotherhood, it seemed, wanted to auction him. To sell him to the highest bidder. Because of this detail alone, the operator felt a measure of reassurance. After all, who could outbid the U.S. government? Of course, there were threats—often made during his beatings— that the Brotherhood would not be bought by American dollars. They'd rather behead the man they all called Chris Gibbs than take a dollar from the infidels.

But this was all bluster. When the operator heard squeals of laughter and cheering and bottles of champagne popping, he knew he had been sold. He would not be killed by the Brotherhood.

His captors hustled the operator out of the shipping container. The hood was kept over his head. Still, he almost wept at the scent of fresh air, even if it was mixing with the smell of aviation fuel. A helicopter waited on deck of the ship, rotors churning. They loaded him on board, the blades whooped, and he was airborne.

Almost immediately, the operator picked up on things that didn't make sense. For one, the operator had been almost certain he was somewhere off the coast of Africa or still in the

Middle East. But the helicopter pilot spoke English with a Latin American accent. The pilot's headset was set loud and the operator's ears had become attuned like a blind person's. He thought he heard the air traffic controllers speak with an American accent. Most telling of all, the operator heard the pilot say they were headed to Greenwich. Was that Greenwich, England? Or were they off the East Coast of the United States?

As the helicopter descended, it was night and the operator could see the rooftops of mansions down below. When they landed, the operator was ushered off, and he felt a soft, well-manicured lawn under his feet, and he could smell distant barbecues and a woman's perfume—expensive perfume. And could see legs, beautiful young legs with small, delicate, bare feet walking on the lawn next to him. All signs looked good. God, he was happy to be back on American soil. But why was he still wearing the hood?

"Where are we?" he asked and the butt of a handgun slammed into the side of his head. The woman with the young beautiful legs, perfume, and delicate feet had been the one to hit him. She hit hard. Men now hoisted him up.

Weak-legged, he was dragged across a lush lawn and taken into a cellar. It became dark again, almost no ambient light. He was led down a series of passageways until he arrived at a room that smelled of sweat and raw meat.

"Take it off," a voice said, and his hood was ripped from his head. The operator blinked hard, but the room was so dark that even his eyes, which had grown used to the dark, struggled to see.

"Give this to him," the voice said.

Then he heard dripping and his hands jerked back when something warm touched him.

"Take it," said the voice. "It's just a washcloth. So you can clean your face and hands after your trip."

The rag, warm and soft, was thrust back into his hands. It smelled clean, like soap. "Thank you," the operator said, wiping away months of grime.

"Would you like another?"

"Yes, please."

He was given a new towel to remove another layer of grime. Feeling a little fresher, the operator finally asked, "Who are you? Why am I here?"

"Because you owe me . . . something. Isn't that what it's always about?"

"Owe you what? I can't see anything," the operator said, his face and hands still tingling from the soap and water.

"Let me increase the brightness on this monitor for you."

And then the operator began to see it. Out of the black, a rectangle came to life—first gray against black and then muted colors transformed into a blinking pixilated screen. The words "Donkey Kong" flashed in the center, above a series of best scores. The highest score was still held by Chris Gibbs. The second-highest was held by Wil Degas.

"You owe me the chance to try to beat you," said the voice, now shaking with laughter. "Why don't we play?"

PART SIX

CHAPTER 34

August 2017
St. Patrick's Cathedral

Blazing hot day. Muggy. Gray and white summer clouds boiled in the sky.
Limousines waited along Fifth Avenue. Dolly, Ebbie, Samy, and
Wyatt fell in with the mourners lining up to enter the cathedral.
The Old Man, Hallsy, and Avi watched in the surveillance
van. Rory lingered across Fifth Avenue, disguised as a skate-
boarder, tracking the ground team's movements, scanning for
threats. All communicated via inductive earpieces.

Ebbie, Samy, and Wyatt donned somber suits, boxy and ill-
fitting to hide their weaponry. Dolly wore a simple black dress,
but on her, it wowed. Tucked into a quick-draw compartment
in her purse was a silver Walther PPK, a gun fit for James Bond.
Loaded with hollow-points.

Yes, they were headed to their friend's funeral. But Wyatt
couldn't stop himself from thinking about how beautiful Dolly
looked, how driven. Revenge looked good on her. Dolly, the only

Blue left in Group-C, ran lead on the mission, entering the church first, and Wyatt found himself wanting to catch up, to walk with her.

"Easy," Samy said, hustling next to Wyatt, touching his arm. "You're speeding up, man. Hold formation."

"Check," said Wyatt, slowing. Trying to clear his mind as he started up the stairs, which were already swarming with mourners, tourists, and even paparazzi snapping photos from across the street.

"Damn, I never would have known," said Ebbie, shaking his head. "Hud . . . a rich kid. Never would have guessed it."

"You kidding me? Looks like he was more than rich," said Samy. "This is rich and famous." He shook his head. "My question is, what was he doing at Valor?"

Dolly glared back. "Have some respect."

Her teammates chastened, she turned, stayed a stride ahead.

"All right, guys, we gotta get our heads straight," Ebbie said as they approached the cathedral doors. "Game faces on."

The cathedral was already packed, thrumming with whispers and gossip. A mousy woman with a clipboard, an expensive hairdo, and an earpiece greeted them with a sneer and said, "This funeral is for close friends and family only. How did you know Hud?"

Dolly gave their cover, "Skiing in Aspen. Our parents have homes there."

The woman's sneer remained in her phony smile, but she motioned them into the chapel.

"In that case, welcome." She directed Wyatt and Dolly to a pew. And as planned, the members of Group-C dispersed, slipping into separate pews, each member of the team growing serious, checking in mentally, heightening their situational awareness.

Wyatt sat in the rear right of the church. Ahead, at the base of the altar, he saw a mass of the preppiest human beings on earth, all in dark tones and somber but somehow still shiny. Beaming, in fact. It looked like the entire cast of *Gossip Girl,* and all the extras had shown up. Beautiful people—buffed, polished, and effortlessly gorgeous. No wonder the lady with the clipboard had stopped them. Even in church clothes, the ruffians from Valor stuck out. Healthy and handsome, sure, but they were like shards of sea glass scattered among pearls. They were broken and polished by friction. Ground into something useful. The New York kids, pearls, alluring by nature, formed in a protective shell. Hud was a black pearl, a crossover. Even Dolly, as beautiful and stunning as she was, lacked the high-gloss affectation easily detectible by the trained eye. She was a stunning MMA fighter, not a ballerina. And Wyatt would have it no other way.

Among Hud's fancy friends, one girl stood out, vastly more dazzling than all the rest. A gleaming egg-sized diamond among pearls. Easily the most stunning person Wyatt had seen in person in his life. Dark eyes, blond hair, she had to be exotic. She sat dead center, next to an olive-skinned guy with a scraggly beard. A field of magnetism appeared to surround her, drawing those in close proximity to her. And yet, there was something dangerous about her too, something sinister.

"That's her," Dolly said into the comms system. "She's the one. The blonde from the roof."

Wyatt nodded, though Dolly couldn't see him, as she was seated in the front of the church. Wyatt knew Dolly was right. The blonde had to be the one. He raised his hand to his mouth as if to yawn. "Good eye, Dolly. Let's keep watching her. Follow close. See where she goes."

"That's the plan," Dolly said, but then, breaking protocol

and clearly discarding all of their mission prep, she stood up in her pew and picked her way over to the blonde.

"Dolly," Samy whispered over the comms. "Where you going?"

Wyatt watched as Dolly reached up and discreetly removed her earpiece and slipped her hand into her purse.

"What's she doing?" Ebbie asked.

"I don't know," said Wyatt, though his mind went to her hand in her purse and the PPK inside. "Changing seats."

"We aren't supposed to make contact," Ebbie said.

"I ain't sure she's just making contact," Samy said. "She's off comms and coming up on the girl."

Hallsy's voice broke in, "Someone stop her. Wyatt, if she draws, I order you to stop her!"

They all watched as Dolly approached the blonde and leaned forward, reaching her hand in her purse. Wyatt knew she couldn't hear him, but he whispered the words anyway: *What if you're wrong?*

Dolly smiled sadly and said something to the blonde, who scooted over, making room.

Wyatt could read Dolly's lips. "Thank you," she said.

"Looks like she's just sitting down next to her," Samy said. "Everyone can breathe easy."

From her purse Dolly drew out a cell phone, typed something, and flipped it shut.

Wyatt's phone buzzed. "Staying close," the message said. "Can't use comms. She'll see. Watch my back."

The service was beautiful and sad. As far as most of the people in the cathedral knew, a boy had taken his own life. He was handsome and smart, surrounded by friends and all the material advantages life could offer. And yet he was troubled, not quite whole. His criminal record and stints in juvenile detention were not mentioned directly, only alluded to in a theme repeated throughout the service—the Prodigal Son. Only those from Valor, and his killers, knew differently.

As the service ended, the priest invited Hud's mother to say a few words. From the front row rose an aged 1990s Video Vixen, a woman with a plastic face and body, an inappropriately short lacy black dress, and a lion's mane hairdo. She teetered on six-inch stilettos that clacked up to the lectern.

"Hi." She breathed into the microphone long and slow. "For those who don't know me, I am Hudson's mother."

Makeup smeared and eyes glassy wet pools, she looked like she'd been both crying and slamming Valium. "My husband and I"—she waved to an elderly man in a wheelchair—"invite all of you here to join us back at our apartment for a reception."

Sniffling, wiping away tears, she staggered away from the lectern. The gray-haired priest retook his place at the lectern and began the final prayer.

"Wyatt," Samy said as the congregation rose to leave, "you're the point now. What's the move? Are we going to the reception?"

Wyatt had not taken his eyes off Dolly and the blonde for the duration of the service. He'd barely blinked. They were talking. Dolly's face teary. They started walking out together.

"Yes," Wyatt answered. "Dolly's onto something and not letting go. Let's see where she takes us."

The reception after the service was boring and weird. Weird in that a boy had jumped from the roof of the building and now everyone was inside, eating hors d'oeuvres and making small talk.

Wyatt, Samy, and Ebbie arrived right after Dolly and the blonde. They'd been inside five minutes when Dolly quickly put her earpiece in and was back up on the comms. "Okay, guys. Listen up, I'm going to talk fast 'cause she's coming right back. Sorry I went silent there, but the earpiece would have given me away. This is the girl. She's invited me to a party at a house she's renting with her guardian. She didn't tell me his name, but he runs a company, a tech company called Glowworm Gaming. Have Avi find out everything he can. They rented a house in the sub-urbs for the funeral. It's close, in Greenwich."

"Dolly," Hallsy interjected over the comms. "We can't change plan that drastically . . ."

"Sir," she cut him off, "with all due respect, I'm going, sup-ported or not. This girl is from the group that killed Hud and almost killed my sister. The group that is trolling Valor. I feel it, I know it, it's real. You have to trust me."

"I'm listening," Hallsy said.

"Okay, here's the deal. I've told her some friends are here, and we had plans. So Wyatt, Ebbie, and Samy will come with me. I'm going to act like I just saw them and we are going to leave together. I'll ride with her to Greenwich. You guys are going to—"

Dolly, catching sight of something, pulled the earpiece from her ear. The blonde approached, a short olive-skinned guy with a greasy, scraggly beard accompanying her.

"Sounds like we're going," Ebbie said into the comms.

"Sounds like we're are going to need transpo," Wyatt added, "and something fast. Hallsy, can you arrange that? A car, out-side the building in five minutes?"

Avi answered, "Hold on, guys, we're discussing options on our end."

Wyatt's earpiece clicked.

"Wyatt, you're the only one on right now," Hallsy said. "I want to know. Do you think Dolly's mind is right on this? Do you think we give her the rope? You're on the ground. Tell me what you think."

"I think we do," Wyatt said. "I'm point now, but she's leading on this. We follow. And we make sure she's protected. That's on us."

"I asked about Dolly," Hallsy said. "Is she right?"

"It's not just Dolly," Wyatt said. "We're a team in this. You told us when we started at Valor that our reputations start now. Well, this is it. Reputations are made now. We're making ours as a team."

There was a pause. "Roger that." Another click and his voice returned in all the earpieces. "Car will be outside in four minutes. Valet will have keys."

"What are we driving?" Wyatt asked. "So we know what to look for?"

"Fast. Look for fast," was all Hallsy said.

Dolly put on her best surprised face and came over to Ebbie, Samy, and Wyatt. "Oh hey, I didn't see you . . ." She introduced the blonde as Raquel. Raquel's friend—the guy with the scraggly beard—worked for her guardian at the gaming company. He was college-aged, maybe a little older. His name was Fouad.

At the ground level, the party stepped onto the street and Wyatt saw a silver 1968 GTO at the curb, aftermarket pipes rumbling. The valet—Avi sporting a red jacket and a fresh layer of sweat—handed Wyatt the keys. "Mr. Brewer."

Hallsy does not disappoint, Wyatt thought as he sat in the front seat, noting switches for a Nitro booster and Guns N' Roses' "Paradise City" playing low on the radio. Yeah, this would do just fine.

"Nice car," said Raquel. "You should have no problem following, as long as you keep your speed up."

A problem keeping up? The GTO was a rocket engine on wheels, Wyatt thought, but then he saw her ride. Like a stealth bomber or a mechanical black panther, the Ferrari F12berlinetta rounded the corner, barreled down Fifth Avenue, and growled at the curb.

Fouad crammed into the Berlinetta's minuscule back seat, the girls slipped into the front. Sun was aglow in the sky. Wyatt called out the open window, "Hey, where are we headed?"

"The Cottage," she called back.

"You want to give me an address? You know, in case, we get stuck at a red . . ."

"Yes, the address is *don't get stuck*!" Laughing, she peeled out, tossing her blond hair back.

Wyatt hurried to shift the car in gear but a truck raced up and stopped, nearly shearing off his sideview mirror. "Move!" Wyatt laid on the horn.

"Don't worry," a friendly voice came in over the comms. "I'm launched. And have you covered from above." Rory was watching from a drone overhead.

The truck blocking him in started to ease forward. Wyatt pressed the clutch and shifted into first.

"Wait," Ebbie said, stopping him before he could let the clutch out. "You'll need these." Ebbie handed him a pair of sunglasses. Vuarnets. Wyatt slipped the shades on, popped the clutch, and slammed down the gas pedal. The GTO fishtailed onto Fifth.

Wyatt stayed close behind the Berlinetta from 62nd to 72nd, then she laid down smoke and rubber and high-tailed it east, shooting over to the FDR before driving north again, a comet's tail of city grit trailing behind and Wyatt's GTO trying to keep up. The girl ran her car hard and fast as she barreled north. The

Berlinetta had way more tech, torque, and precision handling to outrun the GTO.

"I'm losing them," Wyatt said. "Rory, what do you see?"

"Traffic on the FDR is light all the way up to Randall's Island, to 278 and 95. That girl knows how to drive. She's hauling ass," Rory said.

"Can I lay down some Nitro?"

"Be careful. But looks like you have a clear shot."

"Here we go." Wyatt tipped the red toggle switch. The gas pumped into the engine and the car seemed to hiccup, then it shot forward, turning rocket ship, blazing past cars going eighty miles an hour like they were stopping to buy snow cones. And still, the GTO didn't gain much on the Berlinetta. The Ferrari was that fast.

"Got another idea," Ebbie said into the comms. "Rory, you got a magic wand to make traffic appear?"

CHAPTER 35

August 2017
Brooklyn-Queens Expressway

Antoinette "Tony" Johnson drove exactly fifty-five miles an hour on the BQE. She drove it twice a day, five days a week, forty-eight weeks a year. And a good thing, too. She was prepared when the "stuff hit the fan." Which happened. A lot. Like the day she thought she saw a bird flying beside her Buick Acadia.

"What the—" She watched outside the window as the thing got closer and closer. It was mechanical. It was one of those things, those drone things, and it hovered above her car, flying in front of the windshield.

How dare they, those kids. There's some kid or some terrorist flying this thing. She started honking and yelling, "Get outta here!" to the flying object. But it flew even closer. Right up in her grill. She slowed all the way down to thirty-five miles an hour, screaming, "What are you doing? Get! Get!" She didn't see the eighteen-wheeler in her rearview, she only heard its brakes hiss and scream. She hissed and screamed too.

The truck started to slide, wheels wailing against the black-top. It jackknifed, and the trailer swung sideways, slamming into the rear of Tony's car. The car shot forward and smashed into the drone, shattering its propellers. The drone crashed, and Tony's car drove over it, the lady screaming and praying to God until the car came to a rest. Behind her, the pileup began.

In the surveillance van, stuck way back in New York City traffic, Rory watched her monitor go black.

"Hey guys, we have a problem. My drone is down. We're going to launch another but right now, we have no visibility on Dolly's vehicle. I repeat, we cannot see Dolly's vehicle. You are following her without air support."

Wyatt couldn't see her either. He began to panic. Dolly was alone with the enemy. But he could see cars slowing as he caught up to the traffic jam Rory had caused. Coming up almost a half mile behind the pileup, four hundred yards from red taillights, Wyatt saw the Ferrari Berlinetta weave across the traffic.

"She's heading to the shoulder," said Samy from the back.

"Got her," Wyatt downshifted, then swerved so that both cars were in the shoulder. The GTO kicking up gravel, rocks, and cigarette butts. The nitrous was no longer pumping into the engine. Both cars cut alongside the traffic jam.

"I bet she's getting off at the next exit," Wyatt said, putting the hammer down and surging ahead, past blaring horns and a sea of middle fingers. He swerved off the expressway, running up on Berlinetta's taillights glowing at the next stoplight.

"Dolly, talk to me," Wyatt said, knowing she couldn't hear him, but hoping she would know his thoughts. She glanced back through the Berlinetta's tiny rear window, a thin smile. Wyatt could read her. A little on edge but not scared. In it. Wyatt locked eyes with her for a millisecond.

Raquel grinned in her rearview, very red lips the same color as the light. He knew what was coming. She blazed into traffic, zigzagging through swerving cars. A Honda Civic slammed into an MTA bus in her wake. Wyatt swung left, dodging the pileup in the intersection.

Wyatt was not losing her now. Hell, no. He followed the Ferrari through the streets of Larchmont, looking to gain an advantage, to cut Raquel's lead.

Soon the Berlinetta ditched the busy suburban roads for the winding beachside streets of Connecticut, curvy scenic two-lanes that hugged the Long Island Sound, lined with mansions, parks, and beaches. The afternoon light now coming in, slanting, golden and rose colored off the windshields racing one after another. The colors kaleidoscopic, reflecting off the homes, leather, sunglasses, Long Island Sound, rippling waves. Wyatt couldn't help but enjoy the thrill. It was a good time to be not quite sixteen and driving over a hundred miles an hour. And there was something else, a feeling deep in Wyatt's chest, chasing after the girl that meant more to him than any girl ever had. The feeling was both terrifying and electric. He was not going to lose her.

He was just getting in a groove, screaming around wide corners of the walled properties, Wyatt losing the Ferrari for a couple of seconds, then catching up again. This time, he saw the brake lights of the Ferrari twenty yards ahead. Raquel's car jerked sharply to the left, tires chirping, dust rising. Wyatt slammed the brakes and cut in the same direction. But the GTO's cornering ability was nothing like the Berlinetta's. The GTO's wheels smoked and the car fishtailed and went into a slide, laying down streaks of rubber, overshooting the turn by a hundred feet and winding up on someone's lawn. Wyatt spat grass and mud from his rear tires and turned up the driveway, pulling into a massive walled compound.

"We're here," Wyatt said into his comms and read an address off the gate.

Rory's response was a mess of digital distortion.

"Repeat," Wyatt said, the GTO humming up the half-mile drive to the giant, looming mansion. To the left, a formal entrance. To the right, a service entrance wound around toward the back of the Cottage, where there were a couple of service vans and a black limousine party bus.

"Cottage, huh?" Samy said, looking up at a house that would give the Biltmore Estate a run for its money. The Ferrari was parking out front.

"Hey, guys," Wyatt said to Samy and Ebbie. "I'm having trouble getting Rory. Can you hear her?"

"All scrambled for me," said Samy, jamming his finger into his ear.

"Yeah, can't hear a thing," Ebbie added. "Lemme see if I can figure this out." He checked his cell phone and the device connected to the earpiece. "We're not getting any signal." Ebbie had a note of fear in his voice. "I mean, the bands are gone. Someone is blocking all cellular reception here."

Wyatt instantly knew what this meant. They were cut off. The surveillance van wouldn't find them, not unless somehow Rory heard Wyatt read the address aloud, but that wasn't likely.

"We should call the mission," Ebbie said. "Now."

"Too late," said Wyatt, nodding ahead, feeling sick. Dolly was passing through a large brick archway with Raquel and Fouad.

"So that's it. We get her and get out. On our own," Ebbie said.

Wyatt nodded and sped up to the top of the drive. He pulled the parking brake and they got out. Wyatt nodded to Ebbie, "Give me your tie."

"My tie?"

"Yeah. Quick." Wyatt pulled his own tie from his neck, and putting it together with Ebbie's, he made a large X on the hood of the GTO.

"Rory will have another drone in the area," Wyatt explained, hustling toward the house. "Hopefully, she'll see this and come looking."

CHAPTER 36

August 2017, Dusk
The Cottage, Greenwich, Connecticut

The doors to the Cottage were left open. They stepped in, feeling like they had entered a museum of darkness, nearly devoid of furniture. Velvet curtains blocked the light from most windows. Wyatt heard light chatter and laughter somewhere in the house. And heavy electronic music.

"This way." Fouad came up to the top of a staircase and motioned them to follow. "We're in the Game Room." Strangely, none of the light fixtures in the house had bulbs. The only light filling the rooms was natural, dimming fast, and coming in wherever curtains had not been drawn shut over the windows.

Down a stone staircase they went, into a nearly pitch-black Gaming Room, with blackout curtains drawn. The room was empty, save a few ratty snooker tables and stuffed animals hanging on the walls, peering down with dumb glassy eyes. There was a bar in the far corner. A waiter in a tux stood to take orders.

Only candles flickered for light. And a table was set lavishly with food. The smattering of guests dug into piles of caviar, sweets, exotic fruits, and dried meat.

Wyatt tried to look natural, but it was nearly impossible until he regained sight of Dolly.

"Party?" Samy said under his breath. "It was more fun back at the funeral."

"Caviar," Fouad said, motioning to the table, "if you eat the stuff."

"Where's Dolly?" Wyatt asked. "I mean, where are the girls?"

"Freshening up," Fouad said. "Don't worry, homes. She'll be right back."

"Who are those people over there?" Samy jerked his chin out to the guests on the other side of the lawn. There were three of them, attended by a waiter.

"Those people?" Fouad said, as if he was recognizing them for the first time. "Right. They just dropped off a package. They're getting a bite to eat before they leave."

"Hey, Fouad," Ebbie said. "You mind if we use the bathroom?" Ebbie turned and looked down a long hallway. Wyatt knew exactly what he was thinking. Go find Dolly. Or go find a phone.

Fouad, no doubt, also knew exactly what Ebbie was thinking. "Sure." He grinned strangely. "Go straight back. First door you'll come to leads to a hall. Make a right. You're there, homes."

"Thanks, *homes*," said Ebbie, who nodded to Samy and Wyatt. "Back in a jif."

"You want me to show you the way?" Fouad called after him.

"Nah," said Ebbie, not looking back. "I'm a big boy."

That he was, thought Wyatt. And he had a Desert Eagle hidden under his coat.

Fouad, Samy, and Wyatt watched Ebbie disappear down the hall. The three looked at each other for a moment, in silence.

"Good times," Fouad said. "Good times."

Ebbie searched the main floor—no Dolly, no phone. Passing another stairwell, he could hear strange moans. He followed, assuming he was now at the basement level. Noises were coming from the end of the hall. Ebbie passed the bathroom. Not a girl's voice. A man's voice. Low and guttural. Someone in pain for sure. But not acute pain. Ebbie wished he had his NVGs. It was so dark. He'd use his phone to light the way, but the light would draw attention. And he had his Desert Eagle drawn out in front of him as he crept down the hall closer to the door.

The noise stopped. Silence. He heard blood rushing in his ears. And the voice of reason in his own head saying, You should go back, get the boys, call in the cavalry. Still, he walked.

"Who's there?" a girl's voice called from down the hall. Accented. Sounded like Raquel.

But Ebbie didn't answer, stepping as quietly as he could toward the voice.

"Whoever you are, do you mind coming closer? My phone is dead and I can't see." She paused, "Can you?"

Ebbie kept moving.

"Can you help me see?" she repeated and then seemed to laugh. "I guess not. Can you see the Glowworm behind you?"

Ebbie heard the girl laugh as he felt a pair of wet arms, like coiled steel, wrap around his neck.

"You look nervous," Fouad said. "Want me to go find the girls?"

Wyatt was, in fact, getting nervous. He hadn't seen Dolly yet in the house and Ebbie had been gone for at least ten minutes. But he didn't like this kid prodding him.

"You want to go find the girls, go right ahead," Wyatt said. "But I'm coming with you."

Fouad nodded. "Sure, no problem." He smiled through his greasy beard and squinted. "Remind me how you knew Hud again?"

"Skiing," Samy said coolly.

"In Aspen. Yeah, I remember now." Fouad made a face. "But . . . hmmm." He looked around like something was occurring to him. It was dusk, and the sun had just set. The last vestiges of light in the Game Room seemed to instantly dim. From golden to a dull amber. An eerie light. And oddly quiet.

"You mean you didn't know him from that camp where you learn how to spy and kill people."

Wyatt and Samy exchanged a look.

"Kidding!" Fouad said. "Man you two looked crazy just then. Like crazy."

Two loud bangs came from the lower floors. Flat, and familiar. Gunshots. Heads swiveled. Wyatt and Samy had guns drawn in an instant.

"Hey, what's going on," Fouad said, smirking. "You bring guns to our party?"

"Get on the ground!" Wyatt forced Fouad to the floor. "Same with you!" He swung his gun around to the guests and the waiter. "All of you, on the ground."

Neither the guests nor the staff seemed fazed, they just kept on drinking, gobbling caviar, slugging champagne.

"They're poisoned. Or drugged," Samy said. "Completely out of it."

Fouad giggled. "You're completely out of it."

Wyatt zip-tied Fouad. He was still giggling when Wyatt gagged him. The guests didn't even notice.

"You don't even know enough to be scared of the dark."

Wyatt drew his knife and pressed it to Fouad's throat. "God help me, I will kill you. Where are they?"

Fouad's smiled faded. "Killing me would be a relief compared to what they will do to me if I betray them."

"Fine, then." Samy slammed the butt of his gun on the top of Fouad's head. He crumpled.

"Leave him," Wyatt said. "This way." And he took off toward the sound of the gunshots.

They moved in a pair down the long dark corridor, slowly. Wyatt looking forward, Samy watching their backs—swim buddies stepping slowly into the unknown. Wyatt had tried the light switch. But like all of the lights and the switches in the house, none worked. Since the original mission was a day operation in New York City, they had not deemed it necessary to bring night vision goggles, and because of this, they were at a tremendous disadvantage. Wyatt had his cell phone glowing in his hand, but he kept it away from his body, in case someone decided to shoot at it.

Wyatt could not see, but he smelled blood in the hallway. He moved forward, hearing a trickling sound. They came up on a spray of blood dripping from the wall and ceiling. No body. But a trail led down the hall to a door, half-open.

"Ebbie?" Samy asked.

"Maybe," Wyatt said, then made a "shhhh" sound and cut his light.

"What's that?" Samy froze. They both heard it—a buzzing, steady whine. Something entered the hall behind them. Now buzzing clearly.

The buzzing came down the hall, and a wind swept toward them. Samy aimed his gun.

"Don't," Wyatt whispered as a drone hummed into view. "It's one of ours."

"Damn, Rory has some skills," Samy said. She must have seen the GTO marked with an X from above, entered the house, and somehow managed to navigate stairs and hallways without crashing. The drone, about two feet in diameter, hovered in the hall in front of them before settling to the ground. Wyatt could see the model had no speaker. But it did have a camera, microphone, night vision capability, and an LED light.

"Rory," Wyatt said. "Flash your light once for yes, twice for no. Got me?"

The LED glowed, one flash.

"Is the rest of the team here?"

The LED glowed once.

"Are they on their way?"

The LED glowed once.

"Is Avi with you?"

LED flash.

"Avi, can you pair the camera in the drone with my phone so I can see what the drone sees?"

There was a long pause, then Wyatt saw his phone glow. Bluetooth pairing. Then Wyatt was looking at a video of himself and the drone's internal dashboard on his screen. This was good news. Bad news was, the drone's battery was flashing. It would run out of juice soon. "We have to move fast," Wyatt said, looking down the hall at the door. "Stay ahead of us."

The drone now lifted off the ground and flew down the hallway. Wyatt kept one eye on the screen of his phone as he followed. He holstered the Glock and reached around his back to check his ammo. The two grenades were still clipped to his belt. The two flash-bangs were there, as well as the two M67s. Wyatt drew his gun again. The drone reached the end of the hall. The door was cracked open, just wide enough for the drone to enter.

"Go ahead," Wyatt whispered.

The drone entered, narrowly avoiding the doorframe. On his phone, Wyatt saw the room was a torture chamber. Blood was everywhere, reading black on the screen—the floor, the walls. The room was empty, except for a blender sitting on a stand next to a strange pump. It looked like two fingers were inside it. Wyatt looked closer. There was Ebbie's Desert Eagle. And Dolly's purse—both splashed with blood.

"Oh god," Wyatt followed behind the drone. "Where did they go?"

The drone pivoted around the room and then settled on a rug that had been tossed aside. The outline of a door, open wide, leading down into what looked like a wine cellar. The outline of round bottles visible in the greenish glow of the drone's night vision. The drone settled onto the floor to conserve battery.

Wyatt and Samy entered the room quietly. Wyatt picked up Ebbie's Desert Eagle and checked the breech. One shot fired. One of the two shots they heard, he thought.

Samy tapped Wyatt and whispered, "Hey brutha, I think we are being followed."

Wyatt looked back down the hall, his eyes unable to see clearly but, like Samy, half-seeing, half-sensing movement.

"Can we send the drone back?" Samy asked.

"Not enough battery," Wyatt said. "And Dolly and Ebbie are this way."

"Damn, brutha. We are getting drawn into a trap." Samy said.

"Yeah," Wyatt agreed. "But they don't know we have these."

Wyatt drew out his grenades and put them into two piles on the door. "Flash-bangs here. M67s here. If they come on, we go out hard."

Samy nodded, putting the grenades he carried into the separate piles.

"Rory," Wyatt whispered to the drone, "you copy?"

The LED flashed once. Wyatt looked at Samy and pointed back down the way they had come. "Keep an eye out."

Wyatt put his phone down next to the Desert Eagle and his Glock. He checked his Colt, took it off safety, and reholstered the Glock. He had more ammo for the Glock, so he wanted to save that gun. Samy did the same with his weapons. Wyatt held a flash-bang in one hand and an M67 in the other. "Rory, show me what's in the cellar."

The drone descended the stairs, and Wyatt monitored progress on his phone. He saw that the stairs led down to a wine cellar—and a massive one at that. It must have been a hundred yards long, running the full length of the mansion. And it was old, the walls shaped by a mix of clay and dirt and cement. Like a mazelike cave. Barrels and bottles where everywhere. It was pitch-black.

The drone moved into the warren and landed, maybe twenty feet from the room where Wyatt and Samy waited. A few moments later and they saw signs of life. What looked like a vast empty cell now crawled with vermin. Rats, mice, and the worst kind—humans. Maybe forty people dressed completely in black and wearing NVGs came out from behind the barrels and the bottles. A trap indeed.

Through the connection between the drone and his cellphone, Wyatt could hear the blonde, Raquel, somewhere in the cellar. "See what it is," she said.

One of the figures clad in black, carrying a hatchet and an M4, came forward. He wore a black hoodie with "Glowworm Gaming" stenciled on the front. He carefully approached the drone. The people, all with NVGs, focused on the object.

Wyatt pulled the pins from two of the flash-bangs, waited a second and a half, then leaned down into the cellar and hurled them at the creeps in their hoodies.

The cellar lit up in a cataclysm of sound and light. Wyatt could hear screams. In the drone's camera, he could see the guards in the cellar, ripping off their night vision. All were blinded.

Someone must have been pursuing them from the hallway because he heard Samy firing shots.

"Follow me," Wyatt said, scooping up his M67s and pocketing them. He grabbed the Colt and the Desert Eagle and dropped into the cellar. A rack of chemicals near one of the flash-bangs caught fire, casting a yellowish light and black smoke.

Wyatt entered, shooting at targets in black hoodies, anyone he could tell was not Dolly or Ebbie. Samy followed seconds later, and when the ground shook twice from above, Wyatt knew Samy had lobbed his M67s down the hall. They quaked above them.

Wyatt dropped the Desert Eagle and the Glock as soon as he ran out of ammo. Without pause, he heaved the remaining M67s at the bodies down the length of the cellar and pulled Samy aside. "Cover!" he yelled.

The M67s exploded a second apart, sending glass, wine, and all manner of debris, including body parts, flying. Parts of the cellar were caving in. Flames were everywhere. The guards, those who could move, fled the cellar, running like rats for an exit. It was pure chaos—exactly as Wyatt wanted it.

Wyatt and Samy pursued, hot on the heels of the fleeing

guards. If he saw hands up, he didn't shoot. Otherwise, Wyatt put down bad guys, swapping out clips as he ran. As bodies dropped, Wyatt realized he wasn't playing a video game. This was killing. Real kills. Lives taken by Wyatt. The killing didn't feel good, but he did it without hesitation. He had one thought in his mind—Dolly. They had her. If he had to kill his way to her, he would.

The exit that the Glowworm's foot soldiers were fleeing into was a wooden staircase that opened directly onto the grounds. Wyatt's sense of direction, thrown off by the blasts and the darkness, was screwed up, but he was pretty sure the exit was on the east side of the house.

Smoke and bodies poured out. Wyatt could hear heavy machine-gun fire outside the door, and he was almost certain he was running to his death when he exploded out, followed by Samy, shooting.

They saw a line of M4s spitting fire. But it wasn't aimed at them. It was aimed back up the lawn at the house. The Glowworm's guards were pinned down by fire from the house. This didn't make sense. Wyatt looked back to the fire coming from Hallsy, Avi, and the Old Man, spread out on the back deck of the cottage, firing into the giant sloping lawn.

Down the sweeping lawn, Wyatt could see a small group running toward a helicopter landing pad. Wyatt thought he could make out Raquel and, with her, three captives. Dolly and Ebbie were two of them. The other, Wyatt couldn't see. But Wyatt could hear a chopper in the distance.

"They're getting away," he yelled, the M4s opening up on Samy and Wyatt, who dove for cover.

Samy lobbed the last M67 at the M4s, but the explosion did little to displace them. Wyatt and Samy were all but dead.

The Old Man saw this as he came out of the house, an H&K on his shoulder spraying bullets at the guards with the M4s.

"Come get it!" the Old Man yelled. The M4s redirected their fire and the Old Man was lit up, his body jerking back and forth in gunfire before toppling to the ground.

Wyatt and Samy used the distraction to open up on the M4s, taking them down quickly. Samy moved to check on the Old Man. Wyatt could not wait. He replaced his last clip and sprinted down the lawn, unsure if any backup was following.

They were waiting for Wyatt at the helipad. Raquel had Dolly from behind, a knife pressed to her throat. Wyatt almost did not recognize Dolly, her face was so badly slashed. She poured blood. Ebbie was no better.

Wyatt leveled his Glock at Raquel, taking aim between her pretty temples, knowing he could pull the trigger and drop the girl likely before she could shoot or stab Dolly. But was it worth the risk?

"Drop the knife. Or I shoot." Wyatt instructed, knowing he'd lost any element of surprise. His words sounded hollow. He was one guy standing across from at least six armed men and women.

"Come on," Raquel said, grinning, using Dolly's body as a shield. "I dare you."

A voice came from behind Wyatt. "I wouldn't take that dare." The voice was unusually calm.

Wyatt glanced over his shoulder to see a creature out of a horror movie coming across the lawn. He had completely white skin, almost greenish, iridescent, and he wore what looked like a diaper covering his groin and a plastic screw cap on his navel. He was muscle-y, but in a strange, unnatural way. His head had clumps of hair smothered in Vaseline or a similar gel.

The man-thing wore welding goggles, even though the sun had set. A bright moon lit the night. And under one arm, he held a man in a headlock and pointed a sawed-off shotgun to the man's head with his free hand. The prisoner's skin was blackened with bruises, and laced with lacerations and wet blood. Clearly, he'd been repeatedly beaten. The prisoner was semiconscious, one eye completely swollen shut, and blood bubbled up from his mouth. Wyatt noticed that his right hand was missing most of its digits and one of his ears had been chopped clean off, the blood still trickling down his face.

"Wyatt, run!" the prisoner said.

And in that moment, Wyatt recognized not just the voice but the face, beaten almost beyond recognition. It was a face he knew well, one very similar to his own, only older, harder, a face Wyatt hadn't seen in almost a year.

"Dad?"

Wyatt's mind tried to process what could possibly have happened. Why was his father on a Valor mission? Why was he being held hostage? Why was he missing an ear? No answers came, and he had no time to search for them. Or to think.

The helicopter was descending toward the pad. Armed guards perched on the runners. The creature looked at Wyatt, laughing. "Little boy," he said. "I think I am going to take you with me. Take his gun," he said to his guards. "And take him with us."

As the chopper came into a low hover, Wyatt, who had at least eight guns on him, saw one way out.

"Okay, I'll put it down." He raised his gun into the air as if he were going to set it down, then aimed for the chopper pilot, fired, and dove to the ground.

The endless close-quarters shooting training at Valor paid off. Wyatt hit the pilot in the head, sending him tumbling into the controls. The helicopter, which was in a hover, canted forward, the rotor wash now blowing sideways, sending furniture across the lawn. The helicopter's blades whacked into the ground, cutting deep until they snapped and broke off and the rotor whined like a screaming, dying, mechanical monster.

As the chopper fell out of the sky, Ebbie, who Wyatt saw was missing fingers on one hand, managed to overwhelm and disarm the guard holding him. Then Ebbie dropped, unnaturally, like a lead weight had fallen on his head. His legs went out instantly, his face went completely slack. As Ebbie fell Wyatt saw the Glowworm, the barrel of his sawed off shotgun smoking. Wyatt instantly knew one of his best friends had been shot, point-blank from behind and was likely dying if not dead. But he could not think about Ebbie now.

From the ground, Wyatt trained his gun on the Glowworm, who swiveled his guns toward Wyatt's father, saying, "Remember I promised you I'd get outside!"

Wyatt put a tight cluster—three shots—into the Glowworm's forehead. The Glowworm's head jerked a few times and then he toppled over, Wyatt's father falling with him. And then Wyatt heard the scream, an awful shriek.

"No!"

Raquel. She shoved Dolly to the side and ran at Wyatt full speed, knife in hand. Wyatt put his Glock on her and fired. But the gun clicked dry. Then, as if a giant hand swept down and batted her away, Raquel was thrown sideways down the hill, puffs of pink blood in the air.

Wyatt looked back up hill and there was Samy, with an M4 he'd taken off a Glowworm guard, picking off the remaining guards. "Yeah baby, camels can shoot too!" He did not stop shooting until there was quiet.

"Cease fire!" Hallsy yelled. "Cease fire!"

He moved quickly from his position by the house, which was now burning, down to the helipad. Dolly checked Ebbie for vitals and held pressure to his bleeding hands.

Hallsy ran up to Wyatt's father. "Jesus, Eldon, what did he do to you?" Wyatt wondered why Hallsy was calling his father Eldon when his name was James. How did Hallsy even know him? He pushed the thought aside, compartmentalizing. At that moment, there were too many questions, so much to find out. There would be time for that. For now, they needed to evacuate and save whoever could be saved.

CHAPTER 37

August 2017
White Plains Airport, F.B.O.

The interior of the surveillance van looked like a butcher shop, filled with blood and gristle. Hallsy drove to the White Plains airport, pedal pressed to the floor. Waiting for them outside a private hangar at the airport was an unremarkable man in a gray suit. He was average height, balding, his suit coat draped over his left arm, which held a tattered briefcase.

His off-white shirt was yellowing and bore two giant pit stains. His skin was yellow, his expression bland, mop-bucket gray-blue eyes looking out from a grim face covered in a thick five-o'clock shadow. The man never introduced himself. Wyatt thought of him as Mr. Yellow. Wyatt did not need to be told the man was a fixer from the Department of Defense. It seemed Hallsy both knew him and expected his arrival.

In an utterly calm and rather bland way, Mr. Yellow guided the van out onto the runway. "You will not be flying back in the jet that brought you here, but on a plane outfitted with medical equipment—surgical tables, EKGs, and so on. One of the planes that the United States used to fly injured soldiers from Iraq or Afghanistan to Ramstein Air Base." He shifted the van into park. "Get everyone aboard. We're leaving stat."

The plane was effectively a flying hospital. Three of the country's top surgeons were on board, along with a crew of nurses, to attend to the campers and staff from Camp Valor. The medical staff did not wait for the plane to begin taxiing before they began administering care to those who were injured, immediately triaging who could be saved and how.

Ebbie was pronounced dead when they reached the plane. The most gravely injured was the Old Man, followed by Wyatt's father, then Dolly, who had been slashed so many times by Raquel that it looked like she had been dipped in ketchup. She was rushed into surgery, pulse dimming.

Initially, the Old Man rallied and seemed to stabilize, but then he started crashing. Less than forty-five minutes into the flight, a harried surgeon came to the back of the plane, to the waiting area. "I am sorry to tell you, but the Old Man is gone. . . ." He paused, letting the news sink in with the rest of the survivors. "His last words were to tell me to take care of other injured first." The surgeon nodded. "And so, with your permission, I will do just that." He left the waiting area and joined the other doctors tending to Wyatt's father and Dolly.

To Wyatt, this perfunctory news seemed too short for a life as impactful as the Old Man's. But he supposed that was how things worked on a mission. The Old Man and Ebbie died trying to save lives, Wyatt's life and others. That was Wyatt's new reality. Lives were sometimes traded. He had lost a father figure and a best friend, and he hoped his own father wasn't next.

Wyatt's father's injuries were grave and painful but, as the nurse explained to him, "not immediately life-threatening." They were the kind of injuries that would take months to heal.

Dolly's injuries, while gruesome, were tended to cut by cut. She had so many lacerations across her body that surgeons worked in teams of two. Most of the lacerations were stitched normally, and the majority of those on her face, hands, and neck—that is, the most visible ones—were stitched more carefully by the most skilled surgeon of the three. However, this man made strong recommendations for subsequent procedures by cosmetic plastic surgeons.

Mr. Yellow came into the waiting area on the plane and stood in front of Wyatt. "Can we speak? Alone?"

"Sure." Wyatt nodded, following the pit-stained Mr. Yellow toward the front of the plane where there was a small conference room with a table and coffeemaker.

"Take a seat," he said, and Wyatt slid into the small booth. "Can I get you a cup?" He motioned to the coffeemaker.

Wyatt nodded.

Mr. Yellow poured two coffees into Styrofoam cups and sat down across from Wyatt. "Here you go."

Wyatt picked up the cup and noticed his hands were covered in dirt and blood. They shook slightly, but he didn't know why.

Mr. Yellow drew a raspy breath and was about to say something when a voice interrupted them.

"Can I join?" Hallsy stood in the doorway.

Mr. Yellow thought for a moment. "Go ahead," he said and motioned for Hallsy to sit next to him on the bench. "But get your own coffee, if you don't mind. I'm sorry. I just need to sit."

"Not at all." Hallsy poured a cup and settled into his seat. "What's going on?" he asked.

"I just wanted to have a word here with Wyatt. As I understand it, he led the firefight at the mansion and killed the Glowworm." Mr. Yellow turned his muted eyes to Wyatt.

"Yes, sir," Wyatt said.

"Well, you did yourself and the country a great favor. The Glowworm, as he called himself, had his tentacles into our country at the highest levels. We're just now beginning to understand how many politicians have been hacked and blackmailed and how much of our government has been compromised by the Glowworm's organization. You put him and his soldiers down, Wyatt. And I just wanted to thank you."

Mr. Yellow extended his hand toward Wyatt, who shook it and was surprised by the firmness of the man's grip. He pulled Wyatt toward him before letting go. "I can see what's going on in your head, son, and it won't go away immediately, but what you did was the right thing. Try not to second-guess it. That man was a monster and you felled him. Okay?"

"Yes, sir," Wyatt said, and pulled his hand away. "Sir, may I ask you a question?"

"Of course. Go right ahead."

"What about the camp?" Wyatt asked. "What's going to happen to the program? Will it be decommissioned?"

"We'll have to see what the SecDef thinks," Mr. Yellow said. "But I don't think he'll mess with it too much. Valor is way too valuable to our safety. Don't think it's going anywhere."

"With the Old Man gone . . . who will—"

"Lead?" Mr. Yellow smiled, and for the first time Wyatt saw a flash of light in his mop-bucket eyes. "Well," he said. "I'd wanted to talk to your father about that. I'll get to it when he recovers. For the time being, I'll take the rudder."

"My father?" Wyatt asked. "Why would he take over Valor?"

Mr. Yellow let out a long sigh. "You know, Wyatt, I'm going to let him explain that to you, okay? I think you two have a lot of catching up to do."

Wyatt nodded, confused but understanding. "And who did you say you are? Did you go to Camp Valor? Did he?"

Hallsy interrupted before Mr. Yellow could respond. "You don't need to know all that yet, Wyatt."

Mr. Yellow smiled again. "He's right. All you need to know is that, like you, I spent a little time in the woods and in canoes, and I know which end of a paddle you hold and which end pulls water. Now, would you two fellows excuse me?" he asked, nodding to a phone on the plane. "I have some calls I would rather not make."

"Sure." Wyatt and Hallsy stood and returned to the waiting area with the others for the duration of the flight.

Wyatt asked if he could see his father. He was still trying to piece together what had happened and would for some time, but in that moment, he just wanted to know his dad was okay.

"You have five minutes," the nurse told Wyatt as she led him to a small suite about the size of a first-class cabin on a fancy airline. "He needs rest."

Wyatt nodded and sat down next to his father. In the relative calm of the medical unit on the plane, Wyatt could fully observe the ravages of his father's captivity. This once strong, vibrant man now looked like a Holocaust survivor. Skin and bones, his body covered in sores, his ear, fingers, and other hunks of flesh from his body removed. His eyes were hollow, bulging, but there was still life in them. Still a bit of the outlaw.

There was so much ground the two needed to cover, so much Wyatt and his father needed to make up and set straight. But it had to start somewhere.

"So Eldon, huh?" Wyatt said, breaking the ice. "That's your name?"

Wyatt's father smiled. "*Was* my name. Said good-bye to it a long time ago." His father blinked a slow, medicinal blink. "Wyatt, I know you want to ask me about how I got to . . . well, where you found me. And I promise I will tell you everything, but for now, I want to ask you something. Okay?"

"Anything."

"Your mother . . . is she good? And how about Cody?"

"She's good," Wyatt lied. He didn't have the heart to tell his father that his disappearance had devastated his mom. And Cody. Not now. "Narcy came to help us when you went missing."

Wyatt's father came up in his seat, a pained expression on his face liked he'd been poked with a small knife. "Narcy?" he asked. "She's home with Mom?"

"Uh-huh. And by the way she's made herself at home, I don't think she'll be leaving anytime soon."

Wyatt's father eased back into his bed. "Your poor mother. I thought I had it bad watching the Glowworm eat."

They both laughed.

Wyatt could see his father's eyes struggling to stay open just as the nurse returned. "Wyatt," she whispered. "There's someone else who wants to see you."

Dolly had her own medical bay. She lay in a small bed, bandaged like a mummy. Wyatt stood in the door for a moment, and Dolly looked over. The head surgeon excused himself.

"Will you come sit by me?" Dolly said and shifted over on the tiny bed. Wyatt moved around from the foot of the bed and sat next to her.

"Thank you," she said, "for not giving up."

"Never," Wyatt said. "You would do the same for me."

"Sure." She smiled faintly. "It's easy enough to do what they tell you here. To run a drill, to climb a wall, to operate as well as you've been taught," she said. "Although I don't think anyone will say that I've been doing that very well." She laughed. "But the thing that's hard," Dolly went on, "is charting new territory and discovering things that you didn't know existed."

Dolly reached up feebly with her less-bandaged hand, which Wyatt took in his. She looked at him closely. "With you, everything is new. I've never felt like this. And I'm confused. I don't know what to do at every turn. That scares me. Can you understand that?"

Wyatt nodded.

"But today, when that girl was cutting me. And that creature was watching." Dolly was crying now, her tears running down bandages that were bleeding through. "I was so scared. They weren't just going to kill me, they were going to pick me apart. But you came for me."

CHAPTER 38

August 2017
Camp Valor

A few days later, Wyatt found his father wrapped in a blanket at the end of the dock. "Mind if I sit?" he asked.

"Please." Wyatt's father motioned to the chair Mr. Yellow had recently occupied. Wyatt's father and Mr. Yellow had been engaged in frequent talks as they tried to determine Valor's future without the Old Man. "How you holding up?" his father asked.

"Fine," Wyatt lied. Since returning to Camp Valor, it was hard for Wyatt to reconcile any good Valor had done when he considered the catastrophic losses of Ebbie, the Old Man, and Hud. Cass was just then going into her fourth surgery at NewYork-Presbyterian, and it was likely she would never walk again. Wyatt knew these collective sacrifices had made the world safer, but wasn't sure if it was worth the cost. Hallsy would likely agree. Perhaps more than anyone else at Valor, Hallsy seemed to take these recent events the hardest. He'd become remote and despondent, taking walks by himself during waking hours and even at night.

Wyatt's father seemed to sense his son's struggle, but he didn't press. "When you're ready to talk about it, we can talk. Don't rush it."

"Okay," Wyatt said. "But now can we talk about you?"

"About me? What do you want to know?"

Wyatt laughed. "I'm not even sure where to start. I mean, for one, you've been living a double life . . . for how long?"

"'Double life' does not do it justice," Wyatt's father said. "I've lived fifty lives. There is a saying in our business, in espionage, that it's like a wilderness of mirrors. I feel like my life is a wilderness of mirrors and I want to break them all but one. The one that's me."

"And who is that?"

"James Brewer. The one who married your mom. The one who became you and Cody's dad. The rest are gone."

"What about the Golden One Hundred?" Wyatt asked. Wyatt had learned that his father was part of the famed Golden One Hundred, a group of former operators—mostly SEAL—whose work was so secretive (and frankly illegal) that the operators themselves could have no ties to the U.S. Wyatt's father could never tell this secret to anyone, including his wife.

"Are you leaving them?"

Wyatt's father nodded. "I no longer blend in." He held up his hand with the missing fingers and pointed to his face sans ear. "Covert action is over for me. And it's not just that now I'm marked. I don't want to do it anymore. I want to be there, for you, your brother, and your mom."

"Will you tell Mom the truth? About where you've been? Why you were gone?"

Wyatt's father thought about this. "I can't. My cover is that I got some deep gambling debts and agreed to work a dangerous stint in Syria for a defense contractor, driving trucks. I'll tell her I lied about my family details to get the dangerous and lunatic shift, and then when I got blown up by an IED and was hospitalized, I couldn't contact anyone at home. . . ." He thought for a second. "And, of course, I'll just beg for forgiveness."

"What if I wanted to join the Golden One Hundred?" Wyatt asked. "Could you tell me how?"

Wyatt's father chuckled, then saw that his son was serious. "When we get home," his father said. "How about we just focus on getting your grades back up first."

"How do you know about my grades?"

"I have my ways."

Wyatt thought for a second. "Must have been Hallsy?" Wyatt read his father's reaction and guessed again. "No, Mum."

His dad smiled.

"Did Mum tell you all about how I got to Valor?" Wyatt asked.

"She told me enough to know the apple doesn't fall far from the tree," Wyatt's father said.

"Well, I've already started studying," Wyatt said.

"How's that?" James asked.

"All our courses are online. I've been accessing them from the Old Man's office in the Cave Complex. Been feeding his dog, too. Ruger keeps looking at the door. Wondering when the Old Man is going to walk in." Wyatt pushed up from his chair. "I need to get back there now."

"Go ahead," his dad said with a sly grin, "but one day I'd like to know what you're really up to."

Wyatt left his father and headed back to the Caldera. He

had not been entirely truthful about studying. Wyatt was using the encrypted computer connection in the Old Man's office to get online, but he wasn't doing schoolwork. He was trying to solve a puzzle. And he'd roped a reluctant Avi into helping him.

"I'm only doing this because I saw how you handled yourself in a firefight," Avi said, entering the codes that granted Wyatt access to all the drives with information on the Glowworm network.

In the days since his father had reappeared, Wyatt wanted to learn everything he could about Wilberforce Degas, his transformation into the Glowworm, and the techniques and strategies of their network.

"I am not giving you access because I have any respect for your computer skill."

"Got it," Wyatt said.

Avi went on, "You know when you were searching for your father on the Web—deep Web—I was trailing you the entire time. You had no idea, did you?"

"Nope," Wyatt said. "So Valor had been watching me before I was arrested?"

"Of course! As soon as your father was abducted and Hallsy had recovered from his injuries in Jerusalem, he made it his top priority to ensure your father's family was safe. You, of course, were getting into trouble already. So Hallsy convinced the Old Man to let you come here. And I was new to Valor. I left the Mossad to come here. But I too had a personal interest in tracking you."

Wyatt sensed Avi was trying to tell him something. "What do you mean? Why would you have cared about tracking me?

"I hoped to see the sharks looking for you. I will not lie," Avi said. "I would have preferred to use you as bait."

"Avi, I'm lost. What are you trying to tell me?"

"The former Israeli Mossad driver who Hallsy contracted to help get your father out of Jerusalem, he was my younger brother."

"Your younger brother?" Wyatt repeated, now understanding Avi's blatant anger toward Wyatt. "He died trying to save my father."

"Yes," Avi said.

"I'm so sorry."

"It's okay. I know it is not your fault. Nor your father's. But Hallsy, I think, must have been sloppy. He had my brother drive into a setup." Avi now became as emotional as he was capable of, which is to say, he looked mad.

"I know Hallsy must feel terrible. I can't imagine what I would do if my brother died trying to save someone I didn't even know."

"I can tell you exactly what you would do," Avi said. "You would try to get back at the killers."

"The Brotherhood," Wyatt said, now understanding what Avi meant by bait. "You were tracking me, hoping that one of them would be after me as well."

"Yes." Avi nodded solemnly. "They are my next target. And I will treat them exactly as they treated my brother. He was given no warning. He practically drove into a bullet."

"Drove into a bullet," Wyatt repeated slowly, his mind running away to latch on to something. "Wait. Avi, before I leave Valor, I need you to tell me everything you know about my father's capture by the Brotherhood."

"Why don't you ask Hallsy?" Avi asked. "He was there . . .

and to be honest, he risked his life trying to protect your father. Almost died, too."

"Yeah, I know, I'll get Hallsy's story. But I need it from you as well. As hard as it may be for you to tell me."

"Hard?" said Avi. "Details are details. I can share them. What may be hard is the truth in the details. Are you sure you are ready to listen?"

"To every word."

"Do I still look like a mummy?" Dolly asked as Wyatt came up the path. She sat on the same park bench where Wyatt had first seen Rory trying to diffuse a bomb. Like they had each night since she was released from the clinic, Wyatt and Dolly met in the Caldera. After she had her bandages changed, he would walk her back to base camp for dinner.

"More like Bride of Frankenstein," Wyatt teased. Her face and body were laced with zipperlike scars and stitches, the scars glistening with ointments and dried blood. He looked around the Caldera to make sure they were alone. And then he kissed her.

Since their mission, all members of Group-C had been elevated to a new unofficial warrior class. Samy and Rory, as well as Dolly and Wyatt, all had risen into, for now, an untouchable place. It was not a defined group or rank, but the deference paid to those who had fought and was every bit as real as if they had a Purple Heart pinned to their chest. No one dared question Wyatt's right to a romantic relationship with Dolly. Still, Wyatt and Dolly preferred to follow the proper decorum, and if they embraced, it was out of the view of others. Wyatt helped Dolly off the bench and they walked in silence as the sun set. Halfway to base camp, Dolly said, "I can see something is bothering you."

"I'm just thinking," Wyatt said, now lying to Dolly like he had to his father. The truth was Wyatt's mind had begun working on a disturbing puzzle, the kind he wasn't sure he wanted to see come together.

They gathered around the bonfire one last time. The entire camp, all staff, and even some of the Group-A members showed. Wyatt saw Jawad seated among some older camp alumni. Members of the Golden One Hundred, it was rumored. They all knew Wyatt's father and had come from outposts around the world, to say goodbye to the Old Man.

Hallsy conducted the closing ceremony. He looked old and gaunt and troubled as he summarized the summer into highlights and critiques. Hallsy, of course, paid tribute, at times choking up, to the sacrifices made by Ebbie, the Old Man, and Hudson Decker.

The honor of Top Camper was something that Wyatt and the rest of the candidates had wanted desperately throughout the summer, but as the moments drew nearer to the announcement, Wyatt knew that nobody wanted it, least of all him. So it was with a heavy heart that, after all the members of Group-C and B and A had been congratulated, Wyatt was asked to come forward and receive the Top Camper honors, which, in typical Valor fashion, was understated. Wyatt rose and walked to the fire, where Hallsy saluted him and said, "Would the recipient of last year's Top Camper award pass on the stone?"

Jawad now came forward. In his hand, he held a smooth, circular black stone. The stone glimmered slightly on one side, and on the other was carved the letter "V."

"This sharpening stone is the most precious rock on this island and the highest honor Valor can bestow. Take it," Jawad instructed, and Wyatt took the stone, cold and heavy in his hand. "As you begin a life of service to your nation, your family, and your god, may your experience at Valor be like the sharpening stone. A blunt and hard but moveable object that is used to bring an edge to a blade. Take your memories and your training with you always, and you can use those experiences to always cut deep into life."

Wyatt did not listen to the rest. As Jawad spoke, he watched the fire play around Hallsy's face, his eyes dull, black, empty, and colder than the stone now in Wyatt's hand. Wyatt's mind pursued a dark, uncertain path that he instinctually knew would arrive at the truth.

After the closing ceremonies, Hallsy took one of the three torches that had been set up beside him and invited Mum and Rory to come forward. Each lifted a torch and then lit the torch with the fire from the bonfire, and then the entire group of people made their way down to the water, where three caskets, draped with American flags, rested atop funeral pyres. Two of the caskets were empty: Hud's and Ebbie's. Hud was already buried in New York. Ebbie's death would need to be covered up back in the "real" world. Each pyre was lit. Mum lit her husband's pyre, Dolly lit Hud's, and Wyatt lit Ebbie's. Three large fires stretched out into the sky and burned throughout the night until they were just ashes.

Jawad was one of the last to leave the fire. Wyatt stopped him. "Jawad, I can't take this." Wyatt held out the sharpening stone. "I don't deserve the honor. I'm not the best."

Wyatt expected resistance when he tried to give back the award. He anticipated Jawad might be offended, maybe upset. He thought Jawad might even take a swing at him for trying to give back the most precious rock on the island—Valor's highest honor. The last thing he expected was for Jawad to laugh.

"No one deserves honor," Jawad said. "Least of all, the Top Camper."

Wyatt was confused. "I don't understand. Is it a trick?"

"No. God no." Jawad grew serious. "It's a lesson. The Top Campers are never just the best, they are the ones who can be the best. Wyatt, the sharpening stone allows you to work, to get better, sharper. You didn't win the award by being your personal best. Far from it. You have a lot more in you—if you can find it and work it. That's the real reward and honor. More grinding work."

"You take it anyway," Wyatt said, putting the stone in Jawad's hand and walking away.

CHAPTER 39

August 2017, Departure Day morning
Camp Valor

Wyatt had wanted to find time to be alone with Dolly, but it was simply impossible. The summer was ending and a well-coordinated and secret return of Valorians to their lives needed to be executed flawlessly—no exceptions. Dolly was slated for an early-morning helicopter ride off the island. Dolly would be taken to her sister, who had come out of surgery responsive. Cass needed Dolly by her side. And so Wyatt and Dolly could only embrace for a moment.

"I know we are not supposed to see each other during the year," Dolly whispered into Wyatt's ear. "But I need to stay in touch with you."

Wyatt felt a thrill rush through him as Dolly's hot breath tickled Wyatt's ear. She gave him ten numbers and told him her address. Another no-no. "158 Willow Tree Lane, Grosse Point, Michigan. Got it?"

"Yes."

"If you can, come check on me. I love you." She kissed Wyatt on the lips, in front of campers and staff, who all looked away, and then she ran blushing toward the helicopter.

Wyatt's heart swelled and he could think of almost nothing but Dolly and the way she smelled and the feeling of her lips on his until her helicopter had cleared the lip of the Caldera and the sound of its rotors faded out of hearing range. His girlfriend—if he could even call her that—was gone. Like some men and most boys, Wyatt felt a measure of sanity return.

Samy and Rory were on the same flight out and were waiting for Wyatt. Wyatt embraced both of them.

"Brutha," Samy said. "Rory and I are going to be here next summer. Tell me we will see you."

"We'll see," Wyatt said. "I have some things I need to work on during the year."

Samy looked Wyatt in the eye and tightened his grip on his shoulder. "You are my swim buddy. You will be here in June. That's it."

Wyatt nodded.

"Okay. We out." Samy turned for the runway. Rory followed, a backpack filled with a drone kit and weaponry slung over her shoulder and her dingy handmade blue elephant tucked under her arm.

Wyatt returned to his cabin to prepare for his own journey home. He rolled his sleeping bag, packed his duffle, and tossed in personal items he'd accrued over the summer—clothes from Mum, the Buck knife, his belt, and, in a separate bag, some tactical gear—his H&K submachine gun, a pair of night vision goggles, restraints, a Taser, his Glock 26, laser sight, and his communication equipment. The two bags would be given to his father for safekeeping, in case Wyatt decided to return the following summer.

All Wyatt would take back with him on his person was the sharpening stone and the bright orange jumpsuit that he'd been wearing the day he left the County Youth Detention Center in Millersville County.

Dressed like the juvenile delinquent he had been three months earlier, Wyatt went to the lodge to say good-bye to Mum. As usual, he found her in the kitchen.

Mum pulled Wyatt in tight. "One of the things he would have asked me," Mum said, "would be to make you promise that you'll be back in nine months."

"I'll think about it," said Wyatt. "But I can't promise."

"I understand." She wiped away tears. "I hope you change your mind. If you decide to come back, I'll be here waiting." She paused. "Before you leave, I want to show you something."

Mum led Wyatt out into the dining room, where the photographs of Top Campers lined the wall. "See that photograph with the black tarp over it? The one from 1982? Take down the cloth."

Wyatt removed it. It was his father.

"He was all but lost," Mum said. "You freed him."

Wyatt thought about this, then asked a question that had been gnawing at him. "When I arrived at Valor, why didn't you or the Old Man tell me my father had been here before me? Why didn't you tell me he was captured?"

"It's simple," Mum shrugged. "Classified. You needed to become one of us to learn the truth."

Wyatt found his dad on the porch and gave him his bags. The father and son embraced, and one last time they rehearsed how they would act and what they would say when they saw each other in a few short days. Wyatt's father and Mr. Yellow walked him down to the dock.

Wyatt shook Mr. Yellow's hand.

"You may or may not be hearing from me soon," Mr. Yellow said. "For your sake, I hope you don't."

The *Sea Goat* was waiting. Mackenzie was at the wheel, and Hallsy stood in the stern. Hallsy looked awful. Even more remote and distant than the day before this, Hallsy's already dark mood seemed to blacken as Hallsy saw Wyatt's father approaching. "You should be resting," Hallsy said. "Can't have another one of us take a turn for the worse."

"Came to see you off. Make sure my boy gets home safe," Wyatt's father said.

"Think he has proven he can take care of himself, and then some," said Hallsy. "But I'll do my best."

CHAPTER 40

August 2017
Valor to Millersville

The boat ride took several hours, eventually arriving at a dock and a small fishing village not far from a modest airstrip. From there, Hallsy and Wyatt flew south and east, hopping from airstrip to airstrip, making their way across North America.

It was night when they arrived at the notorious Millersville County Youth Detention Center. Before they reached the center, Hallsy drove Wyatt to a parking lot and pulled the cruiser alongside a small van, like the kind a plumber would drive. Inside the van, they found a woman with a small poodle and a tackle box of makeup.

"So I'm understanding this, right?" The woman looked at Hallsy and asked, "You want him to look like he's been indoors all summer? Sickly and pale?"

"That's right," Hallsy said.

Wyatt sat in a chair and the makeup artist went to work.

Forty-five minutes later, Wyatt and Hallsy got back in the cruiser and pulled up to the rear entrance of the detention facility. There was no guard on duty, and the gate rose as they approached. Wyatt and Hallsy passed through into an underground parking garage.

Hallsy led Wyatt back through doors and passageways to the isolation unit and Wyatt's former cell. The key was in the door. Hallsy unlatched it, and pushed the door open. Wyatt smelled the familiar metallic scent of the bed and the sink and the odor of feces and cleaning products.

"All right, kid," said Hallsy. Wyatt hesitated.

"Just one more night, Buddy. Then you're back home." Hallsy said.

Wyatt looked at him. "No tricks? No surprises?"

"I can't promise no surprises will be coming down the pike," Hallsy said. "But I can promise you that at a quarter to seven, you'll be walking out of here with a clean record, just like I said the day we met."

Hallsy and Wyatt shook hands and Hallsy pulled him into a hug and tousled his hair. "Hey, buddy, you know I love you. And I'm proud of you. I know I'm not your dad, but I tried the best I could to look out for you over these past three months."

"Yeah, I know," Wyatt said, feeling his shoulders slump, thoughts distracting him, weighing him down.

"Okay, then," Hallsy said, stepping back into the hallway. "I'll be seeing you soon. I'll come check in on the family. Is that okay by you?"

"Of course," said Wyatt. "Look forward to seeing you."

"Alrighty, then. I'm gonna close the door now."

"Go ahead."

The steel door closed slowly, and then Wyatt heard Hallsy turn the lock.

It must have been three in the morning and Wyatt had not slept. He sat there, alone in the dark, his mind turning over his suspicions, connecting dots.

At a quarter to seven, a lock was unlatched. The same guard who had led him out of the cell three months ago looked in. "Good morning. You ready to roll? Today is your lucky day."

Wyatt rose to his feet and followed the guard down the maze of hallways through the Chow Hall. He knew it was an intentional move, so that all of the inmates, some of whom had been there since the beginning of the summer, would see Wyatt and believe he had been in solitary the entire summer. Wyatt walked slowly. Hawkish faces turned. Hollow eyes watched carefully. Wyatt was a wolf in their midst. He'd changed over the summer. And they could smell and sense it. Perhaps admire it. He'd gone into solitary soft and come out a rock.

He'd almost left the Chow Hall when he saw a heavily tattooed and scarred face, one he remembered. The Spider Kid's black eyes seemed to read something altogether different in Wyatt's. He was, if nothing else, an instinctual animal, a survivalist. No doubt, he had been waiting the entire summer for Wyatt to return, perhaps preparing to strike. But now that they were together again, Wyatt knew the Spider Kid would never again try him. Wyatt was now the more dangerous and cunning and lethal animal and the Spider Kid knew it. Wyatt watched as the Spider Kid averted his eyes and returned his attention to a tray piled with institutional gruel.

Another few short corridors and Wyatt arrived at the prison's administrative offices, where he was given the clothes he'd been wearing when he was arrested. He was provided fresh underwear and socks and told to change in the bathroom. Wyatt signed a few documents, and with a vague sense of uneasiness, was shepherded out of the CYDC into the lobby of the courthouse by the warden, Dr. Sudroc. Little droplets of sweat had formed on Sudroc's forehead and his eyes skittered about the lobby.

"So what now?" Wyatt asked. "What do I do?"

"You walk." The warden motioned across the lobby, wiping his forehead and rubbing his temples as if in pain. "I don't know what the hell you did or who you did it for, but I've never seen this happen. You just walk, and I don't want to see you back here again."

"I don't need papers or a pass or . . ."

"You don't need a damn thing. You're free. Your digital record is erased and all paper copies of your files have already been destroyed. Here, take these." The warden handed Wyatt an envelope and Wyatt checked the inside—mug shots and his arrest report, the original paper version.

By the time Wyatt had looked back up, the warden had turned on his heels and was headed back toward the entrance to the CYDC, through the series of metal detectors. Wyatt watched the warden huff and sigh as he dug through his pockets for coins and a pen and searched for his ID.

Wyatt stepped out from the cool lobby into a wall of humidity, late-August heat. Although he'd spent his summer under the giant summer sun, he'd spent the last five hours or so in darkness, and the bright light pained his eyes and he struggled to see.

He was thinking about how he would get home, now wishing he'd asked the warden if he could bum a couple of bucks for a bus ticket. He then noticed a familiar car at the bottom of the wide stone steps leading up from the city square to the courthouse in CYDC. There was Aunt Narcy's car, significantly reconstructed after Wyatt had practically shaved off one side of it. The paneling looked like it had come off a different car. The paint didn't even try to match, but it looked good to Wyatt anyway.

Looking even better was his mother. Her hair washed, lipstick on, like her old self again. She sat in the passenger seat dabbing her tears with a napkin. His father sat in the driver's seat, his mutilated left hand waving out the window. Ear gone, but smiling. And in the back seat, his little brother, Cody, beamed and tried to open the door to meet him.

Of course he couldn't miss Narcy—all three hundred pounds of her—red-faced in the back seat, complaining about the heat, about the car, probably most of all about Wyatt. This was home, and Wyatt was damn grateful for it.

Wyatt had spent the last three months training how to be an operator, a killer, a spy, a soldier, a weapon for the United States of America. To be constantly sharpened, ground down like a knife. Wyatt reached into his pocket and jerked his hand back as he touched something cold and smooth. It took him a moment to realize what it was. The sharpening stone. Hallsy must have gotten it from Jawad and put it in his clothes. Wyatt clenched the stone tight in his hand. He was a lethal and highly prized asset. But for a moment, he forgot all that and became a kid again, coming home from camp to his parents in their piece-of-crap family car, a little uncertain if he was too old for hugs. And so Wyatt, forgetting himself for a moment, just ran, sprinted down the steps. He hugged his mom first.

EPILOGUE

Early September 2017
Millersville

September arrived golden and hot and the air was still and the days before school began again were all too short. Adjusting to life with his family, and especially with his father at home, was a challenge for Wyatt. His dad had promised to leave the Golden One Hundred. The notion of Wyatt's father at home on a permanent basis was wonderful, but sort of like having a recovering alcoholic in the house in the earliest stages of quitting. James was perpetually in motion, fixing the house, working on the shed, unable to sleep. It was a new day, a better person, a better time. But for the family, it felt like they were living in a house of cards that might fall at any moment.

And Wyatt feared that he knew which card would bring the house down. It was a card only Wyatt could remove—a secret he'd discovered in his last days at Valor.

·   ·   ·

The day before school started, Wyatt joined his dad, mom, and Narcy at one of Cody's baseball games. They sat on rusty bleachers. It was the playoffs, and in the fourth inning, Cody sent three batters in a row to the bench. As the teams traded field position, Wyatt heard the dull roar of Narcy's straw probing the depths of her Coke.

"Hey, Narcy, let me get you another drink." Wyatt stood up.

"Wyatt, don't do that," Wyatt's mother said. "You'll miss your brother."

"Cody's not batting for a while. I won't miss anything," Wyatt said.

"Now, Wyatt, I would like another Coke," Narcy said. "I'm glad to see you've come around. I think that detention center did you some good. Taught you some manners. Not that I didn't teach you before you went in, since we was without your daddy and all, though," she said, patting Wyatt's father on the leg. "It's nice to know James here was supporting our troops and all, driving trucks and doing stuff that shouldn't have gotten him in any trouble at all." It was strange now for Wyatt to hear his father called James, even knowing his real name was Eldon.

Wyatt could see a hint of annoyance on his father's face. Or perhaps it was humor.

"Hey, Dad, why don't you come with me?" Wyatt said. "I think we all need another round, and I'll need another set of hands."

"Sure," his dad said, standing, holding up his deformed hand with a laugh.

Wyatt suddenly felt a little self-conscious for forgetting. Memories of the Glowworm flooded back.

•   •   •

"Dad," Wyatt said, stopping on the way to the concession stand. "Come over here in the shade, if you don't mind? Got something I've been meaning to tell you."

Wyatt's dad grinned. "I've been wondering when you were going to finally come out with it. What's up?" His dad put his hand on Wyatt's shoulder. "What's bothering you, son?"

"Jerusalem," Wyatt said, "your capture."

Wyatt saw his dad's genial expression cloud over. He stepped back and lowered his head.

"Wyatt, we don't need to be talking about that."

"No. We do. What if . . ." Wyatt felt nauseous as he began pulling the cards. "What if the Brotherhood wasn't responsible for your kidnapping?"

"What the hell are you talking about? The DOD, Valor, the Golden One Hundred were all negotiating with them, trying to secure my release and—"

"—and the Glowworm bought you out," Wyatt cut him off. "Drove your price up to fifty million dollars, right?"

"That's right," Wyatt's father said.

"What if I could prove to you that's all a lie? And it was an inside job? What if you were given up by the people you thought were supposed to be protecting you?"

Wyatt's father thought about this, rubbing his hands with missing fingers together. Sweat beaded on his face.

"Would you want to know the truth?" Wyatt asked. "If you don't, I respect that. I will not say another word."

Wyatt's father's keen eyes contracted, like they did when he was hunting years ago. Laser focused.

In the distance an umpire called out, "Batter up."

His father looked to the baseball field. Cody stood in the batter's circle. Wyatt's mom and Narcy laughed on the bleachers.

Wyatt's father nodded to himself. "Maybe later . . . for now, let's get those Cokes, and get back to the game."

The baseball game ended a little before dusk. The family stopped to pick up burgers from the local Irish bar on the way home. They ordered them to go with fries and onion rings and a couple beers for Wyatt's father and his mother. Narcy, Wyatt, and Cody opted for milkshakes. The bags of food and the perspiration forming on the drinks make their stomachs rumble.

As they approached their driveway, a flicker inside the little ranch house caught Wyatt's eye. The reflection of the TV playing in the den.

"Dad, why don't you take it to the end of the block?" Wyatt said. He had not left the TV on.

Wyatt's father looked over. "Everything all right?"

"Yeah, just pull down to the alley." Wyatt said. "TV's on. Wasn't when we left."

Wyatt's father rolled past the house, Narcy complaining, "Of all the silliest things, I am hungry. Heck, I could have left the TV on. Or maybe it's on a timer? Why don't we just pull right up and go on in?"

"Maybe someone's in the house," Cody said, picking up on what Wyatt and their father were thinking.

"I don't care if someone is in the house. I hope someone *is* in the house. Y'all bore me. I wanna eat."

Wyatt's mother looked to his father. "Is everything all right, James?"

"Yeah, it's all fine. Just give us a second. Wyatt and I are going to take a look."

Wyatt's father rounded the corner and parked in a service

alley that ran down the length of the block. "Dad, why don't you pop the trunk?"

Wyatt got out, walked around to the back. Inside was Cody's baseball bag. He unzipped it and pulled out a bat, hefted it, and took a short practice swing, getting a feel for the bat as a weapon.

His dad came around. "Hang on. I got something a little better than that."

Wyatt's father moved the athletic bag to the back of the trunk, opening the compartment for the tire. Underneath were two handguns—a .45 and a 9mm.

"Thought you were retired," Wyatt said.

"You never retire from careful," his father said quietly and handed Wyatt the 9mm. Each checked the breech, tucked the guns into their waistbands, and covered them with their shirts. Wyatt kept the baseball bat and closed the trunk.

"Honey, you sure everything's all right?" Wyatt's mother asked. "If you need a bat, wouldn't you rather just call the police?"

"Nah," said Wyatt's dad. "Millersville PD is useless." He shot Wyatt a look.

"Can I come?" Cody called from the back seat.

"Sit tight, we'll be right back." His father signaled for Wyatt to follow him into the alley. Out of earshot from the car he said, "Let's drop in from the back."

Moving swiftly, the two walked down the alley, which smelled of trash baking in the heat. They reached the dilapidated backyard fence and peered through the slots. The TV was on, and there was a figure, shrouded in darkness, watching the local news.

"You expecting someone?" Wyatt's dad whispered.

"No. You?"

"Nope." Wyatt crept forward, drew his gun, and pushed the safety with his thumb. With his left hand, Wyatt reached

over the fence and lifted open the inside latch. The gate swung
open into the yard, and father and son swept in. They crossed
the short yard, ran up the rear porch, and his father kicked open
the back door. They split up, left and right, both leveling guns
at the figure on their couch.

The person did not move. He didn't even blink.

"Derrick?" Wyatt said slowly, "What are you—" He stopped.

Derrick's face, in a greenish death pose, was contorted in a
painful scream, which had been muffled by duct tape wrapped
around his mouth and neck. His hands and feet were bound in
the same way. And as if making a joke, the TV remote had been
placed in his hands. Cause of death was obvious. Wyatt's Buck
knife was rammed straight through Derrick's chest, through the
cushions and padding, and lodged in the couch's wooden frame.
Blood and urine stained Derrick's lap, and resting delicately on
his knee was an envelope with Wyatt's name printed on it. Wyatt reached for the note, when they heard the sound of distant
sirens.

"Police . . ." Wyatt's father said. "Back to the car. We need
to move, now." Wyatt's father pivoted to the door. Wyatt followed, then doubled back.

"Leave it, son," his father yelled.

But he had a bad feeling. He grabbed the envelope and ran
out into the backyard, following his father down the alley. They
ducked behind the trash cans, catching their breath. The sirens
grew louder. Wyatt couldn't stand it. He tore the envelope open
and there was her face. Her dark hair matted. Her perfect mouth
duct taped like Derrick's. Body and wrists bound to a chair. Bandages still seeping blood. Eyes pleading but alive. Dolly.

ACKNOWLEDGMENTS

We'd like to acknowledge the invaluable contribution of our partner and agent, Ian Kleinert, the tireless work of Marc Resnick, Hannah O'Grady, and Elizabeth Bohlke, and the unending patience of our families.

With gratitude, Scott and Hof.